Scorned Prince

Ringdweller Series Book #1

Brady Hunsaker

Lightfire Publishing

Published by Lightfire Publishing LLC

Cover art illustration by Miblart

This is a work of fiction. Names, characters, places, and incidents either are the product of the author's imagination or are used fictitiously, and any resemblance to actual persons, living or dead, business establishments, events, or locales is entirely coincidental.

Contents

Dedicated to my father. It's his fault I
started writing, and he was my first great enthusiast.
Love you, dad.

FROZEN WASTE
MAZANIB
LAZEEM
HABKAMAL
JEHUBAL
SCORCHED WASTE
DELIBAD LAKE
BANADIL-ATAR
CATABAN
MALORIA
ASMALAM
WANAY
SHIBAN
WANAY LAKE

SCORCHED WASTE
JEHUBAL
DELIRAD LAKE
BANADIL-ATAR
CATABAN

Foreword

Just a little about the world of Malahem—the planet is tidally locked. Here's a quick definition of tidal locking: Tidal locking is **the phenomenon by which a body has the same rotational period as its orbital period around a partner**. So, the Moon is tidally locked to the Earth because it rotates in exactly the same time as it takes to orbit the Earth. That is why we only see one side of the Moon.

So what does that mean for the residents of Malahem?

No day. No night. They live in what's called the "terminator zone," which is the region between day and night.

Time is tracked differently. There are no days or hours, so they use the rotations of the moon to track time, since there is a moon that orbits Malahem. One rotation of the moon around Malahem is referred to as a "cycle." A cycle is broken down into 10 marks (which are about the equivalent of 2 hours. So there would be 20 hours in a cycle).

I hope that helps—have fun exploring Malahem!

Chapter One

Scorn

The queen was going to kill him. His own mother. Prince Migo Rikaydian squeezed his eyes tight. He didn't *want* to be afraid, but the feeling seeped into his soul.

"Migo!"

The voice was distant. Muted. The whirling roar of the storm drowned it out. Thunder echoed with every heartbeat. He huddled deeper into the corner of the room, thick arms wrapped about himself. No matter how hard he tried, he couldn't escape the storm. The voice always haunted him. How childish he seemed. Seventeen years old, but still he cowered.

"Migo!" The voice was closer now.

A sharp pain stung his face. The familiar bite of his mother's nails nipped his cheek. He deserved it.

"Coward! What would your soldiers think if they saw you cowering like a child in the corner? Look at me!"

Migo cracked his eyes open. He needed to be brave. His mother stood over him menacingly, a fierce queen, her fine black hair, glittering apparel, and flawless, light brown skin gave her a regal appearance, marred only by the angry sneer that curled back her lips. The Maedari, a powerful storm tainted with dark magic, sprung up so suddenly that Migo hadn't had time to close a window. Torrents of sand and ice shot through the opening with unnatural force and formed a swirling maelstrom that churned the contents of the room.

"You're pathetic." They locked eyes. "The shamans could take you without trouble, and you're supposed to fight them."

Her words stung harder than her nails. Migo struggled to his feet, cheeks burning with shame. His eyes strayed to the window where the storm thrashed its way into the room.

The queen clicked her tongue and covered her face with a veil. She strode through the elements to the window, forcing it shut with a quick jerk. A painful stillness settled with the dust. She dropped the lock in place then shook her head at him as she pulled her veil down. "Make yourself presentable." She exited the room, leaving it empty. Broken.

Migo let out a shuddering breath and wiped his face where a tear managed to sneak by his defenses. He trembled. Rage and shame boiled beneath his skin.

The room was in shambles. Everything smelled of wet sand. His mother was right. What would the soldiers think if they saw their captain like that—deathly afraid of the storms? *Coward.* He clenched his fists. *I deserve to be a captain. I deserve to be the prince.* Even in his mind, the words felt fickle. They made him angrier. He clenched his fists tighter, resisting the urge to punch the stone wall.

He brushed his arms and face, sand scraping off his skin. The storm raged outside, and he barely suppressed a shudder as he walked by the window, boots crunching. Though it had been eight years, every storm brought with it the same nightmare about his mistake. He would never be forgiven. He saw the spite in his mother's eyes every time she looked at him.

I will make up for it, mother. But what would it take to please her?

A knock rebounded on the door. "Captain?" The deep, friendly voice was that of his cousin, Hatan.

"Come in, Hatan."

The door opened, and Hatan rushed in. "I came as soon as I heard," Hatan said, voice thick with relief. His cheeks were red. "I'm sorry the queen made it here before me. How... how was she?" The man was more than twice Migo's age. He was tall, with the large body of a hardened warrior. It was nice to have somebody who cared.

Migo shrugged. "The damage has been done. Besides, how much more of a shame or disappointment can I be?"

Hatan winced. "There's no shame in it, Migo. Anybody who'd experienced what you had could have reacted the same way."

Trauma. That's what it all led back to. "This was the first time she's come to my room the whole year I've been back. It had to be right then."

"She's been wary of you since your seventeenth birthday."

Migo narrowed his eyes. "What do you mean?"

Hatan placed a hand on Migo's shoulder. "Migo, I don't know how to put this any simpler, but the queen has no intention of abdicating the throne when you turn 18, as is your right."

Migo's mind spun. "How can she do that?"

"There's only one way." Hatan gave Migo's shoulder a squeeze. "I was going to wait for a better time to tell you, but... I have a source within her inner circle. She plans to have you assassinated in seven cycles."

Migo gulped hard. He was out of breath, like he'd been punched in the gut. A cycle was a full rotation of the moon, the only way to track time since the sun never moved. Night and day was a thing of the past. "I have seven cycles to live." That was it then. She'd given up on him.

"I'm afraid so. She's hiring professionals so that it can't be traced back to her, of course."

"Is there any way to change her mind?" Migo asked, closing his eyes.

Hatan sighed and rubbed a hand through his short black hair. "Possibly. But she thinks you are weak. Cowardly. Unworthy to rule."

"Maybe she's right." He'd just been cowering in the corner. It was the same reason shamans had been able to assassinate his father. Because of Migo's cowardice. Sorrow enveloped him like a cold blanket, but he had no urge to cry. What was the point?

"She's wrong," Hatan said, eyes fierce. "You are strong and capable, as a warrior and a leader."

"Then I must prove it to her."

"No, you should flee. I won't let her destroy you."

Migo took a deep breath. "If I flee, then I will only prove her point that I'm a coward. I will not abandon my honor, even for the sake of my life."

Hatan shook his head. "Cousin, please reconsider. How would you prove this to her?"

Migo didn't answer at first, but opened his battered wardrobe, selected a beige and maroon uniform, and threw it over his shoulder. With his left hand, he drew forth his heavy battle glaive. "If there's any chance to redeem myself, I'll take it. I'll find the shamans," Migo growled, grip tightening on his weapon. A calmness washed over him. All of this was the shaman's fault. The shame. His mother's hatred. His father's death. The storms themselves. There was only one solution that remained. "I will kill them all."

Chapter Two

Magic In the Storm

Constant thunder rumbled between the stone walls of the sturdy hut. The Maedari was just picking up.

Katsi Danan welcomed the sound and pulled her veil over her face.

"You're not really going out there, are you?" Damani asked, voice soft as he stepped between her and the thick, brasswood door. His brows furrowed into a frown that made Katsi uncomfortable.

"Of course I am. I've got things to do. I'm protected." She gestured at her stormwading armor. Reinforced with powerful bewitchings, the leather material was much sturdier than it looked. She certainly wasn't about to tell Damani that she was going out to steal from a merchant lord.

Lightning flashed in various shades of pink, white, and orange, brightening the otherwise dark building.

"I thought maybe you could stay." Damani fidgeted, running a hand through his light brown hair. The curves of his young face shimmered into focus under the glow of the lightning.

"And do what? More kissing?" She raised her eyebrows at him. They kissed for the first time two weeks ago and he sought every opportunity since then for a repeat.

Damani raised his hands. "No. Just... stormwading." He took one of her hands, his skin calloused from hard labor. His eyes narrowed. "That's something shamanfolk do."

Katsi grunted and pushed him away from the door. *Well I am shamanfolk.* She couldn't voice the words. They both knew the truth but didn't dare speak it. She undid the heavy storm latch with a loud clunk. "I'll see you after the Maedari."

"Wait, don't open—"

Katsi shoved hard, forcing her way out into the storm. Roaring winds and booming thunder assaulted her senses, drowning out Damani's voice. Sand and ice whirled together, blurring her vision. Katsi shut the door behind her and ran to the north, though north in this case meant sunleft. The sun itself was stationary, never moving from the same spot in the sky. Half of the planet was a blistering Scorched Waste, and the other half was frozen, leaving only an eleven mile wide Ring in between where life could thrive.

Lightning streaked across the sky often enough that Katsi could read a book under its light. Granted, the book wouldn't last very long. *Who has time for reading anyway?*

Damani farmed for a living. Katsi thieved. Simple as that. Another secret she kept from him.

This farming settlement was about a mile away from the city. Her boots padded against moistened clay as sand and ice swirled around her. She could only watch Maedaris through her bewitched veil of sheer fabric, but they were so beautiful. The whole world was glowing and warm. Tingles tickled across her skin—the tell-tale sign of magic in the air. It reminded her of her parents. As pacifists, they'd excluded themselves from the war between shamans and ringdwellers. They wouldn't approve of her current actions, but something needed to be done, and she wasn't hurting anybody.

Her target for this storm was a merchant lord, Nedro Wajek. A ruthless murderer. His private army killed all shamans they came across, looting their bodies. He didn't deserve anything he'd stolen from her people. She still identified with the shamanfolk, even though she hadn't lived among them for years. It was her heritage.

She ran at a steady pace, her body occasionally buffeted by the strong winds.

Thick foliage signaled Katsi's arrival at the small jungle that lay between the marshy farmlands and the city of Jehubal. The jungle trees grew thick and strong. Their massive leaves drooped as if hoping to hide from the storm. Katsi passed beneath their beautiful, thick limbs, her feet treading over the hard moss that blanketed the ground. The sound of the sand and ice was muted, softened by the life around her.

Not everything could find shelter in time.

Katsi dropped to a knee with a gasp as she saw a small scaila trying to wriggle free of a rock that had fallen on the back half of its body. She lifted the rock, but the tan lizard struggled to walk. It could do little more than drag its hind legs.

It was so tiny and young. The thick scales across its body had hardly developed. If she left it behind, it would surely die.

Katsi's heart sank. "Okay, come on then." She picked up the lizard, its small body fitting in the palm of her hand. "Maybe you can stay in here for now," she said, tucking the scaila into a pocket of her thin overcoat. "I'll keep you safe." She didn't know if it would survive the storm from inside her pocket, but she couldn't just leave it on the ground.

She emerged from the jungle, lightning streaking overhead, thunder shaking her very bones.

Through the haze of sand and ice, the rounded buildings of Jehubal were mere shadows. She entered the deserted streets. No ringdweller dared venture out during a Maedari.

When she turned the next corner, her target came into view. She flushed with excitement. Wajek Manor was protected by a wall of thick, red stone. Guard towers rose at every corner of its octagonal shape. The soldiers here were better trained for handling shamanfolk, but during a Maedari, she was immune to them. Ringdwellers would never dare come outside. She crept to the building nearest the wall. It provided a narrow blind spot from the towers, not that she worried about getting attacked, but she simply didn't want to be spotted.

Katsi dashed to the wall. It was just over twenty feet tall. She found the spot she'd previously chosen to climb. Some of the stones protruded from the wall just enough to provide handholds. She took a deep breath, braced herself, and climbed, clinging as close to the wall as she could.

As the wind changed its speed and direction, she held still, but while it was constant, she made her steady ascent. She pulled herself up in one final heave and rolled across the top of the ramparts. The guard towers were still.

Katsi smiled. Excitement boiled in her stomach. She snuck to the railed stairway that led down the other side of the wall. As she sprinted to the manor itself, a rock crashed into her arm hard enough that she felt the pain through her stormwading armor. She bit back a curse as she leaned against the side of the manor. If it wasn't for her armor, the rock might have broken her bone. *At least it didn't hit the scaila.*

Light shone from a window just above her right shoulder. She pulled out the shakestone mallet from her belt, gripped it in her right hand, and struck the armored window. A high-pitched *ping* rang out above the noise of the storm, the only evidence of the tool's magical vibration. The window shattered. Katsi scrambled toward the back of the manor. She came to the next window and did the same thing.

With two rooms in chaos, Katsi was ready to head to the back. The residents of the manor would be scrambling to restore order. That, or they'd be quivering in fear, worried that the shamans had come to spirit them away.

But Katsi had something else in mind.

She returned the mallet to her belt and rounded the back of the manor. A smaller, single-floored section of the manor protruded from this end. She ran full-speed at the building, jumped, and took two steps up the stone surface of the wall and grabbed the edge of the roof. She heaved herself up the rounded surface.

The wind nearly buffeted her into the air, but she threw her body flat against the roof and clung on tightly. Once she got a moment to establish her balance, she crawled forward until she was just below another window on the second story. She drew the shakestone mallet, stretched her hand up, and tapped the window. *Ping*. The glass fell toward her before getting swept away in the wind.

Now or never. She got to a crouch, gripped the bottom of the window, and leaped through the opening with precision, the wind giving her an extra shove inside.

A man shrieked a curse and scrambled out of the room. His flight was so speedy that she had barely caught a glimpse of him. For all she knew, it was Nedro Wajek himself. This was, after all, his private study.

The storm swirled about her as she crossed the room, her feet treading on a soft Malorian rug, imported from halfway across the Ring. The room was precisely what she'd expected. A few shelves lined the walls, filled with books and trinkets from his trading business. Not only that, but, as rumored, she was quick to identify the trophy case where Nedro Wajek kept his prizes. He was known for trade among the ringdwellers, but he was also infamous for his brutality against the shamanfolk, and he always liked to collect keepsakes from his victims.

Katsi used the mallet again, shattering the glass that protected Nedro's trinkets. There were several items inside, but one was wrapped in a cloth. She reached for it instinctively, drawn to its mystery. As soon as she touched it she felt... something. It was like a small vibration that ran up her whole arm. Books and items fell to the floor as Katsi stared at the covered item in her hand. What she'd just felt... Father described that kind of reaction to her once. It meant two things. First, the item was magical, and second, that it was responding to magic *inside* her.

Not all shamanfolk had magic. Only the shamans did. *This means I'm a shaman.* Her heart rate quickened, and a shiver ran up her spine. She shook her head, focusing on the time at hand. She grabbed a few other items for good measure.

Nedro's fancy Malorian rug was getting soiled with muddied sand. *Just the kind of thing Nedro deserves.* A satisfied smile curled her lips. She sprang out the window, back into the cover of the Maedari.

Chapter Three

Threats

Migo stepped onto the floor of the training court, boots scraping against the dusty stone. The massive room was intentionally left unswept in order to simulate a more accurate battleground. A series of thick columns, exactly parallel to the rounded walls, supported the roof. Thick windows lined the circumference to allow natural light to filter in. Lightning flashed outside, but it was growing less frequent. The Maedari was coming to an end.

Still enough time for a match. Migo gave his practice stave a few spins, testing its weight.

He wanted to lie in his bed. To scream. To cry. To let his shame smother him until it boiled into rage. A match would help soothe the pain. He loved the ecstasy of victory. It was his only means of becoming something more than the dirt beneath the queen's boot.

The room echoed with voices. Most of the other Rikaydian soldiers, about 500 of them, had gathered into the room. They waited for the Maedari to end so they could resume their patrols throughout the territory.

"I'm ready, captain," a soldier said as he stepped up before Migo, equipped with his own practice stave.

Migo was one of Jehubal's three captains, a position commonly handed to members of the royal family who'd completed their formal training. The queen had shipped Migo off to a shaman hunting military academy just a few months after his father's death, probably because she couldn't stand to look at him. Fighting became Migo's life.

Other soldiers from Migo's squad gathered around, talking amongst themselves in hushed tones as they formed a circle.

"Take a stance," Migo instructed. The soldier he was about to practice with was a couple years older than Migo, but not quite as tall nor as broad.

The soldier nodded, bending his knees slightly and holding his stave to the side.

A soothing energy trickled down Migo's spine. He leapt forward and made a quick jab, testing the soldier's reaction. Migo's stave was swatted away. He tried it again with the same result, and the soldier smirked.

Here we go, Migo thought, fully anticipating the soldier's next move. The soldier made a quick swing at Migo's midsection, which Migo easily deflected with a downward slash, then switched his stave to the other hand, extending his arm in a sharp jab that smacked the soldier on the top of the shoulder with a thud.

The match was over. Several soldiers in the crowd laughed.

"Inspiring," said a gruff voice with an unhidden tone of sarcasm. The crowd went silent.

Migo turned to face Captain Tarahan. The man was ten years Migo's senior, and he was even a bit taller. He held his glaive in one hand, his brass helmet in the other, leaving his short black hair and blockish head uncovered.

"Perhaps you'd like a go," Migo said.

Tarahan chuckled. "That's quite alright. I would hate to mar your illusion of skill in front of your own soldiers."

Migo clenched his jaw as his grip on his practice stave tightened. He took a step closer to Tarahan. Hatan's hand clamped down on Migo's shoulder, halting his advance. What Migo wouldn't give for a good excuse to pound the smile off Tarahan's face.

"I believe your troop," Hatan said in his pleasant voice, "is gathering over there on the far side of the room, Captain Tarahan."

Tarahan gave a half smile that failed to reach his dark eyes. "Indeed they are, Lieutenant Padarro." He said nothing more, but inclined his head, turned on his heel, and strode off.

Most people knew better than to banter with Hatan Padarro. "I don't need you to step in for me, Hatan," Migo said in a sharp whisper.

"He was goading you, captain," Hatan said. He usually kept his speech more formal when others could hear. After Father's death, Hatan had stepped down from his position as the senior captain just so he could spend more time with Migo. Nobody had yet filled the vacancy as senior captain. Migo could only dream that the queen would allow him to take it eventually.

"Sometimes such behavior requires a matching response," Migo said.

Hatan gave Migo a kind smile. "Not when such behavior is foolish. Fortunately, that behavior is beneath you."

"I don't need to be coached on how to speak with dung heaps, Hatan," Migo said. He retrieved his glaive and placed his black and red cape back over his shoulder. "Form up!"

His soldiers shuffled into order. The sunward windows glowed with direct sunlight.

You're pathetic, Migo.

The words of his mother still rang in his ears. His knuckles went white as his grip tightened around his glaive. At least the storm was finally dying down.

Migo issued his orders. "When the storm ceases, you will search the city for any sign of the shamans. Report anything you find directly to me."

On the other side of the room, the watchers raised a green flag. The storm was over.

"Move out!" Migo shouted. The soldiers had been split into groups of ten. They all hefted their own glaives as they marched out a set of heavy iron doors that led outside. Each soldier was outfitted in tan leather armor. Rounded brass helms crowned their heads.

Migo followed the soldiers out at the rear. Hatan fell in at his side. Only the two of them wore the black and red capes of the officers.

They passed under the arched doorway of the training hall, the rest of the soldiers marching out in front of them. The sun burned over the Scorched Waste as it always did. A myriad of colors rested on the thin remnant of sandy clouds that still hovered over the Ring.

Migo and Hatan followed the soldiers halfway across the courtyard of the Rikaydian Palace where Migo stopped and folded his arms, his glaive held in the nook of his elbow. The courtyard was a large, walled enclosure. Gardens decorated the grounds, boasting a variety of vegetation, including the hardy yellow and orange rockmoss. Thick-trunked trees sprouted at the center of each garden, their fat branches stretching towards the sun. At the base of each tree grew several coral bushes in hues of pink and blue.

As the last of the soldiers exited the heavy iron gates that led out to the city, Migo walked up the stairs of the wall until he was atop the ramparts, looking out over the city of Jehubal. Hatan followed at Migo's heels, watching as the soldiers trickled into the city, which was aglow with the orange light of the sun.

The palace walls were high enough that Migo could see for miles. Directly ahead of him, the Ring, only eleven miles wide in most areas, stretched out in a thin line until it disappeared over the horizon. He faced sunright to the ever-present sun burning over the Scorched Waste.

"How can you pretend like everything is normal?" Hatan hissed in a whisper.

Migo clenched his jaw and cast a sideways glance at his cousin. "I have always felt doom lurking over my shoulder. At least now it has a deadline."

He lowered his voice even more. "The queen... You don't need to prove yourself to her."

"I made up my mind, Hatan. Speak no more of this."

"Very well. If this is to be your last week alive, we'll make it a good one." A frown darkened Hatan's face, but he shook his head and turned away.

Migo let out a staggered breath and leaned into his glaive. *The queen wants me dead*. He'd been stabbed before, but this somehow hurt worse. It wrenched his guts, like something was twisting his insides. Seven cycles of the moon. Was that enough time?

Migo frowned as he saw somebody come running up to the palace gates. *Focus on that. Focus on proving yourself to her*. He swallowed the lump in his throat.

Hatan grunted. "Looks like he's one of Nedro Wajek's servants."

Migo nodded and made his way back down the stairs, keeping a firm grip on his glaive. He arrived at the gate just as the servant came huffing up to the entrance. Like most other Jehubalins, the servant had brown skin and black hair. He wore a dark blue robe, and Migo didn't fail to notice the curved knife sheathed at his waist.

"What's going on?" Hatan asked the servant. Two other soldiers on guard came to stand beside Migo and Hatan.

The servant wiped at the sweat on his brow. He dropped to his knees before Hatan. "I come from Wajek manor. Your humble servant requests a word with Lord Rikaydian."

Hatan thumped his own glaive against the ground and looked to Migo. It wasn't often that people referred to Migo by his royal title. Migo gave him a short nod.

"Speak," Hatan said. "Lord Rikaydian will listen."

"My prince." The servant bowed his head to Migo. "Lord Wajek seeks your help. He was attacked by shamans during the storm."

Migo muttered a curse. Nedro Wajek was one of the greatest supporters of the war against shamans. Maybe this was the kind of lead he needed. "You may return to Wajek manor. Lieutenant Padarro and I will investigate."

"You are most gracious, Lord Rikaydian." The servant bowed deeply once again. "I will return and deliver your response immediately." He turned and ran the way he'd come.

"Fetch mine and Lieutentant Padarro's rangolas," Migo said to a soldier by the gate. The soldier nodded and sprinted to the stables.

"This is the third breakin in a row," Hatan said, folding his arms.

The soldier came hurrying back from the stables with two saddled rangolas. The four-legged beasts were bulky and feline. Their bodies were mostly covered in chitinous, yellow scales, except for their underside where they grew short, white fur. They were magnificent, and beautiful.

Migo took the reins of his rangola, Genda, and rubbed her behind the ear. A rumbling purr thrummed from its throat. The thick whiskers around its nose trembled slightly. Genda bent down just enough that her back reached Migo mid-belly. Migo jumped into the saddle and reined in beside Hatan, who mounted his own. As they rode through the streets, the rangola's claws pattered against the pavement.

"Nedro might even have some of those tari tarts for us to try," Hatan said, now with a full-on grin across his face.

"We aren't going there for treats, Hatan. Besides, I thought you were distressed."

Hatan shrugged, a hint of a smile still lingering. "Treats are always a joy."

The streets of Jehubal bustled as people hurried out after the storm. Most folks often slept during the Maedaris—something Migo had never been able to do. He envied them for their apathy.

There was no way to tell the time while the moon was hidden beneath the clouds. Not even the dim stars at the distant edge of the Frozen Waste could be seen during the storm. Now, however, Migo could see their glistening specks shining in the distance. If he ever had a moment of peace on a clear day, he'd stray towards the Frozen Waste just to watch the stars.

The citizens stood to the sides of the street and bowed as Migo passed. A stupid gesture. One he wasn't worthy of. His cheeks flushed before he could shake the embarrassment.

"The moon rises. A new cycle has begun," Hatan said. The tanned, light brown skin of his face wrinkled as he squinted out towards the Scorched Waste, a bright shape inching its way up the horizon.

Migo barely heard his cousin speak. His eyes were drawn somewhere else at the other end of the city where a thin trail of smoke rose into the sky. More destruction. His grip tightened on the reins. "It looks like the shamans were busy this time," he said to Hatan as he pointed to the smoke.

Hatan frowned. "Should we investigate?"

"Yes, but later. We'll first want to see what happened at Wajek manor."

Migo heeled Genda to move a little faster when they turned down the street that led to Wajek manor. He could imagine all of Nedro Wajek's staff bustling about in a panic. From the distance, nothing looked to be in disarray. Aside from the normal damage inflicted upon them from the storms, the buildings to either side of the street were in good condition. The citizens walking the streets seemed oblivious to the idea that a vicious shaman had been walking among them just moments ago.

When they reached Wajek manor, the gates opened instantly, and a guard ushered them inside. Sure enough, a dozen servants and soldiers were rushing about. The balding, plump figure of Nedro Wajek himself came running out to greet them, his cheeks flushed red.

"It was an outrage," Nedro said in his high-pitched voice, shaking his fist in the air. He wore a loose-fitting robe and a tight red jerkin from his military days that looked like it had been long outgrown. He bowed to Migo. "Lord Rikaydian, it is a pleasure to have you here at my home once again, though I apologize that it is for such an unpleasant matter." He snatched at a passing servant and said, "Bring our guests some refreshment."

Hatan's eyes twinkled with excitement as the servant rushed back into the manor.

Migo dismounted his rangola. "Stay here, Genda," he whispered in her ear as he patted her head. The creature growled in acknowledgement. He turned his attention to Nedro. "What happened?"

Nedro let out a huff. "I'll show you." He started walking into the manor. "I tell you, if I was still young, I would've slain those demons myself when they broke in."

From the corner of his eye, Migo noticed Hatan holding back a smile.

When they entered the manor, Migo's heavy boots tread across a soft rug. To either side of the entryway were statues of Nedro and some of his ancestors. The walls were decorated with frivolous, tasseled drapery and hand-painted murals of jungle trees amidst a sand dune oasis. Shelves, cabinetry, and sofas flavored each room they passed through.

"Retirement from military service has certainly been good for you, Nedro," Hatan said.

Nedro clicked his tongue. "I am indeed one of the fortunate, but I've retired only in service. Still, my private group of soldiers is ever-battling with the shaman scoundrels." He barely stopped as they passed through a room. "Here is one of the windows they broke. No storm would have been able to break my windows."

Migo stepped up to the window and squinted at the remains. The frame was perfectly intact, but the glass was almost nowhere to be seen, save a few tiny pieces that had gotten stuck in the cracks. The room itself was somewhat thrashed.

"Have you been cleaning it up?" Migo asked.

"A little bit," Nedro answered offhandedly as he started walking into the next room.

"Well don't do it. You could be altering what little evidence may remain."

"I assure you, Lord Rikaydian, I merely had my servants tidy it up a bit." Nedro pointed at another broken window. "And here! But that's not the worst of it. I will lead you upstairs."

Migo made no effort to conceal his scowl. When they reached the stairs, they were stopped by a female servant holding a silver platter that was topped with several cream-filled pastries.

"Refreshments, sir," the servant said with a bow to Nedro. She wore the same dark blue robes as all of Nedro's servants.

Nedro snatched one of the pastries off with a quick motion. "Go ahead, help yourselves my lords. Always a pleasure to have you." He started his way up the stairs as he ate his pastry.

Hatan smirked and grabbed one off the top, muttering his thanks.

Migo followed Nedro up the stairs.

"You won't have one?" Hatan asked with a hint of surprise.

"No." Treats were disgusting, pointless food.

Hatan smiled at the servant again. "I'll just grab another, then. I'm sure he'll want it for later." He then scurried after Migo as they continued up the stairs.

Nedro had amassed such wealth. It had been nearly a year since he'd last entered Wajek manor, but the difference was apparent. The stone stairs were now embellished with fine, wooden railings and the wall was spotted with the furs of rare creatures from the southern provinces.

At the top of the stairs, the hallway was lined with cabinets that held fine dishes of glass and silver. There was even a rack that held several ancient weapons. Migo paused to take a look.

"I'm told some of those predate the time before the sun stood still," Nedro commented with a smile.

Migo rolled his eyes at Nedro's ignorance and proceeded walking. "The sun isn't still, our planet is tidally locked."

Hatan smiled at Nedro and explained, "The prince studied with an astronomer for a couple weeks."

"Ah, then I will trust your judgment, lord." Nedro paused at a door. "It happened in here." He wiped at his brow as he drew forth a set of keys from his pocket. When he finished unlocking the door, he put a hand over a small knife that was sheathed at the side of his jerkin. "In we go." He pushed the door open.

The inside of the room was a complete mess. Glass shelves had been destroyed. An assortment of various trinkets was scattered about. A fine Malorian rug was settled at the center of the room, its surface sodden with muddied sand.

A guard stood by a third broken window. He saluted them as they entered, then returned his attention to looking out the window.

"They came in through the window," Nedro said, squinting around the room as if he might find another shaman hiding in a corner. His hand didn't leave the pommel of his knife. "Came in while I was still in here. They were probably hoping to assassinate me. You know, like they always do to people during the storms."

Migo ground his teeth as Hatan cast him a worried glance.

"Fortunately, I was able to repel them back out the window, but not before they snatched up some of my collection. Several other items were simply destroyed by the storm."

Migo strode up to the broken window. The guard saluted him and moved out of the way. Again, the frame of the window was perfectly intact, but the glass itself was obliterated. A small section of the first-floor roofing was just about five feet below the window. "They got in from the roof," Migo said as he looked back around the room.

"That's what we figured," Nedro said, "but we're not sure how they got onto the roof, nor how they weren't blown off by the storm. They were certainly some skilled assassins."

"How many were there?" Migo asked.

Nedro shrugged. His cheeks were a little red. "Hard to tell with the storm raging through the room." He crinkled his brow in thought. "At least three."

Migo grunted. "What did they take?"

Nedro scowled. "The main item was something I took off the body of a shaman chief we killed. My merchant caravan ran into them as we were traveling near Omidan Lake." He gave a smug smile as he brushed at a piece of lint on his jerkin. "I usually like to collect a few keepsakes from my victories."

The queen was very supportive of Nedro Wajek and all of his occasional skirmishes with the shaman people. Exterminating shamans was encouraged throughout the entire empire.

"But what was the item?" Hatan asked.

"Nothing more than a bit of jewelry. An armlet," Nedro said with a shake of his head. He glanced about the room. "It seemed more like a sentimental item than anything valuable." He gave a soft smile that failed to reach his eyes. "Not only that, but it was still covered in a bit of old cloth when they took it. Of all the things in here, it seemed like the least appealing."

"Sentimental items can hold great value," Hatan mused.

Migo rubbed his chin. This was certainly peculiar behavior from the shamans. His experiences with them so far had shown that they were brutal. If they'd had the chance, they would have looted as much as they could from the manor. "Where was it taken from?"

Nedro pointed at a display shelf on the opposite side of the room from the window. That was even more peculiar. "They crossed the entire room without taking any other items," he mused to himself as he approached the shelf. The glass cover had seemingly vanished, much like the windows. Inside the shelf, an assortment of items was displayed across a velvety cloth. A scattering of sand made the cloth sparkle under the light.

Migo bent closer. Some of the items on the shelf were gilded with gold and silver. Most of them looked quite valuable. He rubbed his fingers across the cloth, feeling at the strange, sparkling sand, but it poked his skin with sharp pricks. His hand shot back as blood beaded on his fingertips, a gasp escaping his lips.

"What is it?" Hatan asked, stepping up beside Migo.

"This isn't sand," Migo said, pointing at the glimmering cloth. "It's glass. From the shelf's cover. I think the same thing happened to all the broken windows."

"Interesting. I never knew the storms could do that." Nedro mused.

"Because it wasn't the storm. This glass was broken by magic. They were targeting something, and I intend to find out why." Migo straightened himself. He'd never seen this type of activity from them. "There's not much we can do for now, Nedro." He thumbed the shaft of his weapon. "But I'll make a record of your report. If we can locate the item that was stolen, we'll let you know. We have another issue to look into."

Nedro stopped fidgeting. "Ah, another attack?"

"Perhaps," Migo said, walking to the door. "We'll find out soon enough."

Chapter Four

Burned Bodies

Katsi shivered at the edge of Jehubal's swampy farmland. Insects buzzed around her, and the scaila in her hand watched them with eager eyes. She'd already snatched a couple of the bugs with her hand to feed them to him. Or her? She wasn't really sure how to tell a lizard's gender, and she wasn't too eager to go looking.

The Frozen Waste was only about a mile to her left. She'd headed this way after the Maedari, knowing Damani would be coming to check on his ice floras. The tender plants needed colder weather to sustain them properly, so it wasn't uncommon for some of them to take heat damage during Maedaris.

With her free hand, Katsi touched the newly acquired artifact that was tucked into her pocket. She felt the same tingling sensation she'd gotten the first time, though this time it was milder, like a gentle reminder.

"I'm magic, Scales. Can you believe it?" Katsi said, holding the lizard up closer to her face.

Scales blinked its yellow eyes at her.

"No, I can't show you. I don't know how it works... or what it is," she said. "But my father could make enchanted potions, so maybe I could do something like that."

Scales settled into Katsi's palm with a tiny guttural sound.

"Potions are great. Then I could make something to help your legs get better." Katsi eyed her little friend's left hind leg, which looked particularly mangled, and her hopes for a good recovery faltered.

Motion toward the middle of the marshlands caught Katsi's attention. She looked up to see the farmers approaching, most of them wrapped in tan clothes with veils over their faces. She recognized Damani by the dark blue coif over his head.

Katsi stepped down from the jungle floor. "Let's keep you in here for now," she said, tucking Scales back into the pocket of her overcoat.

Damani saw her approaching and waved her over. She dodged a couple pools of standing water before the two of them stood together.

"See, still alive," Katsi said, gesturing at herself.

Damani rolled his gray eyes, which were just about the only thing visible. That and a small tuft of his light brown hair. "It's not that. I know you can take care of yourself," he said, glancing over at the other farmers who'd continued on to their crops. "I just want us to be able to have a normal life together someday, you know what I mean?"

What? Katsi felt something flutter in her stomach. "I'm seventeen, Damani. I don't think that far ahead," she lied. She wasn't about to admit that she'd thought about marrying him over a year ago. "I'm just here to take some of your food." She swung a playful punch at his shoulder.

He gave a short laugh, eyes sparkling. "Is that all I'm good for?"

"You do have your uses," Katsi said, smile hidden beneath her veil. Their families had shared farmland when growing up, but after Katsi's parents were murdered when she was eight, she'd gone into hiding with the rest of the tribe. The tribe tried to raise her as a soldier though. All they cared about was fighting. She had to leave, and Damani was the only one she could think of coming to. He was perhaps the only ringdweller who might suspect her of being shamanfolk.

Damani breathed a laugh. "Well, why don't you help me prod some of these open." He handed her a hooked rod and the two of them headed over to a large patch of ice floras. The plants were round with several layers of white leaves folding over themselves. Without looking closely, they might seem like little rocks.

Katsi inserted the rod into a tiny hole at the top of an ice flora where the leaves did not extend. Then she pried back some of the leaves until the purplish core was exposed. Damani moved in behind her, doing the more delicate work of extracting the hearts.

Despite the cold, Katsi's brow began to sweat. Farming was painstaking work, and her stomach growled angrily. She hadn't eaten since the storm had started.

"That should do," Damani said. He'd pulled the coif down, revealing the lower half of his face. He flashed her a perfect smile and held out a small sack.

"Thank you." She took the sack from his hand, feeling its generous weight. Her eyes widened. "Damani, this is a lot. Are you sure?"

He held up his hand. "Please, we harvested a lot. The crop was pretty good, and I could hear the storm rumbling in your stomach." His eyes softened.

"Actually," he said, "I wanted to tell you something." Damani took a step closer. Katsi couldn't tell if she was just imagining the heat emanating from his body. "I saw something interesting just a few marks ago. Before the Maedari. I hadn't had a chance to tell you before you left."

He glanced around, and Katsi narrowed her eyes.

"You know how I like to lay on the moss at the edge of the jungle sometimes?"

Katsi's smile was hidden behind her veil. That was where they'd first held hands. She gave a small nod.

"Well, I've seen people out there a couple times now, and I saw them again. They're armed. They wear some of that same, uh," he glanced down at her body, "armor that you do, only they don't hide it under a robe."

Shamanfolk. Likely scoping out the farmlands. The Bayvana Tribe was known for running the occasional raid, usually targeting soldiers. Sometimes they even assaulted caravans, stole the food, and slew the guards. They'd been rather silent for a few months now. "What could that mean?" she asked, knowing Damani was clever enough to guess who they were.

He shook his head. "I don't know. It's not safe. Do you think they have some of that *magic*?" He'd said the word with such disgust that it made Katsi's cheeks burn.

"I doubt they're here for me," she said. "Not all shamanfolk are actual shamans either. Magical abilities are uncommon. Do you think they saw you?"

"No."

"Keep it that way. Maybe you could lay out in the north jungle from now on. It's not protected over here." Katsi always felt unsettled that the southern farmlands were hardly monitored. A regiment of twenty soldiers at the road wouldn't do anything to protect farmers like Damani who lived by the jungle.

"I know." His expression dropped. "I'll stick to the north."

Footsteps pounded toward them from the road. Two boys sprinted towards the farmers, no doubt bearing news.

"There was an attack during the Maedari," said the young man in front with a huff, coming to a halt just in front of Damani as the other farmers gathered around. He brushed his long black hair back from his forehead and blinked at them with widened eyes. The other young man behind him slipped on slick rock and splashed into one of the puddles.

Katsi tried not to laugh as the other farmers muttered concern over the attack. The boys were about to report something that she had done herself.

"What was it this time?" someone asked.

The boys exchanged worried looks with each other then the one in front said, "Murder."

Gasps and curses filled the air. Katsi narrowed her eyes.

"There hadn't been any murders for a few storms now. I hoped they'd stopped," somebody said.

Damani pursed his lips and gave Katsi a questioning look, almost as if he was asking her if she knew about it.

She frowned and shook her head, resisting the urge to slap Damani for even thinking it. Why would she know anything about a murder?

He turned his head away.

Katsi ground her teeth. She stole something during the Maedari. She hadn't killed anyone. "Where?" Katsi asked. She was instantly intrigued and furious. She hated these murders. It was just too bad it was never anybody like Queen Rikaydian that got murdered in the storms. She could only wish.

"Just one street in from the entrance of the city."

Katsi nodded and threw the bag over one shoulder. Her stomach was still aching, but she needed to check this out first. The farmers argued amongst themselves as Katsi walked away. She was so mad at Damani that she didn't even look back as she hurried sunward toward the center of the Ring where the sunlight was a little stronger. It didn't take long before she reached the jungle that stood between the farmlands and Jehubal. Now the Maedari had passed, the thick trees had unfurled their giant leaves, soaking in all the sun they could. Thin clouds were hanging overhead in hues of orange and purple.

"Still choosing to spend your time with the ringdwellers, eh, Danan?"

Katsi skidded to a halt, hand going to her knife. Nobody knew her family name. Not unless... He was a middle-aged man with dark eyes and long black hair that was tinged with a brown-orange shade. The unusual shading was typically a sign of somebody who'd lived too long near the Scorched Waste. In this man's case, he actually lived *inside* the Scorched Waste. "It's still a way to get food," Katsi said coolly. "At least I don't have to kill anybody around here." She added a little heat to her words.

The man's eyes narrowed. He was tall, with a strong body. His name was Manahae. A shaman. He smiled. "Until they figure out who you are anyway. It's only a matter of time, of course. Then it's kill or be killed, and your peace-preaching will mean nothing. You know as well as any how that works." His voice was soft and clear, each word spoken with confidence.

"What are you doing here, anyway?"

Manahae's expression darkened. "Leaving." He took a step closer. "If I were you, Danan, I wouldn't be staying in Jehubal for much longer." Without giving her any time to respond, he disappeared at a run, heading south.

It was true. The shamanfolk were planning something. Manahae coming this close to Jehubal? The city itself was possibly at risk. She sped up to a light jog. A small wisp of smoke came into view before the city did. Her pace increased subconsciously as she ran to the city. Whatever had happened, she needed to see it.

Her mind raced. She'd seen death before—far more than she'd ever wanted—but she intended to learn what she could to make it stop.

As she neared the smoke, she realized she wasn't the only one rushing to the scene. Several other people were running to see what had happened, many of them young like Katsi. She sometimes found it difficult to remember that she was only seventeen years old. Living on her own certainly didn't make her feel that young.

When she arrived at the scene, several people stood in a circle. A two-story home burned in flames. Some people assisted a couple guards that were attempting to put it out. And there, lying in the street, with nothing more than a cloth to cover them, were two dead bodies.

One of the guards turned and yelled at them, "Stay back everybody! Unless you want to help us with this fire."

Katsi stayed hidden behind a couple other onlookers, peeking out from between them. The bodies were mostly covered by the cloths, but an arm was exposed, revealing fire-blackened skin.

"What happened?" Katsi asked aloud.

"Demons."

"Shamans."

"Came in during the storm while the family was sleeping."

"Burned 'em with that dark magic."

"Poor Daniya. She and her husband were some of the nicest people."

"That's probably why the shamans went after them. They don't like any of the decent people."

"Where did they come from?"

"Blew in with the Maedari. That's how they always do it."

Katsi had gotten the conversation started, though much of it was likely just speculation. This whole thing was extremely unnerving. Tensions were already incredibly high. Shamanfolk were slaughtered mercilessly whenever they were found. Katsi knew the shamanfolk had plans to fight back. More murders could even persuade the ringdweller armies to venture out in the wastes. If only she could get a closer look at the bodies to see what had really happened. She edged her way to the front of the scene.

"Everyone clear out!" A deep voice boomed over the crowd.

Katsi hesitantly took a couple steps back with the rest of the people, frowning as she looked up at the newcomers. To her surprise, two soldiers came riding up on the backs of rangolas. She scowled with instant recognition. She barely stifled a grunt of loathing as she fell in beside the other citizens.

The two men dismounted smoothly, both of them bearing the glaives of the army. One of the men was young, and he might have been handsome if not for the seemingly permanent scowl etched into his face. Black, wavy hair hung down to his shoulders. Prince Migo Rikaydian. His captain's uniform fit tightly over his muscular body. He didn't immediately approach the bodies, but instead cast his brown eyes across the crowd, squinting at them as he stood in battle stance, as if suspecting that one of them might have been responsible.

Katsi cringed as his eyes lingered on her for a split-second. Her hands tightened into fists.

"Captain Rikaydian," said one of the guards, rushing over and bowing to the filthy prince. The building was rubble by the time they got the fire under control.

"Keep these people back," Migo said to the guard in a stern voice. "This area needs to be secured for examination."

The guard turned on the crowd immediately. "You heard the captain, stand back. Disperse from here. The army will take care of it."

Katsi half-heartedly took another step back as Migo and the other soldier approached the bodies.

Migo crouched and uncovered the faces of the victims. "What do you think it was, Hatan?" He asked his companion in an undertone. Katsi was barely close enough to hear. Barely close enough to see.

Hatan folded his arms and shook his head. "Shaman magic. Similar to those murders a few years ago, actually. Before you were on the force."

Katsi sidled to the edge of the buildings and inched a little closer. She had to see those faces. The guard didn't notice as she slipped over towards the smoldering building.

"But why these people?" Migo's frown somehow managed to deepen.

"Perhaps the shamans failed at killing Nedro Wajek, so they went for some other people instead."

Katsi was just close enough to see their faces. They were terribly blackened in some places, but something about them seemed oddly familiar. Her mind raced, her heart thumping wildly as a thought occurred to her. For some reason, they reminded her of her younger years, before her parents were taken.

Migo tapped his chin in thought, then looked up at Katsi sharply. "What're you doing? Get out of here!"

"Sorry," Katsi said like a good citizen, though she loathed having a Rikaydian's eyes on her. She bowed her head and took a step back.

Hatan brandished his weapon. "Move along now, miss," Hatan said with a firm voice, though his eyes remained soft.

Katsi nodded and retreated into the crowd.

"Hold on, who is she?" Migo asked.

A sudden panic gripped her chest. She wouldn't let him catch her. Without a glance back, she hurried passed the other people and ran out of the city.

Chapter Five

Mother's Wrath

Migo paced in front of his desk, hands clasped behind his back as he brooded. Shamans were attacking them. The queen wanted to kill him. It made his heart thump with rage. He'd also let the girl get away. His reaction had been too slow. Her image had burned into his mind, though her veil had been pulled down only enough to show her eyes and forehead. Light brown skin, thin, black eyebrows, and penetratingly beautiful eyes. He could almost remember a light hint of green in those otherwise dark eyes of hers. He shook his head, trying to clear the image away.

Hatan shifted in the corner, a sigh escaping his lips. "We should be discussing the queen's plan... but I know you're thinking about the girl. We can find her," he said.

Migo scowled. "You're right. If I can catch her, then perhaps I can redeem myself. Or at the very least, the queen will not think me so useless."

Hatan's jaw twitched. "Perhaps. That girl obviously knew how to slip away."

"All the more reason to catch her." Migo ran after her once she'd slipped behind the crowd, but she'd all but vanished. It only frustrated him more.

"I'm committed to helping you if you think this will work, but it's been a long cycle. The hourglass was already on the fifth mark before we came in to take the reports. I think it's a good time to rest."

Migo realized that meant he hadn't slept for two full cycles. It was hard to keep track of time when he was so busy. But he only had seven cycles to live, so what did it matter? He *was* feeling tired though. His continued frowning gave him a headache. "What if I secreted myself within the public. Perhaps I could glean some information that way. See if there are movements into the wastes." He still didn't understand how the shamans could survive out there. He didn't understand nearly enough about their magic.

Hatan shook his head. "Everybody within miles knows your face. Even I couldn't do it without being recognized."

Hatan was wrong. Migo could easily wear a veil. Finding the girl would be difficult. He questioned himself. Would catching *one* shaman appease his mother? *Some success is better than none.* His pacing slowed as he grudgingly decided something else. "Assign a couple soldiers to do it then."

"Very well, lord."

"We'll also continue our searches near the wastes. We need eyes on known camps that have been abandoned or destroyed. We know shamans filter through sometimes, so they're bound to show up eventually. Issue the orders." He'd gathered some intel this way before. He just had to try it some more.

"It will be done, sir," Hatan said with a nod.

"Good." Migo returned to his desk. He had to think of something better to do.

Hatan made to leave the room, then added, "And you, lord? I hope you will get some rest soon."

"Yes, of course," Migo said with slight irritation, but he doubted that he could sleep until he came up with a new idea. "As soon as I'm done."

Hatan inclined his head with a frown before exiting, the door closing behind him.

Migo dozed at his desk when the door banged open. There was only one person who would enter Migo's office in such a way. His stomach clenched with fear. Without looking up, Migo knew that Queen Rikaydian had just come to pay him a visit.

"Murder. Robbery. The shaman scum wander freely through my city while you sit idly in your office like a coward."

Migo pretended to start writing. Goosebumps appeared on his skin as heat flushed to his face.

"What's your plan of action? Where are the shamans hiding this time?"

"We're still working on a solution." Migo could say no more as his mother gripped his jaw in one hand, her nails digging into his cheeks.

"I expect action, Migo," she said in a sharp whisper. "I'll have no more cowering out of you. These shamans must be eradicated." Her perfect white teeth shone brightly through her sneer. She threw his head back, releasing her grip.

Migo gritted his teeth and held back tears of rage as he looked up at his mother. Small beads of blood appeared where her nails had made a mark. How could she treat him like this? "I'll go immediately. Interrogate every citizen that was there," he said hoarsely. "Imprison anybody who tries to withhold information. I'll search the Wastes myself and kill every last shaman I can find." His cheeks flushed with shame as his lower lip trembled.

Would she really have him killed? He could see the hatred in his mother's dark eyes, but he could never tell who she hated more: him, or the shamans. He rose from his desk, grabbed his glaive, and strode out of the room. It was because of the shamans that his mother had become like this. It was because of *them* that she loathed him. And he hated them for it—with all the passion in his soul. *I will make up for it.* His arms quivered with rage.

Was there any freedom from the storm of hatred that roiled around him? His weariness forgotten, he marched out to begin interrogations.

Chapter Six

The Artifact

Blazing heat burned at Katsi's back as she scrambled down the dark cave before her. Each step echoed with the sound of her boots grinding the dust. She gasped a sigh of relief when she stepped through an unseen barrier that left the heat of the Scorched Waste behind her.

"See, Scales, I told you we'd make it just fine," Katsi said, putting a hand in the pocket of her overcoat just to feel Scales shuffling around. She placed her other hand against the smooth, stone wall of the tunnel as they continued to descend, using it to feel her way through the darkness until her hand gave way at a small recess. Inside were two little stones which she drew out and struck together, whispering, "Linara." The two stones burst into a bright, yellowish glow that lit the walls around her. She hadn't used shaman magic—even a Ringdweller could have activated the magic at the word.

The light revealed a few steps ahead of her where the cave narrowed sharply. She proceeded up the steps until she came into a rectangular room with hollowed shelves in the walls and a stone table in one corner. A woven mat laid at the center of the room. One third of the mat was heavily worn, while the rest had been untouched for years. She couldn't ever bring herself to sleep in her parents' spots.

She averted her eyes and swung the bag of ice flora hearts onto the table, took off the canteen, and quickly emptied the contents of her belt: the shakestone mallet, a pouch tinkling with two coins, a weathered parchment, a small bag with chalkrocks, a little knife, and finally, the items she'd taken from Wajek Manor. One was a metal belt buckle, another was a wooden carving of the life icon. The magical artifact was still wrapped in a cloth. Thinking about her burglary still brought a smile to her face.

Katsi removed Scales from her pocket and placed him on the table. To answer her growling stomach, Katsi pulled the sack of ice flora hearts over as she sat down at the table.

Scales looked at the artifact on the table and then back at Katsi.

"I know, Scales," Katsi said, raising her eyebrows at the lizard. "I'll check it out in a moment, but I haven't eaten all cycle!" She was fighting the urge to bring out the artifact even as she pulled out a heart and bit into it. Its thin skin broke to her teeth, and the inner flesh gushed into her mouth like moistened bread, its starchy sweet taste making her tongue explode with saliva.

Before she knew it, she'd eaten three whole hearts. Scales nipped at the remnants that lingered on her fingers.

Katsi stared at the artifact that sat just within reach. She wiped her hands on the sack, set out another heart for Scales, then slid the artifact in front of her. After removing the cloth wrapping, she held a Linara stone closer so she could take a close look at it.

It was a thin armlet. Something that went on the upper arm. The metal glinted with a dull, bronze color. At the very center of the armlet was a flat, rounded stone, clasped by metal prongs. The stone was a grayish-green hue, and there was a symbol carved into the surface like a rune of some ancient language. A fresh string of leather had been attached for tying it on.

It still gave her a slight tingling sensation upon touch. When she tied it onto her upper arm the sensation went away, but she could still detect a sort of aura about it. From what she could remember, magical artifacts like this were rare.

"Sands, I wish I'd paid more attention when my mother had told me about these kinds of things." She looked at her hands as she thought about her magic. "What a crazy thing. To have something be a part of you but have no idea how to use it. Like a baby not knowing how to use her legs." She flexed her fingers. "Except that a baby at least knows where her legs are. I do not."

Scales blinked at her with drowsy eyes.

"I'm speaking metaphorically. Use your imagination." She let out a long sigh. "I've dreamed about this since I was a little girl though, Scales. About being a shaman. My father did a lot of good for people with his potions. He helped ringdwellers *and* shamanfolk." *Even though it got him killed.* She couldn't say the words—even to Scales. *But didn't father know the risk he was taking? Of course he did, and he did it anyway.*

"Well, if I'm going to learn anything about my magic, I'll need to go back to the tribe." She rubbed her temples. "Damani's not going to be happy."

Scales was passed out on a partially eaten ice flora heart, his bloated stomach rising and falling with deep breaths.

"Good idea, Scales," Katsi said. "I'll take a nap too—but when we wake up, we're going to go visit the Bayvana Tribe so I can learn how to use my legs."

Chapter Seven

Suspects

Migo did his best to ignore the sound of distant thunder rumbling out over the Frozen Waste. He knew it was no Maedari, but the muscles of his lower back tightened with worry anyway.

The cobbled street outside the burned home was almost completely empty. Two of his soldiers had been posted outside the ruined building, but what surprised Migo was the presence of two of Captain Tarahan's soldiers standing guard outside the neighboring home. The smell of smoke still lingered in the air. Soot stains smeared onto the paved street in front of it. The rounded roof was still intact, though blackened in spots by the smoke and flames.

Migo stopped in front of the two soldiers he'd left to guard the building. Four other soldiers followed behind him. "What the sands are they doing here?" Migo said, pointing at Tarahan's soldiers.

One of his men started stammering a reply when the door burst open, a woman's scream piercing the air. Out strode Tarahan himself, followed by eight more soldiers. They escorted two people, a man and a woman, all but dragging them out of the home.

"Ah, Captain Rikaydian. How excellent of you to finally show up," Tarahan said, offering a lopsided smile. "However, you seem to be a little late." His expression changed to a disappointed frown.

"What're you talking about?"

Tarahan's smile returned. "While you went back to the palace to pout, I did some investigation. We got a tip that this couple had a close relationship with the victims, so we searched their home." He pulled a dark brown object from his pocket and held it up between his fingers.

"That's not ours!" the husband cried, throwing up an exasperated hand.

"We've never even seen that before," the wife added. Tears wetted her cheeks.

Migo recognized the item as a shamanic idol, a rough, stone carving of a woman crouching over a large bowl.

"Found hidden behind a drawer," Tarahan said in his deep voice. He tucked the idol back into his pocket. "Convincing evidence of shamanic affiliation, wouldn't you agree, captain?"

Migo clenched his fists. Agreeing with Tarahan was the last thing Migo wanted to do. "Queen Rikaydian will be pleased to see some headway."

"Indeed she will," Tarahan said, eyes narrowing as he pointed at Migo and took a step closer. "And she will have *me* to thank for it." He turned up the street, waving his soldiers after him. "Let's move."

"Where are you taking them?" Migo said, keeping stride with Tarahan.

"To the queen of course."

"They'll need to be questioned," Migo said. "We need to find out whatever they know. In addition to my role as a captain, when I completed training with the Hunters, I was also appointed as the royal inquisitor."

"Of course," Tarahan said. "I'm well aware of your beloved credentials, captain. You can question them once I've safely turned them over to the queen."

Migo stopped in his tracks. He hated how desperate he seemed, chasing after Tarahan like that. His cheeks burned with embarrassment and frustration. Tarahan was right, however. He'd have to wait.

Once Tarahan and his soldiers were out of sight, Migo jabbed the butt of his glaive onto the cobblestones, a dull echo ringing out. How did Tarahan find somebody so quick? He'd made it look easy. Perhaps *too* easy. It was a dangerous idea to think that the evidence was planted, and one he doubted he'd be able to prove.

He turned back to the soldiers guarding the ruined building. "You were here since the storm, correct?"

"Yes sir," the soldiers said in unison.

"Tell me what happened in relation to Captain Tarahan's activities."

The older of the two stepped forward, Nivara, a woman who'd previously served under Hatan. "Captain Tarahan had soldiers go through the area just asking questions shortly after you left. We stopped seeing them about one mark later though."

"They probably hid behind that house to wait," said the other soldier, a younger man.

"Captain Rikaydian is more than capable of deducing things for himself, Jonun," Nivara said. "We just convey the details." She returned to addressing Migo. "After another short while, those residents returned home—the ones Captain Tarahan just took prisoner. That's when Captain Tarahan and his men emerged from hiding and entered the residence. Then you arrived and saw the rest."

"What do you know about the residents, Nivara?" Migo asked, knowing she would have made a point to be familiar with those around her.

She cleared her throat. "Names are Bindom and Shali. Lived here for several years. Both worked at a refinery. They seemed a little frightened. Walked faster than most people. Kept their heads down. Held hands the entire time I saw them. They were supposedly really good friends with the victims. Other neighbors said they'd spend a lot of time together."

Migo tapped his glaive on the ground in thought. "Let me know if you see anybody else frequenting the area. Continue as you were." He turned to the other four soldiers who'd come with him. "I want you four to split up and continue investigating the area for the next two marks, then return and report."

They responded in unison, then dispersed. Now alone, Migo proceeded up the road that led back to Rikaydian Palace, the stench of smoke slowly fading behind him. The road before him was all but empty. Sand from the Maedari still littered the streets.

Two suspects had been captured. Based on what little information was available, Migo already suspected that they were not the murderers. The idol could have easily been placed by one of Tarahan's soldiers, which was concerning itself. *Does Tarahan know the queen wants me dead? Perhaps he's trying to expedite the execution by blocking any opportunity to prove myself.* Migo scowled. Tarahan was instantly hostile once Migo had been appointed a captain. Migo wouldn't put it past him to go to extreme measures. Even if it meant framing people.

However, if they were indeed shamans, then it at least gave him a chance to interrogate them, which would hopefully lead to finding others. Nedro Wajek had reported seeing three shamans, which meant there would at least be one more out there.

The girl.

Migo's pace quickened as the palace came into view. Built on a small rise, and as the only building four stories high, the palace could be seen from miles away. When Migo arrived at the palace courtyard, other soldiers and visitors were talking about Tarahan's captured suspects as if the murder had already been solved.

Migo shook his head and headed through a large door into the palace. The entry hall was an oval room with several smaller, round rooms built along the sides to host visitors and those waiting on various meetings. A few merchants were usually always hanging around. He all but ran through the room to the other end where a soldier nodded Migo through the door that took him into a hallway of the inner palace.

If Migo hoped to redeem himself, he'd need to interrogate the prisoners as soon as possible. His heart pounded in his ears. The tan and maroon banners of House Rikaydian lined the walls, a black rangola depicted at the center of each.

As expected, Migo found the queen at the receiving chamber, where she held most of her meetings. A few of Tarahan's soldiers were just leaving through another door. The room was simply decorated with a few chairs and a large table at the center. Some of the queen's guards were always around her in addition to her attendants.

The moment Queen Rikaydian's eyes shifted to him, Migo dropped to a knee and bowed. This was his first time daring to approach her since returning from training with the Hunters.

"You have other news to report, Captain Rikaydian?" the queen said coolly.

Migo took a deep breath. "My queen. Regarding the prisoners that were taken, I desire, as royal inquisitor, to interrogate them. I believe they may be able to help find the whereabouts of a third culprit."

Queen Rikaydian rose from her seat and glided toward him. Her black dress was trimmed with gold, and tiny golden chains decorated her beautiful hair. Why did she have to look so flawless all the time? So perfect? She stopped in front of him. Even though she was a head shorter, she always seemed to tower over him.

Migo refused the urge to shrink away at her searching gaze. He was *not* a coward.

"You look tired, captain," the queen said softly. "Interrogation can be exhuasting work. I recommend you get some sleep, and then we can talk when you wake up."

Migo frowned and opened his mouth to suggest otherwise. Was she not going to give him a chance to redeem himself? Maybe she was extending a chance to him by showing compassion. Whatever the case, he knew he couldn't question her. Doing so now could be fatal. He nodded. "As you wish, my queen."

As Migo turned to leave, his worry built up even more. It wasn't like Queen Rikaydian to hold off on an interrogation. It must have meant she had something else in mind.

Chapter Eight

The Well

Katsi watched from the trees as Damani emerged from his low stone hut. She couldn't stifle her laugh as she watched him try to smooth down the hair that had matted up on the back of his head. He turned and gave her a flat stare as she went to greet him.

"Yeah, laugh it up," he said with a smile. "Just be glad I don't wait to see you right after you wake up."

"That's because you don't know where I sleep," she said, tapping him on the nose.

Damani shrugged and went to give her a hug, which she was hesitant to receive. She didn't want to draw any undue attention from the other farmers within view. Once his arms were around her though, she couldn't resist his embrace. She snuggled her face into his neck, his warm skin against her nose sending tingles down her spine.

One of the neighbors was watching from the hut several paces away. She was an ugly girl named Thera who always seemed to watch Damani too closely. Katsi withdrew from the hug and stared Thera down, hoping she'd turn away, but Thera only glared back at Katsi harder. As soon as Damani looked over at Thera, she smiled, waved her hand in greeting, and ran back inside.

"She might have it in for you, Damani," Katsi said, poking his rib.

Damani laughed. "I hope not, but you're probably right. Fortunately, there's only one crazy girl I care for, and it's not her."

Katsi's smile faltered as she was struck with a pang of guilt. "Damani, you should know that I might be gone for a few cycles."

"Why, what's wrong?"

"Nothing's wrong," Katsi said with a shrug.

Damani's eyes narrowed. "Where are you going?"

Would she lie to him? Maybe. But it was for his own good, right? Why make him worry unnecessarily. But she couldn't do it. "I need to go see the tribe about something," she said, her voice quiet.

Damani's expression drooped. "No, Katsi." He took a step closer, placing a hand on her shoulder. "I need you here. After my father passed away last year... it was hard. That was right when you showed up." He sighed. "I can't lose you."

Katsi chewed her lip. "I know, Damani. You won't lose me. I just need to figure something out, and then I'll be here for good."

He nodded. "Well, be careful. It's just... with the Rikaydians it's not safe to associate with the shamanfolk. For either of us."

Katsi rolled her eyes, too familiar with how Queen Rikaydian had already destroyed her family. "Don't worry, Damani. Everything will be just fine. I'll figure this out and be back in two or three cycles."

"I still have a bad feeling about it," he said with a shrug, "but I haven't been able to stop you from doing anything before."

"That's the spirit." She patted his cheek. "Also, I admit to being a little worried. How would you feel about leaving the farm for a few cycles and bunking in the city, just in case?"

"Uh, that seems a little extreme. I've got my crops to take care of."

"What if this became a battleground?"

"I can lock up inside my home." He shrugged. "Nothing's getting through those stormdoors."

She bit her lip. "And you try to tell me to be careful."

He smiled and shook his head, but said, "Just come back safe," in a serious tone.

"I will," Katsi said, taking a step away. "You be the safe one. I know you're defenseless without me." She said it jokingly, but she couldn't help but think of Manahae's warning to her about staying out of Jehubal. She gave Damani a final wave before turning and heading sunright toward Delirad Lake.

A sense of unease settled in her stomach. If the Bayvana Tribe was planning something against Jehubal, wouldn't that mean Damani was at risk? He lived directly between the tribe and the city.

She gritted her teeth and focused on the path ahead. Hidden in the branches, various lizards whistled at her as she entered the jungle. Overhead, thick white clouds rolled in from the Frozen Waste and then dissipated as they neared the Scorched Waste, as if they were too afraid to be touched by the heat.

As she walked, the moon continued to drift toward the Frozen Waste. All people tracked time by the passing of the moon, breaking one cycle down into ten marks, but Katsi had never felt bound to that sense of time. One cycle always drifted into another. She could never tell how often the moon had passed, and she scarcely ever saw a calendar.

Katsi walked well until the moon had drifted out of view. She'd since entered a forested area, where the trees had needled leaves. A trail ran near the center of the Ring, but Katsi avoided going near there. She didn't want to run into any shaman-hating merchant group like Nedro Wajek's trading company. They always suspected lone travelers. With coral bushes growing in clusters, the going was a little more difficult, but she stopped to take a break only when necessary. She'd have to keep walking at least one more cycle before she'd reach her destination.

A water well stood near the road, so Katsi shook her canteen, the little water remaining sloshing back and forth. She weaved her way through the trees until she saw the familiar storm-protected well at the side of the road.

Caution told her to wait a moment and check her surroundings before proceeding, so she hid behind a few thick, hanging vines. After several moments, however, the stillness of the forest revealed nothing. She got her canteen ready and sprinted to the well. The spigot squeaked as she pumped it. She held up her canteen as the water came out, her eyes glancing about.

A rustling in the woods drew her attention. She stopped instantly, closed her canteen, and slung it back over her shoulder. She took off at a run back into the sunward forest.

"Get her!" She heard the hurried command sharp and clear through the quiet woods.

A single man materialized in front of her, but he looked large and clumsy. She easily outmaneuvered him and kept running south and west. She'd have no trouble getting away if the rest of them were like him, but there was still the chance that the others could be riding rangola. If that were the case, then they'd have a shot at getting her.

Trees and leaves were a blur. After a while, she didn't hear any sound of pursuit, but she kept going at a jog until she was exhausted. Finally, she stopped at the Ring's wall near the Scorched Waste. Her cheeks flushed. She wiped the sweat from her face and drank deeply from her canteen.

Stupid ringdwellers. It took great effort for her not to resent all ringdwellers. It was only because of people like Damani that she didn't believe they were all monsters. Using absolutes was dangerous. Not all ringdwellers were the same, just like not all shamanfolk were the same.

Katsi walked across the stones. They would make it easy to cover her tracks.

She kept walking until she saw the moon rising. It meant Katsi had been awake for over a full cycle.

Hoping to create more distance, she kept walking for a while before looking for a place to sleep. Her nerves were still shaking at the encounter. She tried not to think the words, but they came anyway. *Nowhere is safe anymore.*

She found a small copse of rockberry bushes at the base of a large tree where she figured she could hide and get some rest. If a Maedari whipped up, it could possibly be a good enough spot to wait it out too. She got on her hands and knees and crawled beneath the bushes, shooing a scaled rabbit from the enclosure. Half of the ground was covered in softened rockmoss, which she settled down on. It was almost more comfortable than the mat in her hideout.

By the next cycle, she'd reach the Bayvana Tribe's base. She feared that a battle was coming. One that would kill innocent people like Damani and the other farmers who helped her survive. She could only hope that her fears were unfounded.

Chapter Nine

Training Ground

M igo had just enough energy to make sure his windows were all sealed shut before removing his uniform and flopping into bed with a groan. He'd closed the red curtains over his windows, shadowing the room in semi darkness. The queen's strange request to have him sleep was still unnerving, though he couldn't remember a time when he'd been more exhausted. His eyes burned, and his muscles ached with fatigue. With now seven cycles left to live, he hadn't really imagined spending any of that time sleeping.

There was another time, just a few years ago, when he'd felt almost as tired. The memory was fresh in his mind as he started drifting into sleep. He was in the training yard, practicing against some of the other soldiers. He couldn't have been more than twelve-years-old at the time, but his mother insisted that he train against adults. It was during one of his brief visits back home, away from the shaman hunting academy.

This was a particular day when Queen Rikaydian wanted to be present for her son's training.

"Continue the boy's instruction," the queen said. "I'd like to see how his learning is coming along. Perhaps he has developed some level of competency."

The sprig of hope her words had given him was equally revolting. No matter how well he performed, could she ever be pleased?

A soldier stepped up to Migo. He'd seen the man around, but never learned his name. Migo was tall for his age, and filled out by hardened practice, but the top of his head fell short of the other man's chin. "Ready your stave then, boy. We're demonstrating the stormwind fighting technique here. You've learned that?"

Migo nodded. "Of course." He gripped his stave at the center position in his right hand and held it before him. He would need to be able to alternate it between hands to keep the movements continuous.

As soon as Migo held up the weapon, the soldier attacked, his stave swinging in high. Migo barely had time to deflect the blow before another came in, lower this time, catching him on the shin. Migo held back a curse.

"There's a continuous motion," the soldier said. "Every stroke has a counterstroke. You must be ready for both sides of the stave."

Migo nodded again and held his stave out. The attack resumed. Migo countered the first attack and was prepared for the second. And the third, and the fourth. With the fifth strike, the soldier spun closer, whipping his stave in from the side, striking Migo's rib and knocking him to the ground. He let out a grunt of pain and rose back to his feet. His mother scoffed.

"Keep your legs wider apart. You need to be able to move when attacks come in at different angles."

Migo took the instruction with a clenched jaw. They practiced the stance several more times, though each instance ended with Migo getting struck by the stave, and the soldier offering more instruction. Queen Rikaydian's expression grew more bitter with every defeat. Migo's anger and frustration matched his mother's bitterness. He was a prince without pride. The shame of his continued failures was mounting.

He and the soldier practiced for a full cycle under the queen's eyes. She wouldn't let them stop. "Not until you strike him, Migo. Strike him, and you may eat. Strike him and you may drink and rest." She said this as she herself took a meal before them. Each word she spoke was like poison to his ears. It might have been the first experience where Migo had truly started to loathe his mother.

But she deserves to hate me. Migo remembered the thought with perfect clarity. It was the same thought he had whenever she spoke to him, a constant reminder of his greatest mistake. A mistake that he could never remediate, no matter how many shamanfolk he killed. It was his fault the shamans had been able to kill his father.

Migo's frustration mounted to the point where tears stung his eyes, his face twisted as he held back sobs. His body was in pain. They'd probably gone through the stance more than fifty times, each round ending with a stave striking Migo's body. His left leg was trembling with the strain. Still, his mother would not let them cease fighting. The soldier was exhausted as well—Migo could tell by his slowed movements—but he was still in better condition than Migo.

The soldier had long since ceased providing instruction. Migo knew that under the watchful eye of Queen Rikaydian, the soldier wouldn't let up or go easy on him. Migo had grown to hate this soldier as well, since he'd become an example of Migo's own failure.

Migo held out his stave. The soldier attacked. Their staves struck again and again. Migo discovered a rhythm to the technique. He'd come to understand the concept of constant motion and that every stroke had a counterstroke waiting to happen. He could anticipate the moves as they came, even the twists and alterations the soldier applied. Migo was exhausted, yes, but his anger and shame brought with them a keen awareness.

So when the soldier's movements faltered, Migo noticed instantly, his own stave moving in ahead of the soldier's. The soldier attempted to restore his assault, but it was too late, and Migo was already ahead of the swing. He almost couldn't believe it when his stave struck the soldier on the knee. The blow was exhilarating, and he followed it through with another, striking the soldier in the face with no reservation. His own face twisted with the pain of his shame and anger, tears gushing from his eyes as he struck again at the soldier's ribs. The soldier collapsed in an exhausted heap, holding his arms up in a weak defense as Migo hit him again and again.

Migo was thrown to his back as other soldiers stepped in, shouting at him to cease. His mother stood, shook her head, and walked away without looking at him.

Migo's rage burned within him. He'd found no relief in defeating the soldier. His shame could never be alleviated. He released a shout that tore at his throat as his mother faded away. The memory ended abruptly as Migo shot up from his bed, his shout echoing off the walls of his room. He held his glaive in a white-knuckle grip. Tears stung at his cheeks as he blinked around his room, loosening his grip on his weapon. He let out a sound that was half sob, half cough, tossed his glaive to the ground, and buried his face in his pillow.

Chapter Ten

Cataban Soldiers

Katsi awoke to gibberings as a flock of scaila glided overhead. Scales watched them from the ground, his own webbing still developing. The small reptiles rode a hot air current that carried them north, toward Jehubal. Their seemingly frantic passing put Katsi on edge. She scooped her little friend up and placed him back in her pocket.

She drew her knife and scanned the area. Beneath a nearby coral bush, a scaled rabbit trembled as it looked from side to side, even more frightened about the scaila's passing than Katsi was.

A sudden movement caught Katsi's attention. She could barely see something at the edge of the trees, no sound betraying its passage. It disappeared for a moment, only to reappear no more than ten strides away from her as something large prowling low to the ground. She caught a glimpse at the face of a wild rangola.

Katsi dropped to her knees beneath her cover of rockberry bushes and started rubbing handfuls of sand and dirt across her skin. Would it really be enough to cover her scent? The sound of a deep sniffing followed by a growl caused Katsi to freeze in place. She leapt away, drawing her knife at the same time. The rangola landed behind her with a thud. She spun around as its claws dug up a clump of moss.

It snarled, lips drawn back to reveal teeth longer than Katsi's fingers. Adrenaline pounded through her body. She swung her knife in front of the creature in warning. Would she even be able to pierce its scales? Probably not. She was sure she was about to die. Would she then rejoin her father and mother to dance among storm and sky as all dead shamanfolk?

Tears blurred her vision. Katsi growled and took a bold step forward, jabbing the knife. The rangola easily backed away, then lowered its head and front legs, preparing to pounce. A flush of energy surged through Katsi's body as she prepared for the attack.

But it never came.

Bits of sand and dirt rushed through the air around her in a strong wind. The rangola cast its head from side to side. The earthen sediments bounced off its armored body harmlessly, but still the rangola let out a moan as it searched around itself, eyes no longer focused on Katsi.

Katsi growled again and swiped at the rangola, cutting at the underside of its ear. The beast snarled and slashed at her with a massive paw, but she stepped back, dodging the attack. The wind and sand whipped about more fiercely, and Katsi wondered if a Maedari was about to pick up.

The rangola may have thought the same thing. It took a step back, bounded over the protection of rockberry bushes, and disappeared into the north.

Katsi's heart pounded as she collapsed to the ground, back against the tree. The knife fell from her hands and bits of sand and dirt collected on her hair and clothes. If a Maedari was coming, her best option at this point was to stay put. But the wind was already dying down to no more than a light breeze.

What just happened? She knew she should have died just now, but something had saved her. A cut in the ear hardly seemed a reason for the rangola to run away. She could only assume that it had suspected a storm was coming. Maybe the answer was simpler. Maybe magic had saved her.

Whatever the cause, Katsi heaved a sigh of relief and crawled out of her hiding place, continuing on to the tribe's ancient base. Birds chirped in the trees, the sky shone blue, and the scent of fresh fruit hung sweet in the air. The tension in her body leaked out. At least for the moment, she let herself feel that danger was behind her. She brushed the sand off her clothes and hair, though she knew it was futile without a proper bath. Living in isolation hadn't instilled in her a great care for cleanliness or appearance unless Damani was involved.

Now, however, she worried about how she might appear to the Bayvana Tribe. After all, she was going to them for help, and she didn't want to seem like she was completely wild.

The walls in this part of the Ring that separated it from the Scorched Waste were in disrepair. Several sections crumbled with age. The nearest cities were either Jehubal or Cataban, and the latter was on the other side of Delirad Lake. For Jehubal, good stone was in short supply, and Cataban didn't seem to care too much about what lay beyond the reaches of its own city. That made this side of the Delirad Lake a great place for the Bayvana Tribe to hide. Plus, the gulbas melons that grew nearby made it easier for them to survive.

Just thinking about the melons made Katsi's mouth water. She dodged around some heavy foliage and saw the caps of the Cataban Mountains come into view further south across the Ring. They were barely visible at this distance. She'd never crossed the lake to get a better view.

A sigh of relief escaped her lips as she realized she was still on track. At the base of those mountains was the city of Cataban. Between her and the mountains stretched Delirad Lake, which spanned the Ring from wall to wall. The Ring was much wider here, reaching something like 30 miles. Caravans had to cross on the frostward section where the frozen water had made it easy to build a bridge. That or take one of the massive barges.

History spoke of water that would run down from the Cataban Mountains into an ancient canyon where Delirad Lake now rested, but the water would simply drain out into the Scorched Waste where it lived a short life by boiling out and evaporating into the air. An old shamanic tribe was the first to settle in the area, and they used their magic to get a bridge across the canyon, and then used even more enchantments to dam the water, forming the lake. Other Ringdwellers, those without shamanic ancestry, had stumbled upon the place, slaughtered the shamanfolk that lived there, and claimed the land for their own. The Ringdwellers had no record of this, of course, and merely claimed that the citizens of Cataban City had been the ones to build the dam.

Whatever the case, Katsi didn't care. What was in the past was history, and what mattered now was what was, and what would be. The Bayvana Tribe, however, would not forget, as they claimed to be the descendants of the ancient tribe that had first settled here. It was part of why they stuck around, warring with Jehubal and Cataban alike.

War. Katsi's upper lip curled with the thought. Thoughts like these reminded her why she couldn't be with the Bayvana Tribe—why her family had left them years ago.

Katsi scanned the area instinctively. From the small rise on which she stood, she got a good look at the surrounding scenery. About a mile away was a massive stone dam on the sunward side of the Ring. It cast a long shadow across the lake. At face value, the structure's geometric shapes made it unclear whether it was natural or manmade, but after so many years, perhaps it was a little of both. On the other side of the structure, a large chasm led deep into the Scorched Waste like a scar across its sandy skin.

Katsi had once stood atop the dam and stared out into the Scorched Waste beside her parents.

"Some say that this gorge leads all the way to the other side of the Ring," her father said.

"What's over there?" Katsi asked with a bounce.

Her father chuckled. "More people like us, I suppose."

"And what's over there?" Katsi asked, spinning around and pointing to the other side of the lake, the part that disappeared into the Frozen Waste.

She remembered the frown that crossed her father's face. "Just cold and darkness, little one—certainly no people could live where the light of the sun doesn't reach."

Her father had been wrong, but it was years after he was dead before Katsi found out.

The memory faded as Katsi made her way down towards a tangle of yellow-green vines sprawled across the ground. The same vegetation covered many of the shorter bushes. From the vines grew small bulbs of gulbas melons. She just wanted to eat one before crossing into the Scorched Waste to find the Bayvana Tribe.

After a bit of searching, she located a melon that looked underripe, but would still do the job. She dug her knife through the top where it had been connected to the vine, scraping away until she got to the inside and punctured the seal. Once through, she tipped the melon over her lips and slurped at the gooey insides. It still had a bit of a salty taste to it, but it was sweet nonetheless.

"What are you doing here? This is the king's property."

Katsi dropped the melon, nearly choking on the contents. She held her knife before her as she regarded the two men who approached her. One was armed with a pike, the other held a short sword.

"Eating a melon. What are you doing here?" Katsi countered, taking a few steps back.

The man with the short sword spoke. His head was shaved, and a dark shadow revealed his receding hairline. He laughed at first. "We must secure our land from foreigners and Outlanders. No citizen of Cataban ever goes hungry or has need to steal the king's melons, so we must assume that you fall into the former category."

Katsi hated the way the man spoke to her. There was a tone that insinuated that he thought she was an idiot. She glanced back the way she had come, prepared to make an escape, but to her surprise, she saw two other armed men walking in to close the gap. There was even a soldier blocking her path towards the wall and the Scorched Waste. "That doesn't answer what you are *doing*," she said, using the same condescending tone that he had.

The man stopped, folded his arms, and smiled. "It must be determined whether you are to be put to death or thrown in prison, so naturally," he paused and waved his hand, the four soldiers rushing in on her, "we'll be taking you into custody."

Katsi dashed towards the Scorched Waste. It was her best hope. The nearest soldier hurled his pike at her, the weapon stabbing into the ground in front of her. She jumped over the weapon, but someone caught her by the ankle. Katsi fell sharply, her arm smashing against a rock. She spun to her backside and prepared to swipe at the man's arm with her knife. The haft of a pike smacked her wrist, jarring the weapon from her grasp.

Katsi gasped from the pain. Her chest tightened, filling with dread as she looked at the men around her. Would they torture her? Put her to death like her parents? She'd *never* been caught, and the possibilities burned through her mind like nightmares.

"There'll be no more need to fight, girl," the bald man said. All four soldiers surrounded her as she slowly rose to her feet. "Justice will be your fate now."

Chapter Eleven

Execution

Migo's hands were sweating as he made his way through the hallways of Rikaydian Palace. Queen Rikaydian requested his presence in the throne room. It had been seven years since he'd been in there. He prepared himself to get scolded by the queen for being lazy. How dare he sleep when there were shamans on the planet? At the very least, he hoped she'd just give him permission to interrogate the prisoners.

Soldiers saluted as he passed. He nodded back, keeping his face as stoic as possible. Even within the protection of the palace's thick walls, he could still hear the subtle sounds of thunder.

The halls of Rikaydian Palace were not decorated with the same elaborate decadence found in Wajek Manor. Still, the walls regularly displayed banners of the Rikaydian family symbol depicting the profile of a black rangola on a red-and-beige-striped back. The rangola was a symbol of power, pride, and cunning. His mother always tormented him for having none of those attributes. At the heart of it, Migo had to wonder if the queen even considered him family anymore. He fought back the lump in his throat.

A couple guards stood to either side of the throne room doors. As members of the royal guard, they wore different attire than Migo or the soldiers in the army. Instead of brass helmets, theirs were cool blue iron, and their shoulders, arms, and shins were plated with the same metal, and blue tufts at the shoulders were the most prominent feature.

The guards nodded, and together they turned and opened the doors. Migo walked in alone as the doors shut behind him. A finely woven carpet led up to a dais, upon which there had once been three great chairs, but since his father's death and the ascension of Queen Rikaydian, there was now only one. To either side of the carpet, pillars rose to the three-story ceiling. The throne itself was of fine polished wood, inlaid with brass, and cushioned with rich, red fabric, but it was currently empty.

Several others had gathered in the room, including Hatan, who gave him a short nod and a smile. The other attendants gave Migo nothing more than a dismissive glance. Queen Rikaydian's venom towards him had spread to everyone else who witnessed her treatment. Only Hatan seemed to be immune to her toxic hatred. Migo went to stand beside his cousin.

Hatan squeezed Migo's shoulder. "Good to see you, captain. I hear congratulations are in order for Captain Tarahan's capture." He gave a smile that failed to reach his eyes.

Migo only nodded acknowledgement then whispered, "Is that what this is about?"

"We will see." Hatan looked towards the back of the room.

From the door behind the throne came Queen Rikaydian. Her dark hair was pulled back from the front while the sides were left straight down. She wore a black robe embroidered with red. She came around the throne and sat down, clasping her hands in front of her. She didn't look at anybody when she asked. "Is Captain Tarahan in attendance?"

Tarahan stepped out from the crowd, barely suppressing his stupid grin. "I am here, my queen."

Her dark eyes shifted to him. "As some of you may have heard, we must congratulate Captain Tarahan, who has apprehended the shamanfolk responsible for murdering two of our citizens." She paused and offered a smile while the other attendants shouted their congratulations.

"At the conclusion of the current Maedari, we will be celebrating with the execution of these two demons. Captain Rikaydian will be tasked with carrying out the execution by beheading."

Migo stepped forward. "My queen, we haven't yet had—."

Queen Rikaydian silenced him with a raised hand. He could see the fire burning in her eyes. "Silence, captain. Retrieve the prisoners and be prepared to meet us in the main courtyard when the Maedari has concluded."

Migo dropped his eyes as his cheeks burned. He could feel the others looking at him, sneering at the way his mother belittled him. "I will do as you command."

She dismissed him with a wave of her hand, and Migo turned to exit the throne room. Hatan followed. They said nothing to each other until they were halfway to the prison. If it was Tarahan who arrested them, why not have him perform the execution? What was the point of making Migo do it?

"What are your thoughts?" Hatan asked.

"There was no interrogation even though I'd requested it. We don't even know if they were directly connected to the murder. If we just jump to the execution, then we will miss the opportunity to try and glean some information from them."

Hatan cleared his throat. "She did have them questioned shortly after they were placed in their cells. Or at least, they were beaten and yelled at." He paused to shake his head. "I don't know what information she was able to acquire, but apparently it was enough for the queen to order their execution."

Migo ground his teeth. "Why was I not informed?"

"I don't know. Perhaps she wanted you to get some sleep. She knew you'd been up for a few cycles."

Migo gulped. "Who did the questioning?"

"A soldier from the queen's guard as well as Tarahan's soldier who'd originally found the idol in the home. I doubt they were as thorough as you would have been."

"What was the consensus?"

"Guilty. There was no reason for them to have the idol. They are either shamanfolk themselves or sympathizers."

"No confession or anything?"

Hatan frowned and gave Migo a sad look. "You know how the queen operates. If she sets her mind to it, her word is law. She has already spoken on the matter. All we can do is agree." He lowered his voice. "Even if we might think otherwise."

Migo could only hope that assigning him as executioner was a small sign of favor. He bit his tongue, tasting the bitterness. It was more than likely a message. Perhaps that he was next. He wondered if his mother's lust for vengeance had skewed her rationalization. *Could the same be true of myself?* His stomach sank with the thought, and he forced it away immediately. They descended a long flight of stairs that took them to the palace dungeon.

Here, beneath layers of earth and stone, the air was cool. The palace dungeon connected to a natural cavern, part of it extending out beneath the Scorched Waste. Many generations ago, the Rikaydian family had eradicated a tribe of shamans that dwelt within the cavern. As a reminder of their victory and power, they'd built the palace on the same location.

A guard let them pass, unlocking and opening a door. Hatan led the way from there. They passed a pool of water to one side, a glowing blue stone above it. After Maedaris, water would seep through the ground and collect in the pool. Having been filtered through the layers of earth, it was a remarkably clean water source—one of the main reasons the ancient shamans had chosen this as a place to live. Clean water was hard to come by.

They proceeded through the cavern. There were only a few cells down here. Keeping prisoners for more than a few days wasn't customary. The Rikaydian family always sought justice as soon as possible. Besides, if people were left isolated in the dark too long, they were prone to madness.

Voices echoed from the caverns ahead. The smell of earth and ancient stone was heavy in the air. The walls also became rounder since this part of the dungeon held more of its natural shape. The voices quieted as Hatan and Migo approached.

Hatan unlocked the door to the cell, the sound of tinkling metal reverberating off the walls.

Migo held his weapon in front of him, prepared for any rash movement the prisoners might make.

"Is this it, then?" Bindom's voice asked from the darkness behind the iron bars.

"Come on out," Migo said without answering the question. Coldness seeped across his nerves as he shifted into his role as executioner.

Shali couldn't suppress a whimper as the two of them emerged from the deepest end of the cell. "Please, lord," Bindom said, his voice shaking. "You must know that we are innocent. We've never killed anybody. You must believe us." Bindom's face was covered in bruises. There were even two long cuts across his cheek that reminded Migo of his mother's nails.

"Your verdict has been decided," Migo said. Despite his earlier thoughts, he could feel his own rage burning its way to the surface. Shamans were the reason Migo lived in pain every day. They were the reason his mother had changed. He grabbed the chain that bound Bindom's wrists and dragged him forward. Still, he avoided looking either of them in the eyes. "Both of you are to be executed for murder and treason."

Hatan led the way back, and Migo took the rear, keeping the prisoners between them. Shali wept openly.

Migo steeled himself. He knew he shouldn't say anything, but he couldn't resist. "Why weep? You should have known the consequences of your actions."

"These are the tears of the innocent who has been misjudged!" Her words were spoken with venom, but Migo found them paltry in comparison to his mother's.

"Lying won't do you any good at this point."

When she tried to deny her lying, Migo jabbed her in the back with the butt of his glaive. But did he really believe they were guilty? His insides twisted with confused thoughts. *This is simple. Perform your duty like the queen assigned. Show her you can do as you're told.* But her sobs still tortured him. The pain in his gut grew sharper.

Bindom cast sorrowful eyes back at Migo as they ascended the stairs. "If only they were lies, Lord Rikaydian. My wife speaks the truth. I understand the implications of the evidence, but certainly that does not always indicate the truth. We don't know where the idol came from, but somebody must want us—."

"Enough!" Migo spat the words. They were trying to manipulate him.

"If we were shamans, could we not break our bonds or call down a storm?"

"I said enough!" Migo shoved them both to their knees.

Hatan turned and dragged them both back up with a gentle hand. "There's nothing to be done now. Judgment has been made."

"But what else am I to do when the judgment is wrong?" Bindom said, his voice shaking and tears dripping shamelessly down his cheeks.

Hatan glanced at Migo just briefly. He wore a face that Migo recognized as a forced expressionlessness. "There can be no falsehood in Queen Rikaydian's decision. If she says you are to die, then it must be so. There is no alternative."

Dread filled Migo's chest. What did that mean for her decision regarding him? There was no alternative for Migo's own fate?

Bindom hung his head in resignation. He held hands with his wife in silence as they were led out into the courtyard. The gates were opened and several citizens entered the open space, eager to catch a glimpse of fresh shaman blood. Low-hanging clouds over the Frozen Waste were glowing with a tinge of orange-red light from the burning sun. The courtyard itself was as beautiful as ever, the rounded plots of vegetation were in full bloom—plants were usually eager to unfold themselves after a Maedari's passing.

They approached an open section of the courtyard, set off by a swirling pattern in the stone pavements. There was a single, rectangular slab of stone that protruded from the ground to about knee-height. Here, the four of them stopped.

Another set of doors opened and everyone turned their attention. Out strode two guards followed by Queen Rikaydian herself, her black hair decorated with silver adornments. She stopped and nodded to Hatan.

Queen Rikaydian addressed the crowd. "Citizens of Jehubal. You see before you two people guilty of shamanry and the murder of their own neighbors. It has long been understood in our city that shamanic involvement within our borders is intolerable. There is no place for their terrible organization. There is no place for their murders. We will not live in fear of their Maedari. All who belong to shamanic descent are to be eradicated from among us, and any others who sympathize with them will suffer a similar fate.

"Let this be a lesson to shamans. We will not be intimidated by their evil magic. No dark storm can destroy us. We are stronger than them, we always have been, and we always will be." She shifted her eyes to Migo. "Captain, dispatch them."

Migo nodded. His heart pumped rapidly as he grabbed Shali and led her to the block. Her tears had ceased, and now she only stared at Queen Rikaydian with a cold rage. In a strange way, he felt similar to her—a prisoner, hated by the queen. *Soon it will be my neck stretched across the block.* More likely a knife in the back. He shuddered at the notion.

A tightness crescendoed in his chest. If he didn't perform the execution, somebody else would. He could not save them. And if he refused, the queen would only kill him sooner for insubordination.

He forced Shali to her knees and placed her head just across the edge of the block. He lifted his glaive, axe-shaped blade held to the back of her neck. In one swift motion, he lifted the weapon and brought it down with immense force, severing the head with a thud. As blood spattered on Migo's hand, he closed his eyes and turned away, trying to ignore the screams of excitement from the crowd.

A sob escaped Bindom's throat, but the crowd continued shouting in rage, already eager to see Bindom slain next. Migo was struck by the image. Anger had come to define them. He knew that he too was filled with that same anger. *Perhaps we can never have joy until the shamans are all dead,* he thought, grabbing Bindom by the shoulder. He hated the queen for making him do this.

"I'm a dead man," Bindom said, just quietly enough for Migo to hear, "so it's too late for me."

Migo ignored the words and set Bindom down against the block. The smell of Shali's blood stung Migo's nose. He resisted the urge to immediately find something to wipe off his hands.

Bindom cast his eyes across the crowd. "The true killers are still out there."

Migo didn't dare say a word, but he felt the same. He raised his weapon, ready to strike, but in that moment, he saw the look in Bindom's eyes. It was a sad look...the look of the innocent. Still, Migo knew what would happen. If he didn't do it, somebody else would kill Bindom. Then Migo would be next. Their blood was on the queen's hands. He'd find the girl, even if it was the last thing he did.

Migo hesitated for only a moment as his heart fluttered, then brought his weapon down, severing Bindom's head.

Chapter Twelve

Rust

Katsi scraped her legs as the guard dragged her to their settlement. The smell of smoke stung her nose. It had been a year since Katsi had been to the lake, and apparently King Gendin of the Cataban estate had since claimed the land.

The base consisted of three low buildings, one old, and two new. The old one was built right against the shore. It was where boats would be dragged in to hide from the Maedaris. There were a dozen guards scattered about, each armed with a glaive and armored with iron breastplates and helmets. King Gendin didn't seem to be sparing any expense for his new expansion.

Katsi tested the strength of her restraints, which were flawless metal braces that clipped over her wrists and were locked in place by a key. They held firm and fit tight against her skin. It didn't seem likely that she'd be able to slip free. Her skin was hot with frustration.

They led her to the center of their base and connected her restraints to a chain held in place by a metal pole. The other guards laughed as they saw her dragged past them, some of them eyeing her too closely. It made her squirm inside.

"Caught eating the king's melons," the bald man announced to the others. They laughed more. She ground her teeth at the course sound. They'd already stripped her of her possessions, which they set on the ground in front of her, just out of reach as if to taunt her. Their rough touch as they tore her items from her was still haunting. The drawing of the rune was included among the things taken, but fortunately they hadn't noticed the artifact strapped to her upper arm and hidden beneath the sleeve of her robe.

The bald man sat on a boulder near her, a casual smile curving his lips. He stared at her a moment longer, his creepy smile making Katsi even more uncomfortable. He rifled through her belongings, taking his time as he unrolled her drawing and looked at the rune. Katsi hoped he wouldn't recognize it as shamanic in origin. He tossed the drawing back to the ground.

"All right then, girl. What's the story?" he said. "You seem quite young to be wandering the Ring by yourself, and from the looks of it, you've been out there for a few cycles."

Katsi had already been formulating a story, but she'd have to play the part as well. She stood as tall as she could and turned up her nose. "I was with a caravan heading south from Jehubal. We'd just stopped at a well after our first cycle on the road when we were attacked by bandits." As she spoke, one of the soldiers started writing on a piece of parchment.

The bald man turned up his eyebrow. "Bandits? Between here and Jehubal—are you sure? Isn't it likely to have been shamans, if anything?"

Katsi gave him a nasty look. "They were bandits. Looked just like you or me, and they didn't dress strangely or anything, and they didn't use any magic. So, yes, bandits." She was playing off a common impression of shamanfolk, that they wore strange clothes and had sun-bleached hair. They did, sometimes, but so did a lot of Ringdwellers.

The bald man said nothing, but folded his arms and regarded her with a slight nod to encourage her to continue.

"There were only a handful of them, but our caravan was smaller than the kind Wajek usually sends out, so we were still outnumbered." Katsi paused to curl her lips just slightly in disgust. "A couple of the guards were killed instantly—run through by javelins." Katsi stole the bit about the javelins from an incident she'd heard about a couple years ago, hoping that this band of soldiers had heard the same thing.

The man had no reaction, waiting for her to continue with an expression of veiled boredom.

Katsi went on. "The guards fought to keep the bandits away from the caravan, but a couple of them got through to me—I was on the caravan, you see—but they didn't seem intent on killing me like they did the guards. I was able to run off through the jungle and hide beneath some rockberry bushes. By that time, I had no idea how long I'd been running, but I was well separated from the rest of my group." She changed her expression, tilting her head down and frowning just a bit. "I don't know if any of my companions survived, but I suppose they may have turned back to Jehubal by now."

"There hasn't been a caravan through here for a few cycles," the bald man said, "but go ahead and continue. What happened after you were separated?"

Katsi shrugged. "Not much. I continued south, hiding along the wall beside the Scorched Waste instead of the road. I didn't want to have another run-in with bandits. I must have been walking for two cycles before I came to the lake and saw those melons—I'm sure you could imagine my relief."

"Indeed." The bald man chewed his cheek in thought. "Why continue south? Why not return to Jehubal?"

Katsi shook her head. "I have the payload. I need to reach Cataban." She tried to say it in a way that suggested his question was ludicrous.

"You have the payload?" the bald man kicked at her belongings, his eyebrow raised in skepticism.

"Yes, the drawing," Katsi said. She could feel her heartbeat quickening. "Wajek Manor was attacked recently by the shamans, and they stole something from him."

A few of the men laughed, and one of them said, "I heard about that."

"Nedro Wajek didn't give me all the details, but he said that the rune had something to do with the object that was stolen," Katsi explained. The story seemed like a stretch, but she was hoping it would get her out of their clutches. "He wanted us to travel to Cataban to see if we could learn more about it, and then onward further south if we needed to. Even the Rikaydian family sanctioned the initiative since it might help to understand something about the shamanfolk."

The bald man chewed his cheek for a moment before asking, "Why would Nedro Wajek trust you with the goods?"

Katsi turned her nose up at him again. "Well, I'm the only one who made it this far, aren't I? Seems like I was his best choice." It was the easy answer, since the caravan did not exist. She could tell by the bald man's frown, and the tilt of his head that he didn't buy her answer, so she hurried to say more. "Though quite simply, I am just the most well-learned of Wajek's followers regarding shamans. Shamanic studies aren't a primary focus for the merchant lord, so even if my knowledge is limited, it's still prime pickings given his options." Katsi had said too much. She was making her story more elaborate than it needed to be, so she stopped there and turned her head away.

"Why did you try to run from us when we caught you eating a melon?"

Katsi shrugged. "I had just recently been attacked and wasn't too fond of trusting the first band of men I came across. I am unfamiliar with the garb of Cataban soldiers. You could just as likely have been bandits yourselves."

One man came and whispered something in the bald man's ear. The bald man spoke to the other soldiers when he said, "She can tell a good story." Many of them chuckled.

Katsi felt a sting of worry. Perhaps she had missed something. They suspected she was lying. She looked around and saw the Cataban banner still hanging from the dock building. Despite what she'd said, she was familiar with the Cataban military uniforms, and theirs checked out. Maybe there'd been a hole in her story, but she couldn't remember all that she'd said.

It was only when she took a closer look at each of the soldiers that her error became clear. The man who'd whispered into the bald man's ear—she'd seen him at the well. He was the man who'd tried to block off her retreat. Her heart sank.

"You want to know what I think?" the bald man started. "I think you're a shaman, and you've been running away, hiding, causing mischief. I bet we could take you back to Jehubal and get rewarded for turning you over to the Rikaydians." He smiled.

"You are welcome to escort me back though you certainly won't receive whatever reward you're anticipating. I'm not a shaman." It stung to say the words, but what did it matter?

The bald man gave her a toothy grin. "I guess we might both be in for a surprise, then, won't we, shaman?" He threw a rock at her, as did several of the other soldiers.

The stones bit at her skin as the soldiers held back none of their strength. Katsi screamed with pain, trying to dodge as well as she could, but the onslaught continued for well over a minute. Even through her stormwading armor, the direct hits were sharp, especially on her uncovered hands and a rock that hit her in the ear. She was huddled in a heap when the bald man came and lifted her face in his hands.

"How does it feel, shaman, to be caught in a storm?"

Katsi tried to pull away, but he held her head firm and spit in her face before he rose back to his feet. Tears burned hot in Katsi's eyes, though she tried to force them away. Her body trembled with pain.

"Get the cart ready. I'll need half of you prepared to come with me to Jehubal by the time the moon sets."

There was a flurry of action as the soldiers went about fulfilling their orders. Katsi wiped her face and curled up on the ground, her body trembling. Tears of rage and pain stung her eyes as she thought about how she'd never been so mistreated. They had no justification. Anger burned within her. She wanted to hurt them all—break their noses, chop off their fingers, anything. Her parents would be ashamed of her.

She *had* to get away. One man sneered at her as she glanced up at them, but he returned to his work setting up a reinforced barrier around their stormcart, made mostly of brasswood with occasional ironwork. She looked for the moon and found it high in the sky. Her things were still left in a pile in front of her.

There had to be a way to escape. If she could just get beyond their reach somehow, she knew she could run to safety. Though her body was now bruised, she was in good shape, so she had confidence that she could run faster than any of these soldiers, especially since they would be bogged down by their uniforms and weapons. All of them were busy setting about their tasks, and the bald man had disappeared into one of the buildings. If only she could break her restraints.

Katsi clenched her teeth as she tried to pull her hands free, but the metal held firm and pulled tightly at her skin. There had to be some kind of weakness in the contraption. She scanned its entire surface. *There must be a weakness.* As she continued to search, her heartbeat quickened, and she noticed small spots of rust across the surface and deep inside. Strange... it seemed flawless just a moment ago.

With renewed vigor, Katsi fought to free her hands again. She couldn't be sure, but the rusted area of the metal seemed much larger than before. The rusty metal burned at her skin as she continued to struggle. She let out a gasp of relief as the metal bent just slightly enough that she knew her right hand could pull free. She double-checked what the soldiers were doing as she kept working on the left hand, leaving her right hand in so as not to alert them. Aside from the occasional glance, it seemed like the soldiers were all avoiding looking at her, as if her shamanic blood might curse them for it. All the better. Whatever superstitions they had were just fine as long as it worked in her favor.

With a painful jerk, she loosened the restraints enough that she was sure she could pull free. She waited for an opportune moment to run for it, but she was afraid to wait too long. As soon as she felt everyone's eyes were off her, she pulled her hands free. She snatched up her canteen, knife, and the drawing, and ran sunward. Making it to the Scorched Waste was her best chance of escape.

The second she started running, the bald man came charging out of the building and bellowed, "After her!" Something clunked off a rock behind her, and a thrown javelin flew just over her shoulder.

Katsi sprinted with all her might, legs burning with vigor. She was vaguely aware that the wind was picking up, the kind of wind that whipped back and forth in every direction. She reached the west end of the Ring near the edge of the lake and started scrambling her way up the stone embankment that stood between her and the Scorched Waste.

At the top, the cliff's edge greeted her. The bald man was at her heels. She kicked at his face, but the bald man caught her by the ankle and twisted her leg so that she fell down. The winds were getting stronger, and she heard the distant rumble of thunder coming from the Frozen Waste.

"A Maedari is coming. What are you doing?" she screamed at the man. She wrested her leg free and crawled towards the Scorched Waste.

"There's just enough time to strap you to a tree, demon!"

The venom in his tone struck Katsi with horror. She readied to jump to the ledge of the cliff in the Scorched Waste when the bald man leapt at her. His hand caught her by the upper arm, but a strong wind hit them just hard enough to tip them over the edge of the wall. They fell, and not towards the ledge that Katsi was aiming for, but into the canyon.

Chapter Thirteen

First Encounter: Nine Years Ago

Migo stifled a giggle as he crouched, hidden behind the archway. Voices echoed from further down the hallway as a small party approached. He clutched a brasswood branch in his hand, brought to him by Hatan from the northern jungle. His father had explained that it was a wonderful gift. Brasswood branches rarely separated from their mother tree, but their wood made some of the strongest glaives and stormcarts. Migo found it most useful for play-fighting his friend Yavasu. Sometimes, even his father would play sticks with him when he had a moment.

The sound of footprints scuffing across the beige carpet drew closer. Migo sweated with the anticipation. He'd been waiting there for at least a full mark, using every last bit of patience he could muster.

The voices became distinct, and he could pick out that of Father's. "...still don't think it's plausible cause. We've been trading with them and living beside them just fine for years."

"But the murders continue. You can't deny the evidence points to dark magic," another voice said.

His father sighed. "Yes, I don't deny that, but if we found a Cataban knife in someone's chest, does that mean that every Cataban citizen is responsible? We must consider this logically."

"We try to consider everything. And we all agree that this dark magic is too dangerous to allow. We must trust in the emperor's mandate; the only way to ensure complete safety is by eradic—"

Migo jumped out at that moment, holding his stick high and shouting as loud as his little lungs could manage.

The man walking beside Father stumbled back with fright, lifting a hand to shield his face. His father's dark eyes glinted in delight as he laughed and charged at Migo with his own roar, scooping him up onto his shoulder. Migo dropped his stick and flailed, trying to wrest himself from Father's grip as he was spun around and then laid flat on his back against the floor.

A grunt from the other man drew Father's attention. He released Migo and rose to his feet, straightening the sleeves of his red robe. From what his father told him, he'd deliberately worn his robe to the meeting instead of his uniform as a "subtle way of opposing the war."

Father cleared his throat. "It's not polite to frighten our visitors, Migo." He smoothed down some of his black hair.

"Not frightened, just a little surprised," the man said, frowning at the offense. The man was big. Almost as big as Father.

"Apologize, take your stick, and go back into the lounge room with your mother."

"Sorry, sir. Won't happen again," Migo said in his sincerest voice, then he scrambled to his feet, snatched up his stick, and ran off to the lounge room, unable to contain his laughter after he'd gained enough distance. The look on that man's face had been priceless, eyes wide, lips curving back as they'd shaken with terror.

Migo was still smiling when he entered the lounge room.

"Slippers off," Mother snapped. She hadn't even looked at him as he'd entered the room. Perhaps *she* had shaman powers. He removed his slippers, bare feet squishing into the lush carpet. The walls of the room were draped with red and gold tapestries. Couches and cushions abounded except for one side of the room where a fireplace burned. On the same wall, a few feet higher, several storm windows let in some light.

Mother and cousin Hatan were playing a game of Ganaueh on a wooden board set across the table. Migo hated when they played it because they wouldn't ever explain it to him.

Hatan rose from his seat. As an officer in the guard, he was wearing his uniform. He gave Migo a wide smile. "What are you smirking about, little cousin?" He picked up his glaive and walked towards Migo with a knowing look in his eyes.

"Something funny, of course," Migo said.

Hatan only shook his head. "I'll leave you two. I've got to head another round through the market."

"Stay," Mother said. "We didn't even get to finish."

"You were going to win anyway, my queen. As always." He gave Mother a bow and ruffled Migo's hair as he passed him to leave the room.

Mother held out a hand. Migo shuffled over, his feet sliding over the too-plush carpet. She spoke after he touched her hand. "I assume your father is on his way back. I'm sure you were trying to spy on him the whole time." She smiled at Migo, revealing a set of brilliant white teeth. He knew his mother was the most beautiful woman in the world. Father said so all the time. Her sleek, black hair was decorated with white, metal rings and yellow tassels. It looked nice, but sometimes it took her over a mark just to get her hair done.

"He should just let me in. It'd be a lot easier that way."

"When you're older, little prince. Everything has its time."

The door opened again, and in came Father, carrying a mug of something else Migo wasn't old enough for. His shoulders sagged, and he wore a frown on his face. Migo wasn't accustomed to seeing Father like that, and he instantly worried that maybe he'd done something wrong by frightening the visitor.

"Kidem?" Mother rose to her feet. "What's wrong?"

"I'm fine, Tilayna. Don't stand on my account." His features softened and he straightened. He took a sip from his mug, frowned, then placed it on a side table and went to sit beside Mother. A sigh leaked from his chest as he sank into the cushions.

Mother's eyes narrowed as she settled next to him. "What was it this time? There's not enough evidence?"

Father rubbed his forehead with three fingers. "I just finished arguing with them, Tilayna, I don't want to argue with you as well. Let us relax for a moment. We're a people at peace."

Migo fidgeted nervously. He stared at the Ganaueh board. He'd heard his parents discuss the war before, but Father was confident that there was no real threat from the shamans. And Migo trusted Father.

Mother laughed. "Debatable, but I'll acquiesce for a moment of peace." She laid her head on Father's shoulder and closed her eyes.

A knock came at the door. Father groaned just before it opened and a guard poked his head in. "Lord, Yavasu has come to visit the young prince."

Migo all but sprinted to the door.

"Stay in the covered hall," Father shouted after him.

Migo barely remembered to put his slippers back on before racing out towards the waiting room. There he found Yavasu, clutching his own wooden stave. He had gray eyes that Migo always thought looked awesome, and even his skin was an interesting shade of orange and brown, lighter than Migo's own. Most everyone Migo knew had the same light brown skin.

"My father let me tag along. Let's have a bout," Yavasu said. His father was a lesser lord of some sort that always seemed to linger around Rikaydian Palace. Migo didn't understand how adults could have so much *business* to do all the time.

Yavasu fell in beside Migo as they headed toward the covered hall where they liked to play. Yavasu was already eight years old, but he was still a little shorter than Migo. Father kept saying Migo would grow up to be a giant, and that they'd have to extend the ceilings to accommodate him once he got older.

Yavasu kept talking about how his father was working on some silver acquisition thing until Migo teased, "Sands, that sounds boring. I hope you don't grow up to be as boring as your father." He heard enough of that boring talk around all the other lords who talked to his father. All anybody cared about was trading.

"It's not boring! Silver's valuable stuff. Father says a hundred people died extracting it from the Frozen Waste."

"Wow, those people picked a stupid job."

Yavasu rolled his eyes. "I think *you* picked a stupid job—sitting on couches all day cuddling your mom."

Migo shoved Yavasu. He knew Yavasu was just joking, but it still made him mad. "I do fighting drills! Then I can pummel you with my stick."

They exited the palace through a pair of open double-doors on the north end of the palace. Columns to either side held up a stone roof leading to a tower that overlooked the edge of the city and the northern farmlands. A calm breeze blew from the Frozen Waste and the smells of food drifted out from some vents to the palace kitchens below.

A couple guards stood to either side of the door on the outside, but Migo told them to stand on the inside. Sometimes, he felt embarrassed to have adults watch him play. The guards knew the drill and didn't hesitate to go inside, but Migo didn't miss the smile on one of their faces.

"All right, well you can be a palace guard, and I'm going to be an invader," Migo said.

"Why can't we both be invaders?"

"How would that work?"

"I don't know. We could imagine we're both guards."

Migo shook his head. "No."

"Then we could both be invaders."

Migo groaned. "Ugh, fine." He preferred being able to fight a real person. He also liked to be able to boss Yavasu around, so being on the same team worked great. What he really needed was a few more friends.

They walked further toward the north tower as Migo discussed a battle plan. The smell in the air turned a little crisper. Migo noticed because he missed the scent of steamed vegetables. The wind from the Frozen Wastes felt slightly stronger near the middle of the covered hallway. With any luck, it would stay that way, because they would sometimes get sweaty from running around.

After they'd been playing for several minutes, Migo hardly noticed a change in weather until he was blown over, a flash of hot rain slapping him in the face. Lightning nearly blinded him as he looked to the frostward. A cacophonous wave of thunder shook the air around him.

Yavasu had blown over as well. The storm had caught them both by surprise while they were on the open balcony. He scrambled to his hands and feet, a look of sheer terror on his face. He didn't even glance back at Migo as he crawled to the hallway and towards the palace door.

The two guards were shouting, but Migo couldn't hear them. He was fixated on the freezing wind that threatened to carry him away. *I shouldn't have left the hall.* He clutched the column beside him. This was the third floor of the palace, but sand and ice still reached him and started to bite at his skin. He knew he needed to get inside, but he couldn't get himself to move. The guards had closed one of the doors, but they regarded him from the distance, their faces twisted with the same look of terror Yavasu wore.

Nobody survived the Maedaris outside. They weren't going to save him.

Migo felt the tears on his face. He inched his way forward, the continuous lightning and thunder sending tremors across his skin. He stopped at a column as the wind grew fiercer, but he wasn't prepared as it suddenly shifted and blew a different direction. He tumbled across the pavement, his back scraping on the stone until he slid just over the edge of the incline that went down to the roof of the next floor. In a spur of instinct, he grabbed the ledge, keeping himself from falling. The pain of sand and ice nipping at his skin was almost unbearable. His screams were lost in the storm. *Why didn't I crawl back with Yavasu?*

Somehow, above the roar of the storm, Migo heard a voice calling his name. He looked back towards the palace doors where his hero stood. Without another heartbeat of hesitation, Father came dashing towards him, his jaw set with determination.

There wasn't really any handhold for Migo to stay in position, only the cracks between the stones, and he clutched at these desperately. Part of him felt a sliver of peace, however, knowing that Father was going to save him. Of course he was.

As Father neared, a sharp wind pressed Migo against the stone, actually easing some of his own weight, but it blew Father to the side. Though the sun was now covered by dark clouds, flashes of lightning kept the sky alight, highlighting the fact the Father wasn't alone on the hallway.

There was another figure in the storm. A black, shadow of a man. He walked through the Maedari with frightening confidence. The figure scared Migo even more than the storm. A long knife appeared in his hands as he approached Father, who was unarmed. That knife was the kind of weapon shamans used.

Migo looked on in horror. He lacked the strength to pull himself back up. The pain from the Maedari was almost unbearable.

Father noticed the other man and gave Migo a tentative glance. Father dodged a swing and a jab from the man's blade. They both moved in Migo's direction, whose grip was getting loose.

Father will win. Father will save me.

Migo blinked furiously to keep his eyes clear and fixed on the fight. The pain of the sand and ice eating at his flesh would go away if only Father could reach him.

Even through the density of the storm, Migo saw with vivid clarity as his Father was slashed across the arm. Blood splattered onto the stone, glistening under the glare of lightning. They scuffled some more, but all Migo could see was a new gash across Father's chest. And the blood. There was another tearing sound as the shaman swiped at Father again and something warm spattered across Migo's face. Father fell to the floor, eyes open wide, and his blood... so much blood.

Migo lost his grip. He crashed onto the stone below and rolled across the roof until he fell again, his body somehow wedging into a crevice. The biting sand no longer struck him with enough momentum to pierce his skin. The respite from the Maedari was no comfort. *Father... Father.* The image of Father's blood spattering on the stones kept playing over in his mind.

Father was...dead. *He was just trying to save me.*

Guilt crashed into Migo like a wave. If only he hadn't been so paralyzed with fear.

Why didn't I just follow Yavasu?

Horror washed over him, drowning out the storm.

Chapter Fourteen

Stormcaller

Katsi started with a gasp. It was dark, and she swallowed painfully against the dryness in her throat. She cast frantic eyes around, trying to figure out where she was. A dim light reflected off sandstone walls, revealing the exit to the cave she was in. The last thing she remembered was falling towards the cliff. Her hands were unbound and Scales nudged at her fingers with its nose. Her things were set beside her. Beneath her, sand gritted against her dress.

Her memory felt fuzzy, but it was returning. After falling from the wall, Katsi had kicked away from the bald soldier. They'd both made it past the edge of the cliff, but she'd somehow managed to land on a small ledge just below the lip of the cliff, while the man had fallen from sight. She'd hit her head on the landing, but she could vaguely remember the feeling as a strong wind seemed to push her, guiding her to the ledge so that she didn't fall further. She remembered *wanting* that to happen.

Aside from that, she wasn't sure how she'd found shelter from the Maedari.

A shadow played across the entrance to the cave. Katsi scrambled to a crouch. She picked up her knife and prepared to attack. Another quick glance confirmed that there was no other way in or out of the small cave.

The shadow moved very slowly. Dust swirled inside as the figure hunched down and entered the cave, revealing itself as an aged woman. Katsi half lowered her knife.

"Good, you're awake," the woman said, her voice clear and strong. Her brown skin was darkened and leathery, her black hair streaked with gray. She was a bit stooped and walked with a cane in one hand, though she didn't seem to lean on it. "You're lucky I saw your scuffle with the Cataban scoundrel before you fell. It's not every day I meet a stormcaller." She stepped closer to Katsi, ignoring the knife, and peered up at Katsi's face. "You're coming of age. Might not even know what you did—probably why it was sloppy."

"Excuse me?" Katsi asked. She swatted the woman's hand away just as she was reaching up as if to pinch Katsi's cheek. "Who're you?"

The woman cackled. "Me? I'm just an old lady. You, on the other hand, are a shaman."

"Old ladies can be shamans too," Katsi said, eyeing the woman closely. She was clearly of shamanic descent. Her thick, dark hair, tinged with orange, was pulled back, and two thin, long braids were tied together over her right ear with a weathered piece of fabric. There didn't seem to be any stormwading armor beneath her robe, which fit closely around the woman's lean frame.

The woman shrugged and nodded at Katsi. "At least you're keen."

"What makes you think I'm a shaman?" Katsi asked, playing it safe. She retrieved her things and placed Scales in her pocket.

The woman gave a rich laugh. "Because I saw you use magic."

Katsi made her way around the woman. "What do you mean?" The woman's words made her curious, but Katsi wasn't fond of talking to a stranger inside a dark cave.

"No need to play it safe here, stormcaller," the woman said. "We're far from the reach of any ringdweller."

Outside, Katsi was surprised to find herself not at the top of the cliffs, but at the bottom of the canyon. Tan and gray rocks rose high above her. The entrance to the cave was covered in shadows, and a light breeze streamed steadily by. Based on the position of the sun, she figured that she was deeper into the Scorched Waste than she'd ever been. There was not another soul in sight.

"Where are we?" Katsi asked.

"Banadil-Atar. This is where the Cataban Tribe fled after their village by the lake was destroyed and taken over by the ringdwellers."

"How did I get here?"

"I brought you. You needed safety from the Maedari. Good thing I did too; a stormcaller getting crushed by a Maedari would be a pitiful way to go. The irony of that would have made a good story. Not that I have anyone to tell stories to." She scratched her head as if pondering.

Katsi tried to imagine this ancient woman dragging her down into the canyon all by herself. It didn't seem plausible. She looked around again expecting to see others, but it was still just the two of them.

"Stormcaller—why do you keep calling me that?"

The woman chuckled and walked a little deeper into the canyon, towards the sun. "It's a pretty self-explanatory title, girl, I'm surprised you can't put it together. It's too bad there aren't any smart stormcallers anymore. Such wasted potential."

Katsi wrinkled her nose in a frown. *She's playing with me.* She couldn't help but remember the sand and wind that whipped around her when she'd seen the rangola. There was also the instance with the cuffs breaking off. *But that metal was just terrible quality.* These things certainly didn't mean that she could call storms.

Katsi was so wrapped up in her thoughts that it took her a moment to realize that the old woman had disappeared. "Hey." She ran forward. Following the woman might be the only way she'd be able to find a way back out of the canyon. After a few strides, she came upon a crevice that ran into the side of the canyon like a massive scar. She hesitated at the entrance before entering the darkness beyond.

It was somehow hotter inside. Katsi was tempted to drink all the water in her canteen. Only years of practicing restraint allowed her to do so now. She could faintly hear the sound of boots grinding against the ground ahead. Her natural inclination was to cease pursuing for fear of a trap. *If she wanted to kill me or something, she definitely could have done that already.* She pressed on, following the sound.

"How do you see in here?" Katsi asked.

"My veil."

"Oh, it's bewitched." Of course. It must let her see in the dark. There were so many kinds of magic and Katsi knew she was aware of only a small fraction of what was out there. This old woman seemed to know a few unique things. Or perhaps she was part of the Bayvana Tribe, but she didn't seem familiar.

"Very astute. There is hope for you yet."

Katsi couldn't tell if the woman was trying to be funny, but she frowned at the sarcasm. "Where is your tribe?"

The woman kept shuffling along, and Katsi stumbled behind her as the ground sloped up. There was no response until they stopped at the edge of a rise, a bit of orange light filtering down through a wind-carved crack.

"My tribe is dead," the woman said, regarding Katsi with her face masked behind a dark veil. "I am all that remains. The emperor saw to that."

"The emperor. You've been here all this time?" Katsi said mostly to herself. The emperor hadn't been down this far south in decades—not since his initial purge when he'd marched his armies around the entire Ring, destroying every shamanic tribe they could find in an event called The Massacres.

"Oh yes. Many years. I was deep in the canyon, receiving my initiation to the Order when the soldiers came. They had been quite thorough. Even the children…" her voice trailed off, and she turned to continue her ascent.

Katsi scrambled after her. There was a large gap in the stone up above, so Katsi could see more clearly.

"What is your name?" the woman asked.

"Katsi."

"Your full name."

"Katsi Danan."

The woman spared a glance back at Katsi. "You've been with the Bayvana Tribe?"

"Not really—are you leading me back out of the canyon?"

The woman nodded.

"And do you know where the Bayvana Tribe is?" Katsi asked.

The woman laughed. "I don't try to keep tabs on them, but this time of year? Probably just near the edge of the Ring a little further north. They've inhabited an old city there."

"I remember the place," Katsi said. Though it had been years, the way there was still distinct.

They neared a ledge that Katsi could tell was just at the top of the canyon. Once there, she'd be able to continue to the Bayvana Tribe. She could almost smile, if only seeing them wouldn't be so bittersweet. Just to be sure she still had all her things, she patted herself down. Everything was accounted for except… the artifact was no longer on her arm. She stopped in her tracks. "I'm missing my bracelet. I had it here on my arm—did you see it?"

The woman had pulled her veil down, and she regarded Katsi with light green eyes. "Oh yes," she said, taking it out from a pocket of her dress. She looked at the artifact, her eyes almost glowing, then held it out to Katsi.

Katsi grabbed for it, surprised to find that the woman held tight to it for a moment before letting go. The woman nodded, offering Katsi a forced smile.

"Thank you," Katsi said, then something occurred to her. The woman was old. Perhaps she knew something. "Have you ever seen that symbol before?"

The woman didn't look at the artifact. "No. Safe journey." She lifted her arm up as if giving Katsi permission to go, offering yet another fake smile.

Katsi strapped the artifact back on. She tilted her head to the woman in a small bow. "You've done me a great service in keeping me out of the Maedari. I can't thank you enough." With that, Katsi hurried off, keeping to the shadows as much as she could. Something about the woman's behavior was strange, and it was also unclear as to how the artifact had gotten off Katsi's arm. *She must have taken it off of me.* It was a chilling thought. She'd gone out of her way to remove it, but then she'd offered to give it back simply by Katsi's asking. It didn't make sense, and thinking about it any more just made Katsi keep looking back over her shoulder, but the woman was nowhere to be seen.

The blazing heat kept Katsi moving at a steady pace. Her stomach grumbled all the while.

Focus. She was risking her life not just to find out what a stolen artifact was. She was saving lives. Saving Damani.

The only safe route to take was to head back to the Ring, travel a little further north, then cross back into the Scorched Waste near the old tunnel hideout where the Bayvana Tribe would be staying. She'd visited the tribe a few times since separating, so she knew the way. She traveled warily once she crossed back into the Ring, but moved as quick as she could until she reached the area to cross back over.

The wall was not well maintained here, so scrambling over its crumbled frame wasn't difficult. She shielded her eyes against the blaze of the sun as she stared out at a field of gray stones, lightly glazed with sand.

This was it. Hidden amongst those stones was a network of tunnels and an open compound that made up the Bayvana Tribe's hideout. There was supposed to be a greenish-black rock that indicated one of the main entrances.

She jumped down and headed straight sunward. Though it didn't happen too often, her skin burned. Too much wandering in the sun this cycle. She needed to find the entrance as soon as possible.

A larger boulder offered just enough shade that Katsi could crouch behind it to hide from the sun and look around. She could see the stone a few strides south, so she left the brief cover and dashed over, finding the gap in the ground that dropped into the tunnels. She stepped down a few rocks that brought her to the bottom and squinted into the darkness that stretched ahead of her. Inside was the Bayvana Tribe, and the past she'd left behind.

The air was cool with magical enchantment, and a slight breeze blew out from the tunnel, like the very earth was alive with breath.

Instead of proceeding, Katsi waited. She was certain she must have been seen. The tribe was always wary of attack and discovery, so they would have had somebody watching her the moment she scaled the wall.

Sure enough, she could see a faint light approaching from the depths of the tunnel. She watched the light with anticipation. It was a good sign. If they'd wanted her dead, they would have struck her from the darkness, but it didn't mean they wouldn't be angry.

Chapter Fifteen

Conspiracy

Migo paced as he thought. Muted voices sounded from the many alcoves that lined the walls of the palace's large parlor room. Even in his own alcove with Hatan, Migo still squirmed inside. It had been some time since he'd been comfortable here. He still wasn't. His body itched to be elsewhere.

Migo rubbed his eyes, still slightly red from having cried earlier. The execution had rattled him. *Even if they were* not *the ones who murdered their neighbors, they were still shamans. Shamans still need to die. Otherwise there will be more murders. More Maedaris. More families ruined like mine.* He had killed before, but none of those experiences had been this jarring. He clenched and unclenched his fist, imagining himself screaming and throwing the couches across the room. The memory of his father's death flashed through his mind. He avoided looking directly at Hatan for fear of him noticing.

Hatan sat on a cushioned seat with his legs up on the short table. He picked at the different treats on a tray in his hand. "My lord, I might recommend one of these puffs—they're still chilled from the Frozen Waste." He popped one into his mouth as if to make a point.

For someone who seemed to like food so much, it was almost a surprise to Migo that Hatan wasn't overweight.

"You know I've never had much taste for sweets, Hatan."

"It's a pity, too, but I still hope to convert you."

Migo shook his head. He couldn't understand how Hatan was always so cheery. The execution was making Migo's guts churn. He couldn't even bring himself to process it. Thinking about it made him feel like he was going mad. Shouldn't Hatan be feeling anxious about the likelihood of Migo's own execution?

Other people in the room steered clear of their alcove. Migo had grown accustomed to the other lords and ladies avoiding him. Queen Rikaydian's usual distaste for Migo was common knowledge since she made no effort to hide it.

Hatan placed down the tray with a sigh. "You seem distressed."

Migo said nothing, but stared down a merchant lord and his wife as they walked by.

Hatan swung his legs down from the table. "All right, what's on your mind, cousin? Let me do what I can to help you."

Migo stopped his pacing and sat beside Hatan. He was unsure of how to voice his thoughts. He lowered his voice. "What if Bindom was right?"

"Lord." Hatan looked around them to double-check that nobody could hear. "It's certainly possible."

"Yes, but... What if they were set up? What if I'm being set up?" How would Migo explain this? *Maybe the shamans really did get to me.* He clenched his fist so tight that his nails dug into his palm. "It almost seemed too easy."

Hatan unsuccessfully wiped cream filling from the corner of his mouth and leaned forward "I wouldn't put it past Tarahan to place false evidence in order to take the praise for doing your job. It would be difficult to prove."

"Then what do I do?"

Hatan shook his head. "You can't challenge him head on. The best you could do is find the real culprit or some other shamans. You don't want him to overshadow you. At the same time." Hatan lowered his voice to a whisper and leaned even closer. "I've got some other ears around the palace. I won't let anyone come after you. Not even the queen."

Migo nodded, grateful to have at least one person in his life who cared. "Then there is still the possibility of course that shamans are the ones who placed the evidence."

Hatan inclined his head. "I wouldn't put it past the shamans to blame somebody else for their dirty work."

"So, the shamans potentially planted that evidence? We might still have murderers on the loose. We know for a fact that there are a couple tribes operating near Jehubal."

"Yes, so what do we do?"

Migo ground his teeth. "They're all guilty, so all we can do is eradicate them. As long as they survive, more murders will happen." It was the same thing his mother and the shaman hunters had preached to him.

Hatan frowned. He popped another treat into his mouth as if to cover up some kind of disappointment.

"Is there a problem?"

"I've seen so much death." He sighed. "It's a shame."

Migo considered for a moment whether he should press Hatan for a better answer, but decided against it. Now wasn't the time. "Well, there was still that girl. I suspect she may have a connection."

"She did act strangely at the scene, but she'll be difficult to locate."

"I have an idea of where to start. It seemed like she fled the city. It's possible she simply crossed into the wastes, but she may have connection with some of the farmers outside the city. There are only a few hundred of them south of the city."

Hatan made no effort to hide his frown this time, but it was gone in a moment as he stood from his seat and smiled at an approaching party.

"Already planning out a way to find more shamans, I assume," Nedro Wajek said, his plump frame lavished in a fine robe. At his side was a servant bearing a plate heaped with even more treats than Hatan's.

Migo had grown accustomed to a life of near solitude. Aside from his soldiers, suspects, and the occasional scorn from his mother, the only person he spent much time with was Hatan. Most others in the court knew to respectfully keep their distance, so he wondered why Lord Wajek made an exception.

Hatan was about to speak, but Migo stood and cut him off as something sprang to his mind. "You saw the shamans who entered your house, correct?"

"Of course, my lord," Nedro said, a smile flashing across his pudgy face. "I fought them off myself."

"You said there were at least three. We only caught two."

"I suppose you're right." Nedro's face twitched with a frown. "I wish you luck in the continued search."

"Of course," Migo said, offering a smile that felt unnatural on his face. "I hope you enjoy the rest of the activities." He dismissed himself and hurried from the room as Hatan followed.

Migo waited until they'd gotten to a more deserted hallway before he spoke. "This is why the queen should have let me interrogate them. We missed the opportunity to find out anything else about other shamans in the area."

Hatan still held onto his tray of treats, popping one into his mouth with every few steps. "But what if we find this girl, and not just her, but all three of the real culprits?"

"What does it matter? If they're shamans, then we kill them and say that they wouldn't come peaceably, simple as that."

Hatan pursed his lips but didn't say anything else.

"I know what you're thinking, Hatan," Migo said, frowning in annoyance, "but this is war. My father would still be alive if it hadn't been for them, and if I hadn't been such an idiot."

Hatan's eyes softened. "Migo, you can't blame yourself for that—that case was never solved."

"I saw what happened!" The images had been burned into his memory. He could still see his father's blood spattering across the stones. "And I was the cause of it."

They'd stopped at the end of the hallway. Hatan gave Migo a sad shake of his head. "Migo, you've always been a good person. I don't want these things to alter you like they did your mother."

"Don't compare me to her, cousin!" Migo resisted the urge to shove Hatan.

"There's more to life than hatred and shame, Migo."

"Enough!" Migo let his voice drop to a serious tone. "You've spoken too freely. Leave. I don't want to see your face."

Hatan swallowed hard, then nodded. "Yes, captain." He turned on his heels and strode away, humming a tune to himself as Migo climbed the stairs to his room. There was no time to consider any of Hatan's crazy ideas.

Chapter Sixteen

Bayvana Tribe

Katsi watched as a face slowly materialized from the darkness that stretched before her. A cool breeze whispered softly against the stone walls when a young woman stepped into view. Shinaseh. She was about a year older than Katsi, with bright green eyes of which Katsi had always been jealous. Now that they were older, and Shinaseh had grown into her body, it seemed like there was even more to be jealous of.

It was always a shock for Katsi to see people she had once known, and it almost made her feel like she could've had a normal life among the shamanfolk. But that was before her parents had been killed.

Shinaseh wore a frown. It surprised Katsi to see Shinaseh armed with a peculiar, curved blade and wearing full stormwading armor.

"You quit bathing now, eh Katsi? I didn't realize two years outside a tribe was all it took to naturalize someone."

"I might be a little messy, but I could still pin you at Chama-Fen."

Shinaseh shook her head, a slight smirk turning her lips. Katsi's muscles relaxed.

"You may want to smooth that sharp tongue of yours if I let you come in. The elder shamans don't have a sense of humor anymore." Shinaseh clasped Katsi's arm just above the elbow. Katsi returned the gesture, a sign of greeting among shamanfolk.

"What do you mean, if?" Katsi asked, raising an eyebrow as she took a step further down the tunnel. She was cautious enough to keep her distance from the weapon Shinaseh held. If it was what Katsi suspected, then she feared for anything the tribe might be planning.

Shinaseh grunted. "Well, what are you doing back here? I thought you left in search of a less violent lifestyle."

"Which is still true," Katsi said with a sigh, "but I'm still shamanfolk, and I do like to visit my tribe." She paused, unsure of how to present the information to Shinaseh. "Also, I came across a symbol, and I was hoping to get some help identifying it. That and... I found out I'm a shaman."

"Really?" Shinaseh raised an eyebrow. "How do you know?"

"My parents taught me that magic artifacts can trigger it."

Shinaseh chewed her tongue in thought for a moment before she said, "Very well." She took the lead, walking further into the depths of the hideout. "Have you noticed what kind of magic you might be proficient at?"

Stormcalling proficiency was rare and they hadn't had one in the Bay-vana Tribe for a couple generations, but that's what the shaman woman in the canyon told her. "Not sure," Katsi lied.

"Is it true you've been living among the ringdwellers all this time?"

"Not for a single day," Katsi answered, the words coming out with more bitterness than she'd planned. "I've been living outside in the Scorched Waste. My parents had a place there, before they died." She gave Shinaseh a worried glance. *Why did I just tell her where I live?* Secrecy kept her safe. "Please, don't repeat that to anyone. I'd rather they not know where I'm staying."

Shinaseh gave Katsi a short smile. "Don't worry, I understand the necessity. It must be lonely out there."

You have no idea. Katsi tapped the pocket where Scales lay hidden, and she thought back on Damani. Shinaseh still held the weapon in her hand, and Katsi couldn't help but ask. She pointed to the weapon. "Is that a secula?"

Shinaseh looked back at Katsi. "Possibly. What with all your peace-preaching, I'm surprised you even know what a secula is."

Katsi held back a snarky remark and tried not to be offended. "I grew up learning about enchantments just like anybody else." Their tribe hadn't made magical weapons in years, and the bewitchment process was supposed to have been lost, but seculas were said to be terribly destructive.

"Uck, you almost talk like one of the elders already," Shinaseh said with a laugh. "You're supposed to be younger than me."

Laughter. It had been a long time since Katsi had made someone besides Damani laugh. It warmed her. Maybe she could stay with the tribe this time... but the weapon in Shinaseh's hand warned Katsi not to get too desperate. She didn't doubt that Shinaseh had been made into a warrior. All the shamanfolk were warriors now.

"Oh, I'm still younger," Katsi said, keeping the conversation light, "but I have to be wise in order to survive on my own."

"But you don't have to be on your own," Shinaseh said in a low voice.

Katsi tried to ignore that. "How have things been here?"

"We've been getting along fine." They turned a corner and went deeper into the ground. "Some Cataban soldiers have been trying to cut us off from the lake. It made things pretty annoying for a while since they took all the melons, but during that Maedari earlier, we liberated it back as Bayvana territory."

"Were they killed?" Katsi asked, reflecting on how those very same guards had tortured her just last cycle. Perhaps that smoke she'd seen rising was from burning buildings and not a campfire.

"Of course. You know how it is, can't leave any loose ends." She lifted her weapon. "These made it easy."

Katsi nodded. More killing. It made sense. She'd always been against killing, but part of her felt relieved to know that her captors were gone. It made her sick all the same, bile churning in her stomach.

They passed a room that was little more than a hollowed-out section to one side of the corridor, but it had natural light that filtered down from a deep hole to the surface. In there, they cultured the mongae and lawean, some foods that could be spread like pastes. There were a few other rooms along the way, but none of them were lit.

The ground evened out, and there was another light up ahead. The large room was the main courtyard. Some of the cave network was natural, but for the most part, it had been carved, smoothed, and reinforced by a class of shamanic magic called alterations.

"When we get in there, Katsi, remember that not everybody will be pleased to see you. Maybe try not to be so bold as you normally are, and try not to do anything crazy. Since I'm the one who let you in, I'd probably take the blame for anything that happens."

"Sure." Katsi rolled her eyes against the darkness. She'd been back to the tribe six or seven times since she'd left, and they never once turned her away. Even though she had left, she was still shamanfolk and kin to the tribe. It was true that each time she returned, she was given progressively colder reception. She detested the separation, but she couldn't support their enthusiasm toward the war. Not all ringdwellers deserved to die. There were good ones, like Damani. *Why can't the tribe see that?*

In Katsi's childhood, this hallway had been completely lit by linara stones. Things had changed so much, but she couldn't exactly tell why.

When they entered the courtyard, Katsi blinked up at the vast ceiling. Six large holes had been bored into the top, each letting in a beam of light that shone on the eastern wall, highlighting different shamanic icons. Wisdom, art, industry, weather, distortion, and life. Much of the meaning behind the icons had been lost, but Katsi at least knew the connection between them and shaman magic.

The courtyard was bustling with activity, though it wasn't as crowded as it had been in Katsi's youth. Despite the relative darkness, many of the shamanfolk in the room were sharpening weapons or prepping them for bewitchment. It struck Katsi with a sense of horror. Perhaps it was just because of their recent raid against the Cataban guards, but she knew there was something deeper. They really were preparing something. Damani had to get out of the farmlands.

"This way," Shinaseh said, prodding Katsi's shoulder as she crossed the courtyard. It was a vast chamber, but it was smothered in darkness. It had once been lit by large linara stones, but now the shafts of light overheard were used as the primary source of light.

"It's different here," Katsi said, her voice drowning in the empty space. Shinaseh gave her a sad look. "Things change."

Groups of people spoke as they passed, though many of them lowered their voices as they recognized Katsi. What Shinaseh had said was right: they looked at her differently, some of them glaring. War had hardened them.

One particular group didn't seem to notice, and their voices carried to Katsi. "I can't believe cousins Bindom and Shali are dead—and killed by Migo Rikaydian himself. What a terrible way to go."

"They should've left once Kinay and Roda were assassinated during that Maedari. Spies living next door to each other was a stupid idea to begin with."

Bindom, Shali, Kinay, Roda. These were names that seemed vaguely familiar to Katsi.

"Well, at least we won't need any spies once we kill Migo and half of the guard. Five more cycles is a long time. We just need—," the voice cut short in a cough as the man set eyes on Katsi.

Katsi swept her eyes away as if she hadn't been looking. She had a feeling that she just overhead something very important. The tribe wasn't just taking back land by the lake, they were planning something against Jehubal as well. If half the guard was dead, then that could possibly tip things in favor of the tribe, though there would still be private soldiers commanded by merchant lords. Perhaps it would be enough to throw the whole city into chaos.

"They just get riled up sometimes," Shinaseh said in a quiet voice, disrupting Katsi's thoughts. "If he could kill half the Rikaydian guard, I'd be quite surprised." She gave Katsi a small smile of assurance.

Katsi wasn't convinced. The man, and those in his group, kept staring at her even after she and Shinash passed. She felt their eyes boring into her back. A fragmented Jehubal would mean an easier fall. Many other people would die. Damani would be one of them. Knowing him, he'd probably join the guard if the city were under serious threat. Her heart started beating a little faster as she worried about what might happen.

"Danan. I can't say I'm surprised."

Katsi started. She'd been so focused on her thoughts that she hadn't realized they were at an open entryway to a room adjacent to the courtyard. Inside, the room was lit with several linara stones, glowing with a soft, yellow light. A dark rug was laid across the floor, and smoothed, wooden furniture lined the walls. A large brasswod table sat at the center of the room, atop which was a six-pronged candelabra with a linara stone in each slot. For all Katsi knew, this room flaunted what was left of shaman decadence.

At the end of the table, an older woman, Mashe, sat with a bowl full of steaming metal shards before her that was garnished with pondei leaves and garaso oil. The metal was undergoing a bewitchment. Another shaman man, Felaha, was mixing something together at a desk on the far wall, but standing in front of her with his arms folded, was Manahae.

Katsi nodded. Manahae and the other two were all shamans. She wasn't sure how many shamans there were in the tribe, but she suspected there were only a couple dozen of them. There used to be a lot more, but for some reason, there were less and less of them with each generation.

"I know when to heed a warning," Katsi said, dropping her eyes.

"Not every time," Manahae said, raising an eyebrow, clearly referencing the time when Katsi chose to leave the tribe.

"Is someone else still watching the main entrance, Shinaseh?" asked the old woman seated at the table.

"Yes, elder."

"You look a little frazzled. How was the trek here?" Manahae asked, still standing just inside the entryway with his arms folded.

Katsi could tell that Manahae's underlying question was really about how she managed to come through the Maedari. This was something she didn't mind telling the truth about. "I actually had a run-in with those Cataban guards, but I managed to slip away and get into the canyon right as the storm hit. In fact, there was a shaman woman who helped me get to safety."

The two other shamans turned their eyes on Katsi, and Manahae glanced back at them. Even Shinaseh seemed to perk up and a frown of thought creased her brow.

"Who was she?" Manahae asked

Katsi shrugged. "I didn't get her name, but she isn't part of the tribe. She seemed to know quite a bit about the Bayvana Tribe."

The shamans didn't respond, but Shinaseh smirked and said quietly, "Few people have seen her. They call her the spirit."

Manahae rubbed his chin. "She's a seer. She only shows herself to a select few. We've gone to find her before, thinking that another tribe might be seeking refuge in the area, but we can never find her when intended. She must be from an ancient tribe that dwelt here many years ago. I suppose it's a good sign that she helped you..." Manahae trailed off, still rubbing his chin.

A seer. Another rare magic proficiency. All Katsi knew about it was that they could see visions of possible futures. In a sense, Katsi came here to spy, but there was another bonus. "I came to ask the elders a question, if I may," Katsi said.

Manahae looked back at the other two shamans, who regarded Katsi with squinted eyes. Felaha wasn't nearly as old as Mashe, but age wasn't what determined who was an elder. At least, it wasn't the only factor. Manahae wasn't an elder yet, but it was only a matter of time.

"The others are seeing to different affairs," Mashe said in her deep voice, "but you may ask us your question."

Katsi bowed her head in thanks. "My parents told me of ways to recognize magic, and I discovered I'm a shaman. The woman from the canyon called me a stormcaller because I manipulated the wind a little during the storm. Would you be able to offer me further insight into this? I'd like to know how to use it properly."

The wrinkles on Mashe's face dug deep as she raised her eyebrows, but it was Felaha who answered. "We haven't had a true stormcalling shaman in the Bayvana Tribe for at least three generations. Much of its art may be lost to us. Have you noticed anything else besides controlling wind?"

Katsi pursed her lips as she considered other bizarre occurrences. "I may have rusted some metal cuffs when I wanted them to come off... and I created a small sandstorm when I was trying to defend myself against a rangola."

Felaha nodded and said, "Rusting metal. That seems like a form of alterations. I see your wrists have marks." She turned and looked at Mashe. "Some of her blood likely got on the metal."

Mashe spoke slowly as she squinted across at Katsi. "Her use of the magic seems to occur quite naturally. The blood was a coincidence."

The reference to blood had Katsi's brain whirling. Blood magic was used for distortions, and it had long been outlawed by the tribe.

Mashe continued, "Though all magic has a sense of instinctiveness to it, stormcalling may require less technical training than brewing or bewitching." She clasped her hands together and leaned forward. "We could teach you what we know: the crafting of potions, bewitching, and alterations. The skills gained there could help you harness your talent for stormcalling."

A chill of anticipation ran across Katsi's skin. The eagerness with which Mashe regarded her was both uncomfortable and exciting. *This makes me unique. Rare.* Even Shinaseh's wide-eyed expression made Katsi swell.

Scales shifted inside Katsi's pocket. But what would it cost to train with the Bayvana shamans? *Would they turn me into a warrior?* They already seemed to be planning an attack on Jehubal. She couldn't support that, and she needed to warn Damani. Maybe there was another way...

"I would be happy to learn," Katsi said, "but I will need to think about this, and there's another reason I came." She looked away to avoid seeing their reactions and pulled out her drawing of the rune. The parchment had been weathered by her travels, but the image was still clear. She placed it on the table in front of Mashe as Felaha came to look as well. "I was wondering if you might be able to identify this symbol."

"Where did you see this?" Mashe asked.

She'd been anticipating this question, but it still made her nervous to answer. "One of the merchant lords in Jehubal is said to have recently acquired a relic with that symbol on it. He picked it off the corpse of some shamans he'd killed, and I was hoping to find out who it belonged to."

The woman grunted. "The shaman who it belonged to is dead now. It no longer matters." She seemed dismissive, but she shared a glance with Felaha.

Katsi took a step forward. She knew they were hiding something, so she pressed. "Even still, I'd like to hear what you know about it."

"It's not important," Mashe said firmly, her cloudy brown eyes fixing on Katsi. "I'd rather not discuss it with you."

"Like you said, Mashe, they're all dead, so what does it matter if we tell her?" Felaha said. Mashe gave him a cold look, but he kept speaking. "That symbol is indeed ancient. It's a combination of all six icons into the word shavaranashi. It's the symbol of the Shavarani Tribe, an old tribe that used to dominate this entire area, but their practices grew less appealing with societal changes. Many of them defected into other tribes. Even some of our ancestors come from the Shavarani Tribe."

Mashe gave a subtle sigh and said, "That spirit you saw in the canyon. She's likely descended from one of them. Where did this merchant lord come across a shaman with that symbol?"

Katsi perked up. They'd given even more information that she'd expected. "I don't know." *The shaman in the canyon might be a connection? No wonder she was weird about the artifact.*

"Someone might have just been keeping it as an heirloom of sorts, the poor soul," said Felaha at the back of the room, his brows creased with a frown.

Mashe grumbled again. "Possibly... but don't go looking into this. Their tribe diminished for good reason. You ought to stay here amongst your own tribe anyway."

Katsi merely pursed her lips. The fact that Mashe told her *not* to just made her want to do it even more. She bowed her head again. "Thank you, elders." She grabbed her drawing and turned to go as both the elder shamans nodded at her.

Manahae followed casually beyond the doorway as if escorting Katsi, Shinaseh walking on the other side. When they'd gone a short distance, he stopped. "Katsi, I'd listen to Mashe. I gave you that warning a few cycles ago because I care about you. Your parents were my friends, and I don't want something to happen to you either." He lowered his voice. "The Shavarani Tribe is said to have used the darker magics—arts that were abandoned generations ago. I doubt they are all dead, but even if they could teach you anything about stormcalling, it won't be worth the cost." The look in Manahae's eyes gave Katsi a chill. "It might be best if you let this thing go." He stood back and nodded to her dismissively as he returned to the room.

"Wicked," Shinaseh said, smiling at Katsi. "I can't believe you're a stormcaller shaman. And I haven't heard that much about the Shavarani Tribe before—I haven't even heard Mashe speak more than a few words."

"Well, at least now you know how to set her off," Katsi said with a wink as they walked back across the courtyard.

Shinaseh rolled her eyes. "Where to now? You're not staying, are you?"

"Of course not," Katsi said, thinking of Damani, an image of his cute smile coming to mind. *What would I do about him if I weren't a shaman-folk.* She sighed with the wistful thought. "You should know that I can't stand to have people tell me what to do."

"Aha, well, I think you should leave, then, and never come back." Shinaseh laughed at her own wit.

"Nice try," Katsi said, proffering a sympathetic smile. She was looking around to try and find the group of men she'd overheard before, but couldn't pick them out. She tried her best to listen in on other conversations, but everyone had since become aware that she was there. She'd made herself an outsider to her own people. At least Shinaseh didn't seem to mind. Perhaps she would return to the tribe one day... but not while she thought Damani might die otherwise.

"The tribe still accepts coins, right?" Katsi asked with a hint of sarcasm.

Shinaseh gave Katsi a flat stare. "Of course. It's not like we've suddenly gone barbaric or something."

"I'd like to get a couple things before I go, then." Katsi had stolen some coins from a previous raid. She had to look after herself.

"Sure. I'll take you to the traders."

After that... Katsi had a few questions for the shaman woman in the canyon.

Chapter Seventeen

Undercover

M igo smoothed his uniform down as he looked at himself in the mirror. He didn't pride himself on very much, but he knew he struck an imposing figure in his armor and maroon cape. *Who wouldn't be intimidated by me.* He took particular note of his muscular arms and thick chest. A knock at the door drew his attention away, and he shook his head, considering himself stupid for the thought. *No time for personal revelry.*

After picking up his glaive, he left the room. Two soldiers waited for him outside—footmen—men who'd only recently joined the guard and were of similar age. He'd selected them intentionally, knowing they'd be more impressionable. He often suspected that many of the soldiers under his command had been manipulated by his mother and were perhaps spying on him.

"Guso, did you send for Hatan?"

"I did, captain, but I couldn't find him. He took a few men on a routine wall patrol."

Migo held back a grunt of disappointment. Hatan was supposed to come with him to the farmlands so they could talk to the farmers. Somebody around there had to have seen shaman activity. *I don't need Hatan.*

Though still, it was unnerving to be without the only person he could trust. *If only he hadn't gone on about that stupid theory.*

"That's good. Hatan will be needed out there," Migo said, covering his disappointment. They exited the palace and Migo mounted up on Genda, his rangola. She hummed with excitement. It had been a few cycles since he'd ridden her, and her company was one of the few comforts that Migo had. He couldn't even imagine what it would be like if another human was excited to see him.

Migo patted Genda's side affectionately as they made their way out the palace gates, the two other soldiers walking on foot behind him.

"How many shamans have you seen, captain?" one of the soldiers asked.

Migo turned back to look at them. The one who'd spoken looked at Migo with a slightly amused expression. He was little more than a boy, maybe only a couple months younger than Migo. *Is he mocking me?* He'd first seen shamans in his parent's court, back before Jehubal had officially joined the emperor's crusade against all shamans. People didn't like shamans, even then, but they were still tolerated. Then he'd seen a shaman when his father was murdered. He'd seen them a few times since, and he'd killed his first one just before he turned sixteen, right after his mother put him in the guard. After a few more slaughters, the shamans all but disappeared, abandoning their villages.

"Too many. But I don't see them as often as I used to," Migo answered.

"Are we going to see one today?" the other soldier asked. He was tall, and about seventeen, but he was thinner and gangly. His wide eyes carried a sense of worry.

Migo gritted his teeth. He hated these questions, and he was tempted to say yes just to see the reaction, but he held back his impatient remark. "If we're lucky, but not likely." The relief that passed over the gangly soldier's face annoyed Migo even more.

People were still cleaning away at the mud or sand that had accumulated from the last Maedari. For now, the sky was clear, but a steady, warm breeze blew in from the Scorched Waste. If he squinted out there, he could see the sand whipping up in the air.

The rounded roofs of the buildings cast most of the streets in shadow. The streets themselves were built in diagonal angles from wall to wall, spanning the width of the Ring. The one exception was the main road that passed straight through the middle of the city. This was the road that Migo always took, since Rikaydian Palace was almost adjacent to it. Also, it gave him a chance to observe the people that went through Jehubal. He wondered if that made him predictable, and that perhaps the shamans avoided this road for that very reason.

Migo nodded to the guards at the entryway as he exited the city. The traffic between the city and the jungle was minimal. Most people didn't travel too far from their shelters. They reached the jungle in just a few strides, and Migo took a deep breath, inhaling the fresh smell of life. However destructive the Maedaris were to people, it seemed that the rest of nature reveled at the opportunity.

Migo laid his glaive across his knees. He'd fought shamans in this jungle and knew to stay cautious whenever he was outside the city. The depths of the jungle cast the road in shadow. Migo had always been amazed at how the foliage in the Ring could change so drastically from one side to the other. He'd heard stories from merchants of a mountainous region in the western edge of Malahem where the Ring was offset by the side of the mountain, its entire slope facing the sun. The Ring was nearly twice as wide there and it stretched a little further into the Frozen Waste, but all the vegetation was consistent from one side to the other because the temperature was hardly any different. Even Cataban, the next city-state to the south was much wider due to its slope.

The farmhouses of the marshlands came into view. Various crops grew from one side of the Ring to the other. Jehubal wasn't rich in minerals or manufactured goods, but it had good land that was perfect for growing many unique foods. They could grow just about anything from fruits and vegetables to nuts and herbs.

From the distance, Migo could barely see the guardhouse further down the road where at least twenty-five soldiers were always on duty. Migo often supplemented this by having regular patrols along the walls. This area was the main source of Jehubal's wealth and stability. If the shamans ever sought retaliation, he was sure this would be their target, but there was no convincing his mother that two-hundred more of the soldiers stationed at the palace should be reassigned here. There were also sections of the wall that were in disrepair, but Queen Rikaydian hated trading for new stone from Cataban. All she cared about was destroying shamans.

Migo steered Genda towards the guardhouse near the edge of Jehubal's borders. He'd done his best to establish a good reputation among the farmers. Perhaps it was because of the distance from the city, but it seemed out here that his mother's distaste towards him hadn't infected the farmers. He waved to some of them working in the field as if to make a point. They waved back, offering him a tiny semblance of satisfaction.

When they reached the guardhouse, Migo dismounted and handed the reins off to the gangly soldier. The soldiers at the guardhouse greeted him with a greater level of respect than Migo normally received within the palace grounds. Here, the soldiers knew who really cared about their safety.

One of the soldiers, a dark brown-skinned, well-muscled man named Falshon, bowed deeply. "Lord Rikaydian, we're honored to see you again," he said. Falshon was the commander of the post.

Migo nodded to him in acknowledgement.

"Patrol, orders, or reconnaissance?" Falshon asked.

"Reconnaissance. I'm sure you heard of the recent murder," Migo said, striding into the guardhouse. It was made of sturdy stone, and the brasswood door groaned as it opened and closed.

"Indeed, I did."

Migo made his way straight to a back room that stored a few extra armaments as well as Migo's disguise. Once it was only him and Falshon in the room, Migo started to change his clothes as he described the plan. "This time, you'll ride Genda and take six men with you to the eastern wall to scope out the Frozen Waste near that old hideout and see if there's been any recent activity. Return within a quarter of a cycle. I should be back in here by then."

"Yes, lord," Falshon said. He removed his own cape and put on Migo's instead, dressing up so that he could pose as Migo. They were the same height and had similar builds.

Lastly, Migo handed his glaive over to Falshon. It was no easy thing to do. He always felt uncomfortable without his weapon. Instead, he hid a knife on the inside of his brown robe and another up his sleeve. Such roguish weapons were beneath him, but he needed something that could be concealed, and a six-foot pole with a silver blade wouldn't work.

Once they were both fully outfitted, Migo dismissed Falshon with a nod. Falshon left the room, posing as Migo, while Migo headed over to a cupboard that swung open, revealing a passageway that led underground. Only darkness awaited. Migo ducked as he proceeded through the dark tunnel, holding a hand against the wall to guide his way. Before long, the ground sloped back up, and he stepped over large roots that laced the ground. He fumbled at a door before him until he located the lock.

He turned the handle on the door and pulled it inward just a crack, listening for any sound outside. He heard nothing, so he hurried and slipped outside, sliding the door shut behind him. He was outside in the jungles south of the marshland. The door had been carved out of the side of a castletrunk tree and had been made to fit perfectly with the seams of its bark.

Migo rushed to the other side of the tree where the road was just a few steps away, and then proceeded to move north to return to the farms. He was undercover. This was precisely the kind of thing Hatan discouraged, and Migo found a small sense of satisfaction in that.

A small troop of Rikaydian soldiers were marching off towards the Frozen Waste, one of them riding atop a rangola. Falshon was right on time. As Migo passed the guardhouse beside the road, he waved at a couple of guards that stood outside, which just so happened to be the young soldiers Migo had brought with him. They nodded to him without further acknowledgement.

Migo made it to the marshes and steered his way toward a particular farmhouse that was closer to the Frozen Waste. He wanted to get this over with. The feeling of cloth against his face was unpleasant, and it stifled his breathing, giving him a slight claustrophobic feeling. *How can they stand these things?* He noticed a few farmers up ahead who were wrapped up even more thickly than he. Migo concealed his identity not for his own sake, but for that of his informant. It could potentially spoil the man's connections if it were known that he was leaking information to Prince Rikaydian himself.

Farmers looked in Migo's direction as he came closer, but none of them paid him any special attention. Random visitors were not uncommon. It was a typical practice along the eastern Ring cities for people to assist in farming. Life in the Ring was rugged, so people made efforts to support each other when possible. Nobody would survive long if they were homeless and hungry.

Migo came to the door of the modest farmhouse and knocked. No more than a couple heartbeats passed before it was open, and Migo's informant looked out at him, a young man with knowing eyes, his skin as uniquely pale beige as Migo remembered. A hint of light-brown hair peeked out from beneath the wrap on his head.

"Come in," he said, glancing around outside before moving aside to let Migo enter.

Migo strode inside. A seat had already been set up for him, so he sat down, and his informant took a chair across from him.

"Interesting that you should arrive, lord. I heard only moments ago that smoke was seen to the south after the Maedari, out towards the Delirad Lake," the young man said.

Migo considered the news, but that was technically unclaimed territory next to the Cataban borders. It could have been fire caused by lightning, but Migo always had to consider the possibility that shamans had been involved. "Good to know. I was hoping you might have some other information for me, Damani."

"What kind of information are you looking for?"

Migo set his jaw. It was always a little perturbing that Damani didn't seem more immediately forthcoming with his information, but Migo let it slide. "I'm wondering if you might have seen someone come through here recently."

Damani shrugged. "Well, I do pay close attention to any visitors, and I've encouraged several to farm with me, so I've seen many people come through lately. Who is this person?"

Migo pictured her in his head, remembering every detail he could bring to mind. "A girl. Black hair, dark eyes. Perhaps just coming into womanhood, though I can't be sure of her age. Her features were hidden behind a veil when I saw her, and her clothes seemed a bit heavier, as if she might have been wearing something extra beneath her coat and pants." He couldn't be sure because of the man's complexion, but it seemed like Damani may have paled slightly at Migo's description.

"Unfortunately, I can't say I've seen anyone that fits that description recently. The last young woman that came and worked among us was a few cycles ago, and her father came with her. They live just inside Jehubal city limits near the Oshe statue. She had dark eyes, but her hair was a light brown, and she wore a thick dress and a scarf that was a little too thin to be working near the Frozen Waste. I don't think she fits the description. How recent might this person have come through?"

"Two or three cycles ago." Migo watched Damani closely, trying to determine if the man was hiding anything. He couldn't be certain, but it seemed out of character for Damani to detail someone before saying they didn't match. However, Damani had provided accurate information a few times before, so it seemed like he could be trusted, but there was no knowing for sure.

Damani looked around in thought. "I haven't seen any other young ladies around that timeframe. Do you think she's still around? Is she a shaman?"

Migo considered whether or not to answer the questions. These meetings were supposed to go the other way around. If anything, it made him feel suspicious. *Is Damani trying to work me? For all I know, he could be trying to glean information from me for the shamans.* Migo rose to his feet, feeling at the knife concealed in his sleeve. "That will be all, Damani."

Damani dropped his eyes. "Yes, lord. Whatever I can do to help."

Migo strode back to the door and let himself out. He didn't like to feel like he was being played. He wouldn't be a tool for shamans—not again. His fist clenched with an episode of his own self-loathing. He walked directly to the next farmhouse, noticing from his peripherals that Damani was watching from his open doorway.

He gave a hard knock at the door. It was opened by a younger woman. She looked to be of marrying age, but her far-apart eyes, large nose, and pinched smile suggested that she didn't have a high likelihood of getting married. Migo jumped straight to the question. "Have you seen a young woman around here lately, farming with the others? Perhaps even working with Damani."

She gave Migo a dark frown, then glanced at Damani and gave him a weak smile. "Damani helps a lot of people. Plenty of girls have worked with him before." She pouted slightly at that, and Migo was almost amused at the obvious jealousy.

"What about in the last few days? Any girls work with him?" If he was right, he assumed that this girl kept a close eye on Damani.

"Yeah, I suppose. There were a couple of them recently. Some twig of a girl from the city, and then there's the regular one. She comes around quite a bit—usually works with Damani."

Migo felt a surge. "Who's that?"

The woman sniffed. "I don't know. Always wears her veil. She doesn't really talk to anybody else that much... Are you courting her or something?" She glanced over towards Damani again.

Migo didn't bother answering. He spun on his heels and barely kept from sprinting as he hurried back towards Damani's farmhouse. Damani looked as pale as an ice flora, frozen in the doorway.

When Migo was only a few steps away, Damani seemed to snap to, and he moved to slam the door shut, but Migo pounced forward and shoved it open, throwing Damani back with the force. There was a scream from outside.

Damani had stumbled against the table, and he picked up a potted plant from its surface and hurled it at Migo. Migo sidestepped, and it flew by harmlessly as he closed in on Damani. In a sad attempt, Damani took a swing at Migo. Migo caught Damani's arm and twisted him around. Damani's face smacked up against the wall as Migo held him from behind.

"You lied to me," Migo said, his voice quiet.

Damani only whimpered. He stopped struggling. It was clear he'd given up.

Migo shoved Damani to the stone floor and stomped on his ankle. Damani gasped with pain as Migo went and closed the door. He didn't need any witnesses.

"I want you to tell me the truth this time."

Damani's face was wracked with pain, and he backed himself up against the wall, eyeing Migo with a look of fear and defeat.

"Who's the *other* girl you've been working with? What do you know about her?"

"It's a lie!" Damani rose to his feet, though he still kept his distance. "Whatever Sanadi said. She gets jealous of anyone."

Migo shook his head, then punched Damani in the eye and kneed him in the gut. The back of Damani's head smacked against the stone wall from the force.

"You would take her witness against mine?" Damani said, eyes wide.

"If I asked the other farmers, would they tell me the same thing Sanadi did?"

Damani glanced sideways, chewing his lip.

"There's another girl, one who labors with you regularly. Your lies won't work now, Damani. You gave yourself away the moment I turned back to you. The horror in your eyes was all the evidence I needed. This is my job." Migo punched Damani again. The familiar pain in his knuckles almost brought a sense of relief. All this time, Damani had been a spy for the shamans. *How had I not seen this before?*

"Tell me who she is."

"I don't know who you're talking about!" Damani had huddled into a ball, holding his arms over his face.

There was still screaming from outside. Soon enough, others would come and his identity would be discovered. The guards would be close behind though. Migo went and threw down the Maedari locks. Anybody would have a hard time breaking through those. It would possibly give him enough time to complete the interrogation.

Migo sighed and sat at a chair facing Damani. "You have a good heart, Damani." Migo massaged the bruises on his knuckles. "All of this is completely unnecessary. Is this really worth being tortured? Are you willing to die for a shaman? She killed innocent people."

Damani looked at Migo with a deep frown.

"I'm willing to look past all this," Migo continued. "I know you've worked well with us before, so perhaps this case is different because you've felt like you can trust her. Maybe you've thought she's different than other shamans—but she's not. I assure you. I'll let you go free, Damani. I'll forgive your offense, even though you deserve to die for your treason. All you need to do is answer the questions. Let's start with her name."

Damani shook his head and covered his face in his hands.

Why is this so hard? He's betrayed other shamans, what makes this different? Something clicked. "Look, Damani. You lied to me, the prince, so I have punished you for your insult and dishonor. I understand you might feel like you are protecting her, but we have reason to believe that she might know something that could help keep the rest of our people safe. I need to ask her some questions—I'm not seeking to harm her. I need you to tell me the truth, or I'll have to put you in prison. If my mother hears about your crime, then your very life is at risk. Just tell me what you know, and I'll walk away from this."

Damani considered for a moment. "Let me talk to her." It was his first admission to knowing the girl.

"No. It can't work that way."

Damani shook his head again and rubbed a hand across his mouth. "Katsi," he said, his voice barely audible.

Migo leaned in closer. "What?"

"Her name is Katsi—I don't think she's a shaman. She's just scared. She's an orphan."

Migo nodded. He reckoned guards would arrive shortly. "Where can I find her?"

Damani cast his eyes down again. "I think she lives in the Scorched Waste, somewhere over the crumbled section of the wall just sunward of here. I've seen her crossing over it a couple times in the last few cycles." He stopped and looked up at Migo sharply. "You won't hurt her, right?"

"Not if she's innocent," Migo said, getting to his feet. He could hear metal clinking as guards were running near. He released the storm locks from the door and opened it just as five soldiers arrived. Migo pulled back his hood, and the soldiers recognized him instantly. "Arrest this man." He pointed at Damani.

"You said you'd let me go!" Damani rose to his feet, eyes wide with horror.

"You committed treason, Damani. How could I let that go?"

Three of the soldiers rushed in and bound Damani's arms behind his back.

"Don't hurt her," he cried, repeating the phrase as the soldiers dragged him off. "Please."

Migo only shook his head, appalled that Damani had been so easily fooled. He would rot in prison until he died, all because he'd let himself be seduced by a shaman. A tragic fate for a young man who had once seemed promising.

Now, to find this Katsi.

Chapter Eighteen

Snitch

Katsi unrolled a small square of aged cloth and looked at both sides of it. The trees above her groaned under a steady wind, and Katsi released a heavy sigh. She'd gone back to see the old shaman woman in the canyon to inquire more about stormcalling, but her answer was less than favorable. There was nobody around that could teach her. *All she did was give me this stupid letter that I'll never be able to read.* The words on the parchment were supposedly hidden with an enchanted magic, but Katsi doubted she'd ever be able to activate it. Learning to stormcall without training seemed like the only real option.

The best she could do now was save Damani and the other farmers from getting whipped out. She tucked the letter back into her belt and headed north through the jungle. A few farmhouses, including Damani's, were visible through the foliage. The jungle grew thick at the edge of the farmlands, feeding off the rich soil.

As she approached Damani's home, her pace quickened. She'd been away a cycle longer than she'd intended. He'd be anxious. A few farmers went about their normal work outside, but other than the sound of insects, an eerie silence welcomed her. She wasn't typically so blatant, but she knocked lightly on Damani's door. She at least hoped to check in with him before she attempted one of her craziest deeds yet.

No response came.

It's okay. There are plenty of places he could be. She sighed and turned away.

The girl who lived next-door stared at Katsi with a twisted expression. She looked like she was on the verge of screaming or exploding in tears. Katsi shook her head as she turned away and headed for the road. *I knew she was jealous, but wow.* She'd just have to check back in on Damani later.

Few others walked the road when Katsi arrived, but she followed a few paces behind a group of three heading toward the city.

It was easy to hide among ringdwellers. Aside from some old hairstyles and traditional shaman markings, there were no significant differences in appearance, no differences in speech or mannerisms, yet they'd all hate her if they knew what she was. It was unfair. She lived a life of loneliness and obscurity because leaders like Queen Rikaydian chose to sow hatred against the shamans, blaming them for anything bad that happened.

"At least I've got Damani... and you, Scales," Katsi said, patting her pocket as she approached the open gate to Jehubal. Her pocket felt empty. "Scales?" Her heart sank as she looked around, patting her other pockets.

Something nipped her ear. Katsi jumped and muffled a shriek as she reached into her hood and pulled Scales from her hair. "What're you doing?"

Scales licked his eye and released a high-pitched croak.

Katsi groaned. "I'll get you some food in a moment, we just have to reach our spot."

"Everything good?" said a deep voice.

Katsi tucked Scales into her pocket and smiled at the guard who'd approached her. She didn't think carrying a scaila around as a pet was a very ringdweller thing to do. Best to keep Scales hidden. "I'm well! Just heading in, thank you." She hurried to get inside before the guard could say more.

Traffic thickened once Katsi got a few steps into the city. This was where money flowed through Jehubal. She'd long-since mapped out Prince Rikaydian's usual path, which had been fairly easy since he always went the same way, unless he was heading to an incident within the city. She always figured it would come in handy.

More and more people milled about the road as Katsi proceeded. A few traders seemed to have arrived from the north. Most of them would be buying some of the unique foods in Jehubal. It almost felt embarrassing to Katsi that Jehubal's most popular product was its pastries. *Or was it sugar?* She couldn't remember.

She reached her destination, an abandoned warehouse that bordered the road. It sported six exterior doors and a "secret" passage that she could use to escape into the back street. She'd only used it once before after she'd swiped a pastry from a merchant that was paying more attention than she'd thought. Sure, she dropped the pastry on the ground in her haste, but it still tasted fine when she ate it.

Katsi settled down beside the open entryway, leaning against the wall. The door had been missing for a couple years, so it was open to the weather during a Maedari. That made it feel all the more comfortable to Katsi. Shamanfolk didn't use doors on their shelters. There were other angles to use to keep the storms from throwing everything around, and being able to feel nature in action was just... well... more natural.

She pulled out a small pomay fruit that she picked on her way in and started peeling it apart to reach the crunchy inside. Now it was all a waiting game. In an ideal setting, Katsi would have a perfect idea of Migo Rikaydian's exact schedule. She'd know what he was going to eat, where he was going, the names of the other soldiers that accompanied him, who their families were—all the detailed stuff behind a master plan.

But no. She had no time to plan, and no way of knowing when the opportunity would even arise, so all she could do was wait. She was anticipating waiting for half a cycle, thus it came as a surprise when she saw a giant young man marching down the road, a black and red cape fluttering behind him with exaggerated flare. She rolled her eyes. *Does the prince have any idea how pompous he looks?* He was heading north, returning to the palace. Two of his cronies followed behind him, brass helmets gleaming on their heads. Katsi shook her head. If the Bayvana Tribe was truly armed with seculas, then the Rikaydian soldiers wouldn't stand a chance.

Migo Rikaydian watched everyone around him, his brows furrowed in his perpetual frown. From what she'd learned about him, he'd been seeded with a hatred towards the shamans as deep as his own mother's. Katsi hadn't spent much time in his presence, but she'd never seen any other expression on his face. *I suppose a murderer doesn't deserve to feel anything but shame.* If what she'd heard at the tribe's hideout was true, then Migo had recently killed two more shamanfolk, accusing them for the murder of their shamanfolk neighbors. It didn't make any sense.

It's now or never, she thought as Migo walked in front of the warehouse.

"Hey rangola dung!" She threw the core of her pomay fruit at Migo's head, fully hoping to hit him in the face. If only the tribe knew the crazy things she did to try and keep the peace.

He dodged the volley as if he'd been expecting it, his dark eyes locking onto her in an instant. She was struck by how intimidating he looked, tall and powerful. Others in the road hurried out of the way. Migo headed for her, not rushing like she thought he might, but slow and deliberate in his stride. At a signal, the two other soldiers spread to either side, prepared to approach at different angles.

Katsi retreated inside, starting at a sprint. She ran up a flight of stairs near the back of the room. At the top, she rolled on her side across the floor, slipping under a gap in the stonework. This section had been hollowed out for some kind of ventilation, or something. Whatever it had done, it provided good cover for Katsi. The equipment at her belt was barely able to fit. No soldier would be able to squeeze in there. She made sure not to squish Scales as she shimmied along until she reached a spot where a small gap left a fist-sized hole to the first floor. From there, she could peek at the entrance.

Migo was already inside, the light from outside silhouetting his large figure. She couldn't see the two soldiers. That worried her. They'd likely gone to secure other entrances. Despite her confidence earlier, she felt a twinge of fear that perhaps they knew where this shaft led out to.

There was no going back from here. The moment of betrayal. She gulped. "The shamans are setting a trap for you, mad-face," she said. She couldn't bring herself to call him by his name.

"Is that so?" Migo looked about the room. He held his glaive to the side, almost casually. "I don't think anybody else is here, Katsi."

Katsi felt like she'd just been smashed by a house. *How does he know my name?* Her heartbeat pounded in her throat, ears burning. What else could he know? She wanted to get out of there—now. It was all she could do to keep from crawling away. But she needed to do this to keep Damani and the farmers safe.

"Not here. In three cycles," Katsi explained. "They're planning to kill you and half the guard somehow. That would leave Jehubal with weak enough defenses for them to take over."

Migo stopped at the center of the room, far enough in that Katsi could see his face a little better. He kept from moving his head as if to portray a sense of nonchalance, but his eyes darted about. "That comes as no surprise. They've always been planning on killing us."

"Not like this. There's something serious about what they're planning. They have new weapons." Her voice echoed through the room, making it a little more difficult to locate the source, but Migo looked in her general direction. His frown had deepened when she mentioned the weapons. That appeared to be language the brute understood.

"What kind of weapons?"

"Terrible things. They can break through stormguards. Look, just don't fall for anything stupid. Protect the farmlands and everything, but if you hear of something coming, pull the people back into the city. Your main priority should be to keep the people alive. Defend the walls. Don't try to fight the shamanfolk in the jungle. They'd slaughter you."

"I know what my job is," he growled, taking a few steps forward. Katsi heard a foot shuffling in the room above and beside her. They were closing in on her position.

"Then prevent people from dying—don't cause it." She sounded angrier than she'd intended, but then again, she was surprised she had a whole conversation with one of her greatest enemies without yelling curses at him. Maybe she'd throw one in now for good measure. "You don't know anything about what shamans are capable of, milaweed, so you better take this seriously."

Milaweed? I couldn't do better than that? It was a weed that killed other plants around it, but it grew small purple flowers. Migo probably had no idea what it even was. She groaned. *Ugh.*

She crawled further into the recess, away from the hole. Footprints echoed near the landing where she'd rolled under. She didn't want them to find where she'd gone so that when she came out the other end, one of them wouldn't be waiting for her.

When she got to the end of the shaft, the hole widened. She peeked into the alleyway and didn't spot any soldiers, so she slipped out feet-first and fell to the floor, landing lithely. She pulled her veil over her face and entered the street. She ducked into the crowd, catching a glimpse of a soldier still watching the side of the building. She'd weave her way between a few more streets and alleys in case they were trailing her. Then, she'd head home for some much-needed sleep.

Chapter Nineteen

Worth

"Do we try to follow her?"

"No," Migo said, addressing his two soldiers. They stood at the back of the warehouse in the alleyway, noting the air shaft that she'd likely used to escape. She clearly knew the area well.

"We know where she'll end up anyway," he added. He'd posted two guards to hide near the crumbled wall that Damani had told him about. It would eventually lead them to Katsi's hideout.

It had been two cycles since Damani confessed to Migo. They hadn't caught sight of Katsi at all, and he'd been close to giving up hope that she was even around or that Damani had lied. Migo turned to head back to the palace, the soldiers following at his heels.

This supposed attack was coming in four cycles. The same time Migo was destined to die. A ripple ran across his skin. Would it be the moment he could prove himself?

Perhaps he was being manipulated. He ground his teeth as he remembered the look in Bindom's eyes right before he killed him. He tried to blink it away, but the image remained. It was seared into his vision. There was so much blood on his hands.

His fists clenched with frustration. There was a pit in his stomach that made him want to scream and punch someone in the nose. Perhaps Katsi would be the last key to finding the rest of the shamans. If he could kill them all, this whole nightmare would end, though once he captured Katsi, he'd have to keep her alive long enough to question her.

When Migo reached the palace, the queen was in the courtyard, wearing light armor over a more practical, thigh-length dress with slits up the sides. She often trained with a select group of instructors, and Migo was never privy to those sessions. All he knew was that she trained with a variety of weapons, and that she, of her own right, was an extremely dangerous warrior. There'd supposedly been multiple attempts on her life, but each would-be assassin had been met with disappointment.

He hurried to the nearest palace door and went inside. Further interaction with her was out of the question until he had more to report. Katsi's ominous warning wasn't enough to go on. "Find the lieutenants," Migo said to the two soldiers who accompanied him. "Tell them to meet me at the training yard by sixth mark."

They ran off to fulfill his orders, boots echoing through the stone hallway.

Migo turned toward his room to find Hatan walking in his direction. He hadn't seen his cousin since their disagreement two cycles ago.

"Captain," Hatan said, throwing in a salute and a beaming smile, as if nothing was amiss in the crumbling world. "I was hoping we could have a word."

"Very well," Migo said, leading the way down the hall to his room. "How were your patrols?" He tried not to sound bitter.

"The lands are as beautiful as ever. I didn't find anything amiss in our northern borders." He said nothing else until they had entered Migo's room and closed the door.

"The queen hasn't deviated from her plan to have you killed. You have three cycles left."

Three cycles. What would come first, his assassination, or the shaman invasion? "I am aware," Migo said as he unclasped his cape. "If it's her will."

"Migo," Hatan shook his head and placed a hand on Migo's shoulder.

"Should it concern her majesty that you seem to have a man in every place you shouldn't?"

Hatan snorted. "Not at all. It just means that there's another organization looking after the welfare of Jehubal. But Migo, I know you were intent on proving yourself to her. Do you still feel that this is the best option?"

"Not at all." Migo accepted Hatan's help in removing his armor. "I don't deserve to be king anyway. I think she knows what's best for Jehubal."

Hatan's eyes widened in protest. "That's not true. You care about the people and go through great pains to keep the lands safe, with more wisdom than Tilayna has had. It's only her lack of respect for you that taints your name. She should have been your mother, but you were raised by soldiers instead. She poisons you with her own hatred."

Migo let out a deep sigh. "Cousin, I know you mean well by this, but I accept my fate."

"Well I don't," Hatan said. Migo thought he saw tears forming at the corners of Hatan's eyes, but they vanished in a blink. "You've been nothing more than a tool in her eyes. Don't forget yourself, Migo. Your father knew who you were. That's why he was willing to die for you. Any true father or mother would do the same."

"My father did not make the mistake. I did," Migo said. "I will hear no more of this, Hatan. I do have a chance at redeeming myself, however. As circumstances would have it, there will possibly be an attack on the city within four cycles. The Bayvana Tribe has apparently forged some kind of ancient weapon."

Hatan blinked. "How did you come across this information?"

"The girl."

"You found her?"

"Not exactly... she found me. She threw something at me, and I think she called me a flower." It was like the whole interaction had been a joke to Katsi. "She tried to give me a warning about a shaman army that may be attacking the city soon."

Hatan was dumbfounded. "Did she invite you over for treats as well?"

Migo rolled his eyes, though he was glad to have Hatan back in good spirits. "I'm not sure what to think of it, of course. I had scouts sent to Delirad Lake to investigate some smoke that was seen out there. We haven't heard back yet. I'll be meeting with the lieutenants to discuss a strategy. The girl made a point of ensuring I protect the outlying citizenry. I suppose she doesn't know yet that I've imprisoned the traitor who's been harboring her."

"A lot has gone on," Hatan said with a nod.

"And this might sound insane, but," Migo said, flexing his arms. "I hope the girl's right and that the shamans do attack. It would be just in time for me to prove myself in battle." That, or die trying. Both were better options.

Hatan sighed. "Hurting people does seem to make you happy sometimes." His face darkened. "Why would the girl say all of this to you? Why betray her people like that?"

Migo rubbed his temple. "It's probably part of their plan. They want us to pull everyone into the city so the lands are unprotected, then they can pillage all the crops."

"I could see that," Hatan said. "I'll send word to Lieutenant Falshon at the south road tower. We should still pull the citizens back so they don't get caught in anything."

"Agreed. We still have a few cycles to prepare. I'll meet with the lieutenants, and then we can coordinate with the other captains. In the meantime, I've posted some men near where the girl supposedly bunkers down. With any luck, we'll catch her and interrogate her before the invasion."

The plan would work. It had to. And the queen would call off his assassination. But in the pit of his stomach, he knew it was flawed. Something would go wrong. He could never anticipate the unexpected.

Chapter Twenty

Where's Damani?

"So, what about the Rikaydians? I heard they might be a little..." Katsi paused, glancing around and lowering her voice before adding, "off." She was seated at a table in one of the few sleephouses within Jehubal. There were only a few other patrons, but they'd all been commissioned to clean up the mess from the burned home. She slept there for a few marks, which wasn't something she normally did, but she felt too tired to go back home.

"They're not too bad," said one man with dark brown skin, his hair a unique shade of red, peppered with brown. He was maybe from the other side of the Ring on the west of the planet, like Damani. "They kept the shamans out for a good while."

The other man rolled his eyes, his hair a solid shade of black. He leaned closer and said, "Yeah, but apparently the prince is a criminal or something."

"That's just sleet and sand, Kasan," the red-haired man said.

Kasan shook his head. "It's true, Domi. Everyone knows the queen hates him. It's because he murdered his aunt when he was a kid or something. He's not right in the head. That's why he goes about with such brutality all the time."

Domi muttered a curse under his breath and looked back over at the door. Speaking out against the royal family was a crime, but plenty of people did it. The gossip Kasan was sharing wasn't anything Katsi hadn't heard before, but she was hoping to get more information about the recent execution.

"She beats him up, you know," Kasan continued. He'd glanced up when he said 'she,' referring to the queen. "I saw it before, a couple years ago. She just hit him right in the face. I never heard of royalty doing that."

Domi barked a laugh. "You've never heard about that kind of thing because apparently you don't know things about stuff. I've heard plenty about royalty killing their own family." He gave Katsi a reassuring nod. "A hit in the face is of little consequence. I'm sure she was just giving him some sort of growing opportunity."

"How about I smack you in the face and see how much you grow?" Kasan said, giving him a look that called him an idiot.

Katsi found herself impatient with the conversation. "Does the queen still treat the prince like that?"

Domi perked up, flashing Katsi a smile that missed a few too many teeth. "I doubt it. Hard to imagine somebody beating a big boy like him. We haven't heard anything nice about their relationship though, we'll put it that way." He looked down at his hands and his face dropped in disgust as he noted a bit of black filth in one of his nails.

"You better wash that out, Domi. Never know what that dark magic stuff can do," Kasan said, his face very serious.

Domi excused himself without a word and rushed off. Katsi resisted laughing at him. Ringdwellers were so inundated with superstitions about shaman magic, she was surprised anybody had agreed to clean up the residence at all. She decided the conversation was getting her nowhere though, so she dismissed herself as well and went back outside. She'd probably been stalling long enough.

What she really needed now was to see Damani. Some semblance of normalcy would help to ease her mind. Too much worrying about the tribe attacking. *Besides, maybe Shinaseh was right, and those men were just throwing out ideas of bravado.* If she was fortunate, then her warning to Migo would be unnecessary, but the chances were slim.

Sleet and sand. Katsi drew a sharp breath as a terrible thought occurred to her. Migo knew her name. What if word got out that she'd tipped him off? She would never be able to go back to the tribe, and furthermore, they might go after her as a traitor rather than a deserter. Then she'd be hated by both her people and the ringdwellers. *I'm an idiot. I should have just let things play out on their own. Why do I think I need to interfere?* She had to remind herself that this was going to keep Damani safe. That was worth it.

Katsi made it outside the city walls without any undue attention. There was a small bit of traffic ahead of her heading back to the farmlands, and that always helped her feel like she wasn't so out of place. She followed them all the way to the farms, where she slowed and waited near the outskirts, hoping to catch a glimpse of Damani, but she couldn't spot him. Perhaps he was sleeping, but that added to her sour mood. She marched to his home, preparing herself to tell him what horrible trouble it was to keep him safe.

A few farmers were outside their homes, but none of them looked in her direction.

When she got to Damani's door, she knocked vigorously. There was no answer, and she started to panic, knocking even harder.

"He's not there, they took him!"

Katsi spun at the voice to find that neighbor girl looking at her. She frowned at Katsi with a face that somehow managed to make her look even uglier.

"And it's your fault!"

"What are you talking about?" Katsi demanded, taking a couple steps towards her and placing a hand over the sheath of her knife.

The girl stumbled back a bit, fear flashing across her face. "You're a shaman, aren't you? That's why he came looking for you."

"Who?"

"The prince, of course—the one who hunts monsters like you, who would use Damani because of his kindness." Her eyes drooped with a surprising sadness.

Katsi wanted to be snide about the girl's emotions, but her own heart lurched at the news. *Damani was taken by Migo... because of me.* Everything faded. Damani was the last thing she had—the only person she had ever been able to trust.

"Shaman! Guards! Shaman!" The girl screamed.

Katsi growled, took two quick steps, and punched the girl straight in the jaw, knocking her to the ground. She couldn't have imagined a better hit, and the girl wasn't moving. Katsi bent over and felt the girl's breath.

A couple of people stopped to look at what happened. "She's fainted!" Katsi said to them. "Too much excitement or something. Can you find her family? Help her get out?"

One of them was a chubbier woman, whose eyes went wide as she screamed, "I'll find Fennom," and ran off to one of the houses.

Katsi didn't wait to see what anybody else would do. She jumped up and headed back to the road, mixing in with a few other people that were ambling towards the city. She wondered if what the girl had said could really be true. Damani was taken by Migo. It didn't make any sense, though. *Why would Migo have taken Damani?* He must have connected Damani to her somehow.

Katsi burned with frustration. She'd wanted to keep Damani safe, and yet now she was the reason he was in danger. She shook off her tremors. If Damani was being held prisoner, then she would find a way to release him.

Chapter Twenty-One

Invasion

Migo awoke feeling only mildly refreshed. Good sleep and a healthy body would be vital for peak performance in battle.

His conversation with the lieutenants had gone well. They all agreed: defending the farmlands was critical. Now he needed to share a plan with the three other captains. He quickly got dressed in full uniform. A full entourage of ten soldiers accompanied him to the mess hall, arriving just before the second mark to meet with the other captains.

Migo ate while receiving a report.

"We've identified several key locations where we can secrete soldiers along the border and marked them on a map accordingly," said one of the soldiers.

"Very good," Migo said.

The doors opened, and the other three captains entered the room. Captain Tarahan, Captain Seba, and Captain Akailen. Captain Seba was in his young twenties, and Captain Akailen was the oldest of the four, his black hair peppered with gray.

"I'm glad you called us together, Captain Rikaydian," Akailen said. "We haven't had much opportunity to council together since Hatan Padarro stepped down as senior captain. It has left us disorganized."

Migo decided to overlook the insult to his cousin. "I'm glad you would come."

"What did you want to discuss?" Seba said, leaning forward on his elbows, eyebrows darkening in a frown.

Tarahan leaned back in his seat, arms folded, amusement glinting in his eyes.

This was Migo's time to shine. At least among his peers. "We need to discuss the city's defense against a potential shaman invasion from the south."

"Potential?" Tarahan said, a smirk lifting one side of his mouth. "I've heard nothing of this."

"Naturally, Captain Tarahan. That's because your soldiers primarily do city policing and northern border patrols," Migo said with a flat stare. "I've had a source inform me of a potential invasion coming very soon. I sent a scout party to investigate a fire near Delirad Lake. Those scouts returned recently to report that the soldiers at the Cataban outpost there were slaughtered, and their buildings were demolished and burned to the ground. This attack occurred three cycles ago."

"The entire outpost?" Seba said, eyes widening.

"Yes," Migo said, letting the words sink in.

Akailen grunted. "We haven't seen that level of aggression in years. We're not sure very many shamans remain to pose a big enough threat."

The door slammed open and Hatan came rushing into the room. He saluted the group of captains and approached Migo.

"Lord," Hatan huffed, "we've just received another report."

"Speak freely," Migo said.

Hatan nodded. "There have been multiple sightings. Armed shamans in the jungle. A cycle's march from the border. Sightings came in from around Delirad Lake. All the locals around there have fled up to Jehubal. Some crossed the lake to Cataban."

Migo shot to his feet. "How many shamans?"

Hatan shook his head. "We couldn't get a good count from any of the witnesses, but one woman said the jungle was alive with them."

A chill went down Migo's spine. The timing of the report was impeccable. He looked to the other captains. "We already have a plan in place," he informed them. "The citizens need to be withdrawn to the city. The shamans purportedly have weapons that can break stormguards. We need to set up a defensive perimeter along the farmland to ensure they don't steal or destroy the crops. We simply need more men to hold the line."

"Most of my soldiers will be too far to reallocate them effectively," Tarahan said.

"That's fine," Migo said. "Your troops can remain along the city wall and in the north in case the shamans have something else planned. Captain Seba and Captain Akailen, between the two of you, if we could allocate another three-hundred soldiers to the border that would be sufficient to cover the area we need to, especially along the flanks since we don't know where the shaman force will approach from. My two-hundred soldiers will be placed at the road outpost and along the border to either side."

"I agree with this approach as long as we are not spread too thin," Akailen said.

"Agreed," Migo said. "Keeping your soldiers in squadrons with horn alerts for point of contact would be most effective."

Akailen slapped the table and stood up. "Very good. I and my lieutenants will report to the south road outpost within two marks. Captain Seba?"

Seba scowled. "150 soldiers to kill shamans." He rose to his feet. "We'll be there."

"There's more, sir," Hatan said, gripping his glaive before him as if preparing to switch into a fighting stance. Migo nodded for him to proceed. Hatan continued, "One of the reporters claimed to be part of a merchant caravan that was attacked by them, and then he'd managed to hide long enough to run away. I don't know how true that account is, but he claimed to have overheard them planning to seize the lands between here and Delirad Lake. They'd said something about fortifying the border."

"And where is this man now?"

Hatan shook his head. "He ran away after giving his hasty report. Said he didn't want to be anywhere near the mess."

Migo nodded in acknowledgement then shook hands with the other three captains as they dismissed themselves. He leaned the flat end of his silver glaive against his forehead, the metal cold on his skin. The weapon had killed several shamans. It would continue to do so. He strode off down the halls, his soldiers close behind as Hatan walked beside him. "We have a dilemma here, Hatan."

Hatan gave Migo a knowing look. "The warning. The shaman girl knew this was coming."

Migo nodded slowly, tension building in his gut. "What troubles me is the lack of subtlety. Like they want us to know. They haven't operated like this before."

"True," Hatan said, rubbing his chin. "And there's been no sight of the girl?"

"None. Damani may have set us up. I don't know. I'm not sure we have time to investigate it anymore. We need to set up in the jungle. If we move quickly enough, we can perhaps catch the shamans by surprise as they attempt to settle in. We'll attempt our own ambush."

"Very well," Hatan said with a nod. "We'll need to move quickly, then."

"We need to keep our people safe, and I think the best way to do that is to eliminate the threat before it has a chance to get too near our people."

They reached the large training room where the remainder of Migo's soldiers had gathered. He strode to the front of his soldiers, now ready to address them. "We're at war," he shouted. "Be prepared to defend your people. No shaman army will step foot in our city." There were a few scattered roars of approval, mostly from younger troops, but the main bulk of the army was impassive. Migo had an unspoken understanding with them. They had been nullified by the wrath of the queen, their brutal taskmaster. All that remained was to do their job. "To the end!" he shouted, and the soldiers shouted it back.

Migo took the lead, riding Genda, and Hatan came behind him, followed closely by a flagbearer holding aloft the Rikaydian banner of a black rangola. The bulk of the soldiers marched at the rear. It had been too long since they'd fought in full force.

Chapter Twenty-Two

Rescue

Katsi finished tightening the straps of her stormwading armor. Their familiar, aged scent offered little support as she glowered ahead. She stood a block away from the gates of Rikadian Palace. It seemed more like an impregnable fortress now than it ever had before.

Scales croaked and peeked its head out from her pocket.

Katsi stroked under his chin. "Everything will be okay," she said, though she felt more as if she were addressing herself. *I can get him out. I can do this.* The words gave her no comfort. That twisted feeling hadn't left her gut since she'd learned Damani's fate.

What she really needed now was a plan. If Damani had been taken prisoner, there was only one place for him: the palace dungeon. She'd spoken to a few people who'd been there before, though what they'd shared didn't offer much insight. She knew the dungeons were a series of natural caves beneath the palace and some long staircase led down to them. That was it. She had no knowledge of where the staircase was.

But I'll find it. Her vision focused straight ahead as she pushed off from the wall and approached the palace gates at a light jog. Messengers often approached in the same manner.

And the gates were open.

Guards watched her from atop the wall, and two others stood just behind the gates. Were they ready for her? Had they battled stormcallers before? She was about to find out.

The relic on her upper arm felt tingly against her skin as she summoned her magic. Stormcallers of legend had been able to do marvelous things. Powerful things. Destructive things. Calling lightning, shaking the earth, summoning waves of water. She knew none of those skills, but she at least knew how to call upon the wind.

The guards screamed and shouted, one of them falling off the wall completely as a burst of air gushed over them. Particles of dust and sand from the last storm caught in the wind, creating a small cloud. Katsi ran right past the stumbling guards. She entered the courtyard at a sprint.

A set of doors were gaping open, and Katsi entered unhindered. Lordlings screamed and scattered. Some guards here had enough sense to brandish their weapons, but in the open, round room, it was easy enough for Katsi to simply run around them in the chaos.

Guards trailed behind by the time Katsi reached the far end of the room where she found a long hallway that went either direction. She chose left, but soon found a blockade of soldiers barring her path.

"Stand down, shaman," one shouted.

Without missing a beat, Katsi stretched out her arm, the artifact warm against her skin. A fierce wind tore through the halls. It left Katsi unharmed but ripped a few massive Rikaydian banners from the walls. The banners and wind struck with enough force to blow over a couple soldiers, and two other ones ended up wrapped in banners.

Katsi ran with the momentum. She rolled past the soldiers in their disorientation, some of them even scrambling away from her with widened eyes and mouths agape. Were they protecting anything in particular? She threw open the nearest door, and the next, and the next, but they were only rooms.

The soldiers were slow to follow her. *Maybe they can tell I have no idea what I'm doing.*

Hot pain burst through Katsi's shoulder. She spun away to find another soldier attacking her—one brave enough to get close to her. He'd managed to graze her with the tip of his pike. Shouldn't the stormwading armor have protected her from that?

The soldier looked different than the others from earlier. His uniform bore dark blue patches on the shoulders and he wore a round, silver helmet. Three other soldiers in similar uniforms approached her, two coming from the opposite end of the hallway. Something seemed familiar about those uniforms, but she couldn't remember why.

Katsi's heart pounded. The soldiers approached her with steady steps. Not rushing. Not stalling. Confident. One of them even had a smile on his face. She took a deep breath, the magical artifact on her arm flaring with warmth. With a scream, she thrust her arms out at the soldiers to either side of her. The stonework rippled and an explosion of wind erupted all around her. She had no idea what she was doing, she only knew that it felt... natural.

But the soldiers stood their ground.

One of them jabbed his pike at her. She skipped back to dodge the attack. *Trapped.* Her face flushed at the thought. Her back bumped against the wall behind her, a doorknob poking her rib.

Keeping her eyes on the soldiers, she tried the knob and leaned back. The door was unlocked. She pushed the door open and jumped inside. It was nothing more than an elaborate, but tiny bedroom. At least it gave her a little more room to figure things out.

She created a swirling maelstrom as two soldiers entered the doorway. A single, strong burst was all she'd need. Controlling her magic felt easier by the second. With a grunt of physical and mental exertion, she swung her fist at the soldiers from several paces away, calling on the magic to deliver the blow.

The maelstrom burst with enough force to slide the bed right by Katsi. It smashed into the two soldiers, sending them tumbling back into the hall. She followed them out. A soldier still stood to either side of the hall, and she wanted to scream as the trapped feeling pressed against her again. Would they force her to fight? This wasn't something she'd prepared for. She brandished her knife as they lowered their pikes at her.

Katsi rushed the soldier to her left. *I have to find Damani.* A force of wind at her back pushed her forward. She leapt, her body lighter as the wind carried her up.

Instead of jabbing forward at her as she'd expected, the soldier drew his weapon back and stabbed upward. It was barely quick enough to catch Katsi on her lower rib.

Katsi dropped and rolled across the floor with her momentum. She gasped, eyes wide. Shouldn't that have hurt a little more? She placed her hand on her side and felt something a little damp. It was the pocket where she kept Scales. Her heart clenched and tears burst to her eyes. *Stupid. I'm so stupid.*

A couple new uniformed soldiers approached from behind. There had to be another way to free Damani, but if she didn't leave now, she'd never get the chance. These soldiers knew what they were doing. Fighting wasn't an option.

She summoned her magic once again, calling forth torrents of wind that whistled through the hallway. The artifact warmed against her skin, and the hair on her arms and neck bristled up.

The wind burst with such explosive force that it toppled both soldiers, but Katsi was ready for it. She jumped forward, letting it carry her over the shattered bed, the other two soldiers still pinned beneath. She traced her steps back the way she'd come. The wind carried her with such speed that it felt like she was flying. Was this how it felt to be a Scaila? Gliding in the wind?

Scales would never get that chance.

Her vision was so blurred by tears that Katsi wasn't sure how she managed to get back outside. She soared over the palace walls. Enough sand caught in the wake of her storm to create a cloud of cover. She skipped across rooftops until she settled in a crevice between two walls.

She held back her sobs just long enough before Scales popped his head out of her pocket and made a croaking sound.

"Oh, Scales." Katsi's chest and throat rose with excitement. "I thought you'd been hit. I should have known my pocket wouldn't be a good place for you." She drew him out and cradled him in her hands, wishing she could squeeze him close. He certainly wasn't bleeding, but when she looked in her pocket, she did find it wet with the lizard's urine.

His body stopped trembling and he nipped Kasti's palm softly. He looked up at her with beady black eyes and tilted his head.

"I'm fine, Scales, I just..." She sighed. "I failed."

Chapter Twenty-Three

Messengers

Migo walked down the line of his soldiers. They stood in a cluster at the base of a castletrunk. He gave out final instructions then ordered them to their posts.

Several soldiers shifted with anticipation. Migo too was writhing inside. Battle was not something he looked forward to, but when it was fast approaching, he couldn't help but experience the surge of adrenaline. He was almost thrilled when he saw a messenger soldier running up to him.

Migo nodded as the soldier saluted to him, catching a breath before delivering a message.

The messenger's face looked nervous. "Captain, sir. The shaman girl never returned, but she attacked the palace."

"Elaborate." Migo cocked his head. *Is this all some massive scheme?*

"It was a very peculiar attack. She ran in, got repelled by some of the queen's guards, then disappeared in a flash."

Migo's grip on his glaive tightened. "She attempted to assassinate the queen?"

"No, sir." The messenger shook his head, eyes wide. "Once she entered the palace, she went the opposite direction of both the court and the queen's quarters.

Migo blinked. "So, she had some other purpose in mind?"

"We don't know, sir." The messenger shrugged.

"Any other details?"

"That's it, sir."

Migo dismissed the messenger with a wave. He'd never heard of such a thing. The shamans usually carried out pristine objectives. She was being careless. Reckless. *Perhaps she's desperate for something.* He still couldn't think of a connection between infiltrating the palace and the warning about the attack.

But he couldn't really do anything about that now. Besides, he'd already posted a couple soldiers to watch the place Damani had indicated. He started off toward the guardhouse.

Did the shamans know that each of his soldiers had been armed with silver-tipped weapons? Perhaps they were mad enough that they didn't care. His only thought of caution was born of Katsi's warning though, and that frustrated him even more. What weapon could the shaman's possibly have? Why would they have held back until now?

Migo nodded absently to a group of soldiers that were sequestered beneath a collection of bushes as he strode by. As instructed, the soldiers said nothing. They would make no sound until ordered to attack.

The wind blowing in from the Frozen Waste was both refreshing and nerve-wracking. It had been going for a full two marks. It reminded him that there were things much more frightening than war. Battle was something he could understand. He just hoped something else wouldn't get in the way. Defending his people from invasion was something real and tangible that he could actually focus on and understand.

He arrived at the guardhouse and received stiff salutes. His men were getting nervous. Hatan had just arrived as well. Migo entered the guardhouse, where a handful of his lieutenants waited for him. "Everyone is in position?"

The men gave their affirmations.

"We've also got the contingent of scouts running further south to get some more information on the enemy position," one of them reported.

Migo nodded. They'd spent most of the cycle getting the soldiers set up. He hadn't had as much time as he'd liked to devise a plan, but he felt confident things would go well. The other captains had delivered on their promise of soldiers. Still, there was something that made him worry, and he just wished it wasn't the shaman girl's warning to pull the soldiers back to the wall.

He ground his teeth. *What would a shaman girl know about battle tactics?*

Hatan saluted to Migo. He was acting more formal than usual. "I wonder if I might also have a word with you, lord, in private."

Migo tried not to roll his eyes, and led his cousin into one of the rooms and shut the door.

Hatan let out a weary sigh and regarded Migo with a shake of his head.

"What is it?" Migo asked, feeling alarmed at the sadness in Hatan's expression.

"Today is the final cycle, cousin." Hatan leaned his glaive against the wall, and he folded his arms, looking at Migo the same way a father might before telling his son that their pet scaila had died.

Migo sighed. "I'm aware."

"My source scrambled to get here, if you return to the palace after this battle, assassins are ready to kill you."

Migo set his jaw. "So it's settled then. No proving myself."

"She must be stopped, Migo. I can't let this happen."

"Well, you don't make choices for the queen." Migo exited the room, ignoring Hatan's protestations as if he didn't care. Hatan's passion made Migo's throat catch, but his ears burned. His heart groaned at his mother's loathing. There was nothing to do about it now. Migo couldn't count the number of times he'd contemplated his own death, anyway. Perhaps death at his mother's hands would be a mercy. She would finally get the vengeance she'd so long desired.

He clenched his fists. But she didn't deserve the satisfaction of killing him. Better to die in battle fighting the shamans. Dying that way would maybe give the queen one last honorable impression of him fulfilling his purpose.

When he stepped outside the guardhouse, Hatan at his back, he found the two guards by the door crumpled in a heap, dead.

Chapter Twenty-Four

Trade

Katsi sniffed as she bent down and placed Scales' little body beneath one of the coral bushes surrounding a castletrunk tree. This particular bush coalesced in shades of purple and blue.

"This will be a great place for you, Scales," Katsi said. "People throw fruit husks and things in here all the time." She swatted at a swarm of insects. "Plenty of food for you to eat, and the bushes should keep you safe from storms."

Scales licked his eye and shivered, the color of his head shifting to a deep shade of blue. She'd heard scailas could change colors, but hadn't ever seen it happen. He sniffed at a dried seed beside him then took a couple steps toward Katsi.

"No, you'll need to stay here. It's a lot safer, trust me. I'll come back to see you." She stood and let her lungs fill with warm air.

In the middle of the city, this was one of the few small plazas built with any consideration for aesthetics. It was the best place she could think of. A token of peace in a harsh environment. That was how her parents often referred to their pacifism.

Footprints drew her attention. Ready to sprint, she blinked away tears and looked over her shoulder at a couple hurrying across the plaza. Others were coming behind them. Perhaps a factory shift had just ended. She gulped and glanced at Scales one last time before heading south.

Her heart burned. She couldn't free Damani by force. There was something else she could try, but it seemed crazy. She'd already spoken to Migo before. Maybe she could try again. Damani was innocent. He didn't *know* Katsi was shamanfolk. Surely Migo would believe that. But she instantly doubted herself, punching her thigh in frustration. Migo would never release Damani solely based on Katsi's explanation.

It would likely be much simpler. A trade. Katsi's life for Damani. If Migo hated shamans so much, there was no way he'd be able to deny the offer.

She slid her way through the streets of a manufacturing district, avoiding the highway. There were usually less guards but still decent enough foot traffic to keep well under cover.

Her throat caught as she thought of being Migo's prisoner. The *queen's* prisoner. She'd likely get executed by Migo directly. The queen would watch it with eager eyes... Katsi's stomach bubbled painfully. *If it keeps Damani safe, it's worth it.* The words didn't ease the pain growing in her stomach. She'd broken out of captivity once. Maybe she could do it again. She had a better chance than Damani at least.

A steady wind whistled through the streets, its temperature moderate. It had been blowing for a couple marks, and nobody seemed too worried. Most people still went about their business as normal. Wind was not uncommon.

Katsi walked by a few shops that were selling some of the goods manufactured inside. They made various pastries for the most part, but one shop sold crafted wood—a rarer commodity usually reserved for wealthier citizens. It was difficult for many trees to reach full adulthood, and it was almost completely illegal among ringdwellers to destroy natural trees, thus farming trees and harvesting their branches could often be a lucrative business. However, not many families could afford several years of investment to do so.

As Katsi neared the wall, a small crowd of ringdweller citizens came into view. A couple men held clubs as they looked south and chatted animatedly.

"Did you hear how far away they are?" A woman said, her brows furrowed in worry.

"We might not see them till the next cycle," a man answered.

Katsi stopped and stood beside them for a moment, looking out beyond the wall. Amongst the crowd, a couple people glanced at her, but gave her no further attention. She scanned the jungle beyond. Aside from the winds from the Frozen Waste, nothing felt amiss. *But they're planning something. The tribe wouldn't move in so boldly without a plan.*

She looked at the walls. Not nearly enough soldiers. She cursed under her breath. Migo hadn't taken her advice. The soldiers were probably out in the farmlands. Didn't Migo realize how easy it would be for the shamans to sneak around through the wastes?

Migo was her only chance of freeing Damani. She couldn't imagine trying to bargain with the queen. The idea was too sickening. She'd be impossible to reach anyway. Migo was the only option.

Katsi went to the entrance of the gate. "When they come, you should get inside and bar your homes," she told the crowd. Most of them ignored her, and a few even made derisive comments, but Katsi went through the open gate and made her way towards the jungle. Shouts of surprise came from behind her, and someone even bothered calling her back, but she picked up her pace instead.

Her mind was made up. She would attempt to speak with Migo. She didn't make it much farther before she could faintly hear the clash of metal and men shouting. The battle had started.

Chapter Twenty-Five

Two Storms

Migo was a storm among the shamans. He wasn't sure how it had happened, but the shamans were somehow attacking his soldiers from both sides. They'd been much further ahead than all the reports had said. A force of them must have already been hiding around the farmland, but he still couldn't fathom how he and his soldiers would have walked right by them without noticing. It baffled him, but the pressing assault left him no time to think.

Several of Migo's men lay dead. Katsi's warning seemed completely true. Even worse, the weapons the shamans used were as terrible as she'd predicted. They treated shield and armor like they were merely another layer of skin. His men had fallen simply by trying to block the blows of the weapons but failed due to the strange magic of it. Migo had escaped a similar fate by using a fighting stance that used the advantage of his glaive's long reach.

Two shaman warriors closed in on Migo from the front, curved, cursed weapons in their hands. Migo weaved between a couple strikes, stepping further away from them as he did so. He spun away from an attack, wary of another shaman that approached from behind. Most of his soldiers nearby were already dead, but there were a few of them fighting in clusters. He needed to reorganize them.

The two shamans moved together, trying to get close enough for their weapons to reach him. Migo spun to one side, whipping his glaive overhead in a long sweep, the tip of the silver glaive catching one of the shamans on the top of the head. It pierced the shaman's leather cap, gouging into the flesh beneath. Silver metal had a quality that ignored shaman magic, making their magical armor not so unique at all, but nothing more than plain leather armor. If not for his weapon, Migo would have had a hard time taking any of them down.

The wounded shaman stumbled back, and the other shaman hesitated, half turning as if to help his companion. Migo used the momentum of his swing to move a little closer, risking the edge of a weapon. He bashed the butt end of his glaive against the uninjured shaman's chest, forcing him to stumble back. With another jab of the silver glaive, the shaman collapsed with a sliced gut.

Migo rolled, dodging a shaman who'd approached from behind. He was in his element. The impervious shaman weapons merely presented another challenge. It filled him with the thrill of achievement whenever he struck one of them down. There must've been over a dozen of them now that he'd slain. If one thing had ever qualified him as the greatest Rikaydian captain, it was his prowess on the battlefield.

The shaman came at a full sprint, and even though a strike with his weapon missed, he kicked at Migo, scoring a hit on Migo's thigh. Migo almost laughed at the blow, as it caused the shaman to trip and fall beside his wounded companion. This shaman was small. Migo was positive that he was at least twice the size of the little attacker. He shamelessly hacked down at the shaman's neck, ending his life. The blow displaced the shaman's veil, revealing a face that was undoubtedly feminine.

He staggered. Their women were fighting as well.

There was no time to consider. Two of his men were pinned down against the side of the guardhouse, fending off four shamans. Migo hadn't imagined that there were this many shamans left. He'd thought them thoroughly exterminated, but it was clear that they were far from it. He sprinted to the aid of his men just as one of them took a stab in the thigh, right through his plated mail.

Migo cursed. His conscience burned. He should have listened to Katsi and had his men fortify the city wall. Hiding his troops in the jungle and hoping to ambush the shaman's seemed like it had fit perfectly into *their* plan. She'd been speaking truthfully after all.

Migo's sprint to his men was just fast enough to let him hack down two of the shamans and injure a third. The fourth shaman fell to the weapon of Migo's uninjured soldier, which, to Migo's utter relief, was Hatan.

"Sleet and sand, captain, your timing is impeccable!" Hatan said, now supporting the other injured soldier.

Migo finished off the shaman he'd wounded, then turned his back to Hatan. They'd gathered a moment of peace, which he greatly needed in order to assess their next course of action.

"We're losing, captain," Hatan said.

Migo ground his teeth. "I know. We ought to pull back. Can you route the men and retreat back into the city?"

"Most of our men will be blocked off from retreat," said the injured soldier. "For all we know, this is the only spot where we've managed to butcher our back end free."

"I'll do as you command, captain," Hatan said. "I'll get every man I can back to the walls."

Another Rikaydian soldier came running over to them, and Hatan ordered him to support the injured soldier back to the city. "He should be able to limp along with you."

Hatan turned to Migo. "What of you, sir? Shall I head frostward and you sunward?"

"Yes, go!"

A sad look crossed Hatan's face. "If I don't see you after the battle, I'll assume you made it off to Cataban." He dashed away, stripping his helmet off and tossing it to the ground.

But Migo already knew he wouldn't make it out alive, and he certainly wasn't fleeing to Cataban. He ripped his helmet off. He would fight and kill the shamans as long as he held breath. He'd free up whatever men he could until the shamans took him down. It was his only option left. The price for his failure. For failing his father. Failing his mother. And now, failing his soldiers.

His self-loathing stung his eyes with tears as he rushed toward the sun, finding his nearest soldiers. He switched into Rangola Stance, pouncing at the shamans with targeted sweeps of his glaive. In a blur of blood, he'd secured the safety of another one of his soldiers, informing the man to retreat to the city. The frazzled soldier took off at a lopsided jog.

Migo couldn't move fast enough as he saw another of his soldiers die, a shaman's weapon sliced straight though the man's helmet as though it were nothing more than a sheaf of paper. He bellowed, stepping over the bodies of his fallen men as he charged the shamans. One of the shaman's blades slipped past Migo's defenses. The blade cut through his breastplate and slashed him across the chest. It didn't seem to hurt. Migo pressed on, hacking down his assailant with a single swipe.

He moved to dodge another attack, and to his surprise, found that the silver blade of his glaive caught the edge of the shaman's weapon without breaking. With a kick, he drove the shaman back, then finished him off with a blade to the face. One of his men lay on the ground, shouting in pain, his arm completely severed at the elbow.

This is your fault, Migo, he told himself as he reached down and dragged the soldier to his feet. He tore a cloak from a dead man's body and tied it over the soldier's arm. "Hold this in place and head back to the city."

The man's eyes were wide, and he took ragged, sharp breaths as he stared at his arm. There was no telling how much blood he'd lost, but he could still live. Medics had been told to wait near the jungles just outside the city. Perhaps now they'd be rushing out to help the injured back.

Migo gave the man a nudge to get moving and then proceeded sunward. More shamans were coming, but he just needed to free as many of his men as he could before he got killed. It was then that he noticed the wind had gotten stronger. A quick glance upward showed that the sky was obscured by clouds and debris. A burst of thunder rippled through the air.

Panic gripped Migo's chest. He stopped moving completely and stared at the sky with horror. *A Maedari is coming.* Run. He took a couple steps towards Jehubal, but nearby shouts shook him. Two of his soldiers were running from the battle, but another dozen men were still trapped by a group of shamans, their numbers dwindling with every heartbeat.

Lightning flashed across the sky, and Migo turned to flee. He had to get away from the storm and hide.

Coward!

His mother's voice rang in his ears, louder than the thunder that rumbled around him. She was right—he was a coward. He could face shamans, but at the first sight of a Maedari, he had to cower in a corner. Despite his fear, his legs stiffened. The cries of his soldiers brought him to a stop. They were dying.

You're a coward, Migo.

Migo set his jaw. "Not this time," he shouted. He couldn't watch his men fall while he yet drew breath. Wind buffeted him as he sprinted back to his cluster of soldiers, now down to eight. He roared a battle cry, drawing the attention of several shamans, who regarded him with apparent surprise.

Perhaps they didn't anticipate a ringdweller to charge back at them during a Maedari. He sliced one across the chest and rammed the other end of his glaive into another shaman's face.

He was a whirlwind among the shamans, spinning his glaive with devastating precision. Five shamans were down before they were able to collect themselves and form a line, standing between Migo's troops and the city to block off retreat. Fifteen strong, they outnumbered Migo's men.

I don't have to kill them all, I just need to get my men a head-start so they can make it back to the city. If they survived the Maedari, anyway. Two of his soldiers' glaives had been sliced in half, and one of them didn't have a weapon at all. They wouldn't be able to do much.

Migo jabbed at the shamans, using the length of his weapon to keep them at bay. He used the advantage of his silver-tipped weapon, parrying the occasional attack. He made a bold strike that pierced a shaman's shoulder, but he too was cut across the forearm. One of his soldiers jabbed a shaman in the face, but he lost his weapon in the move.

They were running out of time. Pebbles and ice swirled around them, and flashes of lightning flared left and right. Migo's determination was all that held back the panic. So much blood was already on his hands.

"Retreat to the city when I break through," he hollered to them over the roar of thunder.

He wasn't sure if his men heard him, but he charged forward, swinging his weapon in a wide arc, causing the shamans to step back. He spun, dropping to a knee and continuing his momentum so that his blade sliced at shins. Two of the shamans dodged, but two others were caught in the attack, dropping with cries of pain. One of his own men backed him up and took down another shaman.

That broke the shaman line. Migo's men rushed through the gap, one of them getting hacked on his way while Migo was holding one side of shamans back. He fought furiously, jabbing and swinging with a rage that had built up over years of torture, shame, and anguish. He was almost in a trance. A Maedari thrashed around him, and shamans fought to kill him. It was his worst nightmare—one that had haunted him—and yet he still stood there, fighting. He'd refused to cower. It was a small victory to him, even though his father was dead, even though most of his men had been slaughtered. At least he would die well, knowing that in the end, he'd finally made the brave choice.

But my father is still dead. And now it's my turn. A strong wind buffeted against Migo just as a large rock crashed into his shoulder. It tore him away from the battle, tossing him across the ground until he stopped against a thick coral bush. He squinted through the haze. To his surprise, only one shaman remained, crouching low to the ground as the strong wind persisted. Corpses littered the ground. Had he really killed all but one of them?

Migo struggled to his hands and knees, his weapon still clutched in his fist. Sand got in his eyes. He blinked constantly, which only made things worse. He crawled across the ground in the direction of the last shaman. His shoulder throbbed. The cut across his chest stung more than he remembered.

Sand and ice grated against Migo's skin. It had been a long time since he'd felt that stinging sensation. Not since the moment his father had died several years ago. Migo clenched his teeth and spared a glance towards the shaman, who was slowly approaching Migo at a crawl as well. It was all his eyes could bear before he clamped them shut again.

The wind was stronger than Migo expected. In fact, he'd thought the shamans immune to them, but seeing the shaman crawl with equal diffi-culty was reassuring. The wind picked up. It kicked Migo back into the air. He skipped across the ground like a pebble on water. All senses failed him then. The only sound was the roaring of wind and thunder, and the crashing of debris and rocks. He could hear nothing else. His nose and mouth seemed so stuffed with sand that he couldn't taste or smell. His eyes had been so barraged that he couldn't see. He grew numb to the ice and sand that tore at his body. The only sensation that remained was pain. The same pain that had been there ever since his father died. That was the moment that had come to define his life, and now it would be the only thing left as he died.

Chapter Twenty-Six

Saving an Enemy

Distant thunder groaned as the storm drew closer. Katsi drew her knife and sprinted through the jungle. It seemed peculiar to her that as fast winds blew in from the Scorched Waste, the clouds overhead moved the opposite direction. She saw the last few animals as they darted for cover. Even though the magical tingle wasn't yet in the air, she knew that a Maedari was coming. Like her, the animals would pick up on those first subtle signs, giving them ample time to find cover.

Unlike the animals, however, this was where Katsi felt comfortable. Soon enough, the winds would pick up, and the swirling debris and moisture would provide her with a shroud of cover. It was a disquieting idea to think that she felt most secure while isolated. Even being with Damani hadn't given her that same sense of security.

Katsi moved to hide as a cluster of Jehubalin soldiers ran by, heading towards the city. They'd clearly seen her, but made no attempt to intercept, their eyes wide with panic. They were running away. She didn't even find it surprising. Once the soldiers witnessed the damage of the tribe's seculas, Katsi was sure they would've just turned and ran in terror. With the combination of stormwading armor and seculas, she'd be surprised if any of the ringdwellers had stayed to fight. It would be a bloodbath, and if they didn't get shelter before the Maedari hit, all of Migo's men would die. Just like the tribe had planned.

She had to convince Migo that Damani had no idea that she was shamanfolk, and that she'd simply used him. Perhaps now he'd believe her after he'd realize that she told the truth about the shaman attack and their weapons. That was, if Migo even survived.

She didn't see any other ringdwellers until she reached the farmlands. Getting there felt like it had taken ages. Shouts echoed from the jungle on the other side. Towards the middle of the Ring stood a group of shamanfolk, cutting off the retreat of several ringdwellers. A few ringdwellers managed to make it past, but most of them were cut down with flashes of wicked metal. The tribe had become a well-equipped army.

If Katsi hadn't left the tribe, she'd be one of them. Killing defenseless soldiers who were only trying to maintain their land. *Well, it used to be our land.* That was how the tribe justified it. She passed a fleeing soldier, who clutched at the nub of his severed arm. His face twisted in pain, and his eyes swollen from sobbing. Katsi's guts twisted with disgust. How could such torture be justified? He started when he saw her and veered away to keep his distance. To him, she would look like another shamanic warrior.

The winds picked up with immense speed. There was a brief gust from the Frozen Waste, then a continual stream from the Scorched Waste. That was a bad sign. It posed a risk not only to the ringdwellers, but to shamanfolk as well, stormwading armor or not. Katsi was grateful her veil allowed her to see better in the storm. Sand was almost as thick as fog. The full Maedari would be upon them in mere moments. Anybody fleeing the battle now wouldn't make it halfway across the marshes.

Rain poured like needles. If not for her armor, that rain would have stung her skin. Her armor did nothing to shield her from the intense heat that blew in. Sprinting in the hot air left her drenched by the time she reached the other side of the marshes. Here, the air was noticeably cooler, and it blew westward. She spared a glance up, where she could barely pick out what looked like a column of cloud weaving its way towards the ground.

Sand and ice, if Migo's not dead already, then I don't think I could save him now. A few steps further into the jungle and Katsi stumbled into a scene from a nightmare. The bodies of shamanfolk and ringdwellers alike were strewn across the ground. Most of them were soldiers from Migo's guard. At this point, the shamanfolk had probably been wise enough to withdraw and find shelter.

To her surprise, Katsi noticed a group of ringdwellers sprinting across the marshes. She hadn't seen them before, but they were near the wall of the Scorched Waste. She must have been so focused ahead of her that she hadn't noticed. Perhaps one of them would be Migo? From the distance, there was no way she could tell. The wind at her back forced her to stumble forward. She moved with the wind, making her way sunward. She almost didn't have a choice of where to go. Would her magic help her in the storm? Likely, but she wasn't sure what to do with it yet.

Her best course of action now was to bunker down and hope that Migo survived the storm. She knew a couple spots near the Scorched Waste, so she jogged with the wind, dodging between trees, bushes, and dead bodies. She tried not to look at the bodies, knowing she'd recognize them, though she did think to glance at some of the ringdwellers just to make sure that none of them were Migo.

The winds were getting strikingly cold and a little too strong. She tumbled and rolled a couple times before grabbing onto a coral bush and reassessing her situation. Nearby, a wiggling pillar of cloud touched base with the ground. The tornado was in full force. Near-constant flashes of pink and violet lightning lit the scenery with a brilliant beauty. Katsi would have loved to watch it from the shelter of her hide-out, but now was no time for gawking.

She sheathed her knife—there'd be no need for it now—and continued sunward at a crouch. If that tornado came too close before she reached her shelter, she'd risk getting torn from the jungle and thrown out into the Scorched Waste. Shouts up ahead caught her by surprise. *What could somebody possibly still be doing out here?* She found it upsetting. Even shamanfolk would know not to be out this close to a tornado.

It was a massacre of bodies. The ground was soaked with blood. Both ringdweller and shamanfolk littered the ground in equal numbers. The bodies were slowly rolling to the west, occasionally catching in the wind. Katsi felt bile building up in her stomach. Surprise stopped her from vomiting. There was a single soldier yet alive, a massive ringdweller who was untangling himself from a collection of coral bushes. His skin was ravaged and bloody, but even still, Katsi would recognize that stupid face of his from across the whole Ring.

Migo Rikaydian.

Katsi wouldn't have believed it if she hadn't stumbled across the scene herself. He didn't seem to recognize her, but crawled towards her on hands and knees, shouting against the wind, words lost to the storm.

Perhaps she'd be able to get him to safety. She crawled as well, keeping herself low to the ground, but the wind was incredible now. Even Migo was thrown back, and she watched him bounce across the ground, dead bodies flying with him. Katsi couldn't imagine a more terrible setting. She ran a short distance, then stopped against a castletrunk. One of her shelters was nearby. She'd have to convince Migo to go with her.

Though not sure how it would help, she summoned her magic. She peeked around the tree and located Migo's body, the only one still moving of its own volition. He was rolling across the ground, but the winds could pick him up at any moment. She sprinted around the tree, making her way towards him. The storm somehow felt calm around her, like she could understand its movements. It distracted her just long enough for Migo's body to get flung into the air. He smacked up against the wall of the Scorched Waste. The crack of thunder that shook the air could have been the sound of his head as it connected with the hard stone.

Her stomach sank. She wanted to punch herself in the face for regretting the thought of Migo dying. It was a moment she'd silently hoped for, but not when he was her chance of freeing Damani.

He has to be alive. The idea of touching his dead body disgusted her, but she had to be sure. Migo's body slid up the side of the wall, threatening to get carried out into the Scorched Waste. Once past the wall, there'd be nothing keeping him from getting cast out leagues into the desert. There was no getting back from there.

Was she ready to seal her fate as a traitor? She shook her head. She'd already made her decision. For a brief moment, the wind was her ally as she jumped to her feet and ran to him. Just as she reached Migo's body, both of them got swept up in a powerful gust, carrying them over the edge of the wall and out towards the Scorched Waste. She felt a strange sense of calm, directing the wind to carry them down.

They landed hard on the sand. The storm around her had stilled. She could feel the artifact on her arm like a warm pulse.

Panting, she leaned over Migo's body. His eyes were closed. He made no movement. She removed a glove and placed a hand over his throat. Even then, she could feel a burning desire to end him right there. Her own heart thumped loudly in her ears. Tighten her grip. Squeeze. Dig her nails into his neck. The thought disgusted her. His raw skin already stained her fingertips with his blood. Instead, she searched for a pulse and felt a weak thumping from his veins.

He was alive. However bittersweet, he was alive.

Katsi heaved a sigh and checked her surroundings. Now she needed to find shelter from the rest of the Maedari. And somehow, she'd have to drag Migo's body with her. She had a feeling she was going to regret this.

The Orphan: Nine Years Ago

Steam curled up towards the ceiling, slipping around the wooden support beams and vanishing before it touched the stone above. The sharp scent of vante roots mingled with the more bitter smell of dried cozsh leaves. Katsi's father, Gindaba, hummed to himself as he stirred the concoction. The cozsh plant wasn't native to this side of Malahem, but Father grew many unique plants in order to brew some of his more specialized potions. As a potions shaman, Father could imbue his potions with the magic needed to finalize their function.

As shaman classifications went, a potions shaman was at the bottom of the chain, and that annoyed Katsi to no end. At least her father *was* a shaman. There were very few of them in the tribe. She hadn't counted, but there weren't many. The smells did get old pretty quick, though.

Their home felt empty, cleansed of all their shamanic items. After the assassination of King Rikaydian, most known shamanfolk around Jehubal were rounded up and executed. Father was smart though. He'd anticipated some kind of fight, so he'd kept their shamanic blood secret from ringdwellers. Right when they heard about the king's assassination, Father took any kind of shamanic item they had and either destroyed it or put it in their hideout in the Scorched Waste. Then they fled back to the Bayvana Tribe and lived with them for another eight months.

In all that time, nobody had searched their home here in the marshes around Jehubal's southern farmlands. All that caution for *nothing*. Now they had no linara stones, no heating or cooling pads—nothing. Unless you counted the bewitched veils, and that was only because they looked just like any other bit of clothing.

Aside from Damani, all of Katsi's friends were in hiding or dead. She wasn't even sure what that word meant. Surely, they would come back—where was it they'd even gone?

Katsi heaved the loudest sigh she could, hoping Father would hear.

Father looked back and gave Katsi the smallest smile. He waved her over with a tiny motion from his sun-darkened hand.

Katsi slid from her seat at the table and approached her father just as her mother, Sirandui, came in the door carrying a basket of vegetables.

Mother frowned at Father. "Another potion, Gindaba? That's the third one in just a few days. I hope you don't think things can return to normal."

Father's smile faded. "Of course not, Sirandui. But there's not much difference between one potion and three." He handed Katsi a ladle.

Mother shook her head and placed the vegetables on the table. "Who's it for this time?"

"Jalnam. This will help her to get some mongea growing on the rocks in her home. She's had trouble getting enough food to grow since she's been in hiding."

Katsi followed a direction from Father to stir at a particular speed.

Father lowered his voice as he bent down to speak in her ear. He wasn't tall compared to other adults, nor was her mother, but they were both tall to *her*. "Now repeat the words, *geyna sham ba kalaswe denm*."

Katsi did so, repeating the words in connection with her stirring pattern.

Father smiled. "Good. Those are the words that activate the magic in the potion. I've already imbued it with the energy it needs. Now it just requires a little more time on the heat and a bit of cool water. I'll keep stirring if you go fetch us some water to finish it up."

Katsi nodded and handed back the ladle. She snatched up the water bucket and headed out, catching a few notes of the song Mother was humming to herself before she made it outside. Katsi hummed the song as well, passing by Damani's family farm as she made her way to the well. Lots of the other girls in the Bayvana Tribe said mean things about the ringdwellers, but Katsi thought these other farmers were really nice, and they were good at sharing their water and other produce rather freely.

She pulled her veil over her face. Mother cautioned her that even though they'd returned to Jehubal, they still weren't safe. *Don't talk to strangers, wear your veil, and don't ever talk about shamanfolk, even with your friends.* Really, it was quite annoying. She still wondered why they didn't just stay with the tribe. It would be a lot easier that way—then they wouldn't have to hide all the time, and they could actually *use* some of their useful shamanic stuff rather than hiding it in the Scorched Waste.

Before they left the tribe this time, her friend, Shinaseh, kept saying Katsi should stay. If only she could have listened. A seven-year-old wasn't really at liberty to disobey her parents. Both Katsi's parents had insisted that the tribe had some violent ideas that they didn't agree with, whatever that meant. Katsi hadn't ever been abused among shamanfolk or ringdwellers, but at least she didn't have to be afraid when she was with the shamanfolk.

She made it to the well and had to wait behind a couple other people before she could use it. Her little body was just strong enough to pump the spigot which brought cool water gushing into her bucket. She let it fill up about halfway—any more would maybe be too much for her to carry back. Some people talked, and a couple other children played nearby. Katsi made no move to interact with them. A year ago, she might have been able to play with them, but not anymore. *Stupid rules. Stupid queen.*

Katsi didn't want to follow her parents' rules, but a part of her secretly hoped that her good behavior could give her an edge when trying to convince them to give her a baby brother or sister. Then she'd have somebody to play with and teach how to catch scailas or show where all the best hiding places were at the edge of the jungle. She smiled as she thought about bringing it up again and made her way towards home.

Just as she was passing Damani's house, she stopped in her tracks, the bucket of water slipping from her grasp, sloshing water across her pants as it bounced off the ground and rolled to a stop in front of her. There were people at her home. A lot of them. They were wearing beige-colored uniforms, and they all carried those halberd-things.

That was exactly what was *not* supposed to happen.

Katsi started running home when someone grabbed her arm and jerked her to the side. It was her friend, Damani. He placed a finger over her lips and pulled her into a crevice at the side of their home where they usually stashed a barrel of seeds to protect it from the Maedaris. Katsi squealed in protest and pried at Damani's arms.

"Katsi, please stay quiet." His eyes were wide with fear.

She didn't care, she still tried to break free. "Let me go, Damani. That's hurting me."

"If you go, they'll take you away, and you'll never come back. Please, just hide."

Katsi's resistance diminished. "But my parents."

Damani shook his head. "It's too late. The soldiers already know."

Know what? Oh, sand and ice. Tears gushed from Katsi's eyes. She let Damani pull her under cover as realization dawned on her. *But we followed all the rules. We hid all our stuff and didn't tell anybody who we were.* Damani laid a hand on Katsi's back while she wept in deep, silent sobs. She couldn't believe what was happening—this was the same thing that happened to the other shamanfolk in the city—the ones that hadn't returned to the tribe. Shinaseh was right, they were all right. Now her parents were going to die too?

A woman's stern voice carried over to them. "Caught in the act of making one of their potions as well." With the way the woman spoke, Katsi could easily imagine spittle flying from her mouth. "Gather the farmers. We'll make a scene of this."

Katsi wiped her face and crawled on hands and knees from their hiding spot.

"Katsi, no," Damani said, reaching to grab her again.

She kicked his hand. "I'm just going to look."

Damani groaned and crawled out after her. "Just don't go running out there—and don't say anything. I'll tackle you if I have to."

"Like I said, I'm just looking. I'm not stupid."

Katsi peeked around the edge of the house. There must've been thirty or forty soldiers, maybe even a hundred. Counting them while they were all moving was too hard.

The woman who'd spoken was gorgeous. She seemed like one of those princesses from stories. Her black hair was decked with silver and gemstones, and her dress was covered in fancy decorations of red and black. Tinkling bracelets almost covered her whole left arm.

Several of the soldiers bustled away at her command, ordering the farmers to come gather around as Katsi's parents were dragged out of the house. Father was pulled out first, a gash split into his forehead. He held his head high, but he wore an expression that usually meant Katsi was in trouble.

Next came Mother, whose shoulders sagged. She looked like she was about to cry, which brought fresh tears to Katsi's face.

Katsi took a step out from her cover, but Damani held her hand. Mother noticed Katsi and shook her head at her. Katsi held back a sob as she stepped back to Damani.

Other people started to gather around, the air filling with murmurings. Apparently, the princess-looking lady was the queen. Her guess had been close. Everyone seemed surprised that Queen Rikaydian had come down herself.

Katsi had heard about the queen's cruelty already and knew that her presence was no treat. She'd been the cause for all the shamanfolk being put to death. Her heart fluttered with a new flood of panic.

It only took a moment for a large crowd to gather around. Her parents were forced to their knees in front of everyone. The queen sneered at them. To Katsi's surprise, a young boy, perhaps only a year or two older than her, tried to hide behind the queen as he cast fearful eyes at Katsi's parents. Without hesitation, the queen slapped the boy with the back of her hand and shoved him towards a pair of soldiers. That kid had acted like the queen was his mother.

"Two shamans, discovered right here in your own neighborhood," the queen shouted. Her voice demanded attention. The murmuring among the crowd ceased instantly. "Even as we caught them, they were making a potion that very well could have been used to poison your water or destroy your crops."

Father shook his head, eyes closed.

Even with her brow creased, the queen looked both terrifying and beautiful. It gave Katsi a shiver. She always thought monsters would be hideous.

"Fortunately, some of your good neighbors were suspicious and reported questionable activity, allowing us to arrive just in time. Let it be known that *this* threat is extinguished." She pointed at Katsi's parents, and a pair of soldiers hefted their weapons and stood behind them. "Report anything you might find. These demons cannot be allowed…"

The queen's words failed to reach Katsi's ears as her parents were beheaded right in front of her. They were gone. Katsi couldn't process what happened. She stared at their heads, almost expecting them to look back up at her. They didn't. Her body trembled. A weak squeal escaped her lips. She watched as their remains were carried away by soldiers. Damani squeezed her shaking hand with his own.

Katsi took a couple quick steps forward before stumbling to her hands, her knees suddenly weak. She tried saying the names of her parents, but the words were lost on her lips and she could only groan. The pain in her chest was unreal and unrelenting. Tears gushed from her eyes in a sudden wave as she was overwhelmed with the aching loss. She wanted to scream and wail like a Maedari, but all she could do was cry.

Mother… Father…

Hatred bloomed against Queen Rikaydian, but Katsi was too tired, too grieved to even think about it. Her parents had been taken from her.

Chapter Twenty-Eight

Knowing

Pain. Sharp, like ice stabbing through the skin. Overwhelming, like coal pressed to flesh. It pulsated with every heartbeat, as though blood was poison.

Was this the abyss that awaited after death? Migo's punishment for his mistakes? Perhaps it was fitting that he suffer eternally in pain—the anguish of his soul fully manifest as a physical sensation. There was nothing but darkness all around him. He'd never thought much about any kind of afterlife. Perhaps it had been a vain hope for him to think that there might be peace after death. If anything, he'd at least saved some of his men. They would live to fight another day.

No... besides the pain, there were other sensations. In addition to his painful heartbeat, he felt his lungs filling with air as he breathed.

Also, there was some kind of sound that filtered through to him as though it were coming from behind a wall. It sounded like an occasional scraping of fabric against fabric.

The rancid stench of rotten coda milk permeated the air. The taste in his mouth was even worse. Bile built up in his stomach. He tried to spit, but his mouth was completely dry. He could barely even pucker.

The scraping sound stopped and was replaced by two short crunches, one of them very close to his ear.

"Stop that. I won't have you puking in here. That would make it smell worse than it already does. You should really try bathing before you go to battle or something."

That voice was somehow familiar. It was strong and feminine, but not harsh like his mother's. He tried to respond but couldn't form any words.

"Yeah, don't do that either. You shouldn't move. I'll give you a little water to drink, but we don't have a lot to go around. I might have to ditch you for a couple marks to go get some more, but I need you to promise you'll stay still. On second thought, I'll just wait till you fall asleep. Who knows what other stupid ideas you'll get if I leave you here conscious."

Migo felt something press against his lips.

"I'll just do a little."

Some water poured straight to the back of Migo's throat. He sputtered, inhaling some and nearly choking, water rocketing back out of his mouth as he coughed and gulped.

There was a muffled curse. "Wow, how stupid can you be? Isn't swallowing supposed to be one of the first things people learn to do? Sand and ice, princeling."

Migo coughed some more. It took a moment for the itch in his throat to go away. The coughing was unpleasant, and something on his chest felt a sharp sting with each movement. He tried opening his eyes again, but there was only darkness. *I guess I'm not dead, but perhaps I'm blind.* He remembered the sand pelting his eyes like needles. But, to his deep regret, he was alive. He survived. A lump welled in his throat. He'd failed. And now his mother would have him killed with a knife in the dark or a glaive to the neck. Killed by his own mother... He couldn't think about it. A flush of emotion flooded through him: anger, despair, exhaustion, fear, shame.

He hadn't gone to a dark abyss of death. This was worse. He lived.

His shoulders rocked with a dry sob.

The dark memory of his father's death was fresh on his mind. He'd been reliving it over and over until he'd woken up to this woman who'd tried to choke him.

"All right, we'll try this again, but swallow it this time."

Something pressed against his lips again. This time, Migo was ready for it, and he closed the back of his throat in preparation. Warm water filled his mouth, almost to the lips, then stopped. He gulped it down. It scratched its way into his stomach. How could drinking water be painful? Was it some kind of poison? The process was repeated four more times, but it didn't hurt so much for the following gulps.

The woman sighed. "That's all the water for now. I'll have to get more—and I don't have any more food on me, so when I sneak back into the Ring, I'll find something to eat. I'll use something to help you sleep."

She paused for a moment and touched his chest ever so lightly. There was a bit of pain when she did so, but it was hardly noticeable compared to his continual throbbing. He didn't seem to be wearing any armor or clothes on his upper body. "You've suffered some pretty bad injuries. If you have any semblance of a brain, you would heed my warning not to move this time."

There was another pause and some rifling about. Migo didn't let her words slip by unevaluated. From what she'd said, Migo could devise that he was *not* in the Ring. Gauging by the intense heat, it was safe to assume that he was in the Scorched Waste. This was far beyond death. He'd been taken prisoner by the shamans. He couldn't imagine a more disgraceful turn of events.

"I should be back in a couple marks—sooner if things go well. Try to get some sleep."

He felt a bit of air flutter around his face, carrying with it that same rancid stench. Somehow... it made him feel lighter, his pain disappearing as he slipped from consciousness.

* * * * *

Dry air baked its way into Katsi's lungs as she took a deep breath. The crisp parchment crackled as she pulled it out from her belt and unfolded it. The single page was as blank as the day she'd received it. Its contents were hidden.

Katsi's face ached from the frown that had etched its way there ever since a new idea had sprung to mind. There was supposedly only one way to unlock the contents of the parchment. But it was a terrible, horrible thing. Her frown grew deeper, and she shifted her eyes from the paper to look at Migo. His form lay limp on the other side of the small, dark cave. He'd remain asleep for at least a couple more marks before the effects of the herb wore off.

He won't even notice.

She bounced over to kneel beside him. Her own eagerness frightened her, a shiver climbing up her spine. If this worked, it would sure make things easier for her. Everything was dead silent as Katsi pulled her knife out. Migo's chest wound would be the easiest place to draw from.

Katsi placed a finger on either side of the gash and used slight, even pressure to tug at the skin. Blood leaked out immediately. She brought out her knife and held it against Migo's skin, picking up a bit of the blood as she lifted it. She held up the parchment in her other hand. After tilting the knife, a drop of blood fell and spattered on the parchment, staining it a deep red.

She watched expectantly, though nothing happened. Did she ruin the parchment? Her chest tightened as her heart sank.

Then, the blood faded as if soaking into the paper. Words formed on its surface, reading simply, "There is only one way to reveal, Danan. You know the cost." The words vanished a moment later.

Katsi sighed. *Well... it was worth a shot.* She folded the parchment and returned it to her belt.

* * * * *

Pain awoke Migo. Not the undulating kind that had encompassed his whole body before, but this time it was sharper, more exquisite. It pinched across his chest. He jerked, a groan escaping him.

"Whoa, watch it. I almost poked you with this needle. Sands, princeling. I would've thought a warrior could handle a bit of stitching." The woman muttered another curse and there was a tinkling of equipment.

"I can finish that when I knock you out again. Maybe I'll use a rock next time instead of fumes."

Something touched his lips, and Migo opened his mouth again, familiar with the process. After drinking some water, Migo dared to speak. "You talk so much," he managed to mumble.

There was a cluck of disappointment. "Yeah, well you stupid so much. I'd take my foible over yours any day."

That was all the confirmation Migo needed. "Katsi," he sighed.

She hummed an approval. "I knew you'd recognize my signature insults."

He tried to open his eyes, but it came to no avail. "What's on my eyes?"

"I covered them with some ointment and tied a cloth over them. You had some serious eye damage—probably from staring at a Maedari without any eye protection. Another testament to your endless display of intelligence."

Migo ground his teeth. Nobody but his mother had ever insulted him so blatantly. He tried clenching his fists, but found his muscles weak, and his skin sensitive to even the slightest movement. "I was supposed to die," he said through clenched teeth. As soon as the words left his mouth, he wished he could take them back.

"Well, I saved you."

"Why? I'm your enemy. Don't you hate me?"

A few seconds of silence slipped by before Katsi replied. "Sometimes, yes, but... I need you."

Chills ran across Migo's skin, mingling with the anger that still boiled in his chest. He hadn't felt needed or wanted in years. Quite the opposite. "What for?"

"I'm not sure I'm ready to bring it up," Katsi sighed. "What were you still doing out in the storm? Why didn't you run away?"

Migo didn't know how to answer. Why was she even asking that? Why did she care? He kept silent. He still wasn't sure what kind of situation he was in. All that was certain was that she had the upper hand. He was severely injured. The feeling of the sand and ice burning across his flesh was no distant memory. It was the same feeling he remembered from his youth during the Maedari where his father was killed. A spike of pain surged at the memory.

"What of the battle?" Migo asked.

"Too much death," Katsi said with a sigh. "I wish you'd kept the soldiers at the walls like I suggested."

"But what about the city?"

Katsi shook her head. "I don't know. I haven't seen anybody since the storm. I spent all my time gathering food and water to keep you alive."

The city could have been overrun. His people slaughtered. There might be no home to go back to. Hatan. Falshon. Dead. He clenched his fists and tried to sit up, but a hiss of pain escaped his lips.

"Don't try," Katsi said. "I'll look into it when I go back to the Ring next time, but you won't be saving anybody in your current condition."

Migo laid back, seething. She helped him drink some more water, and even put some food in his mouth, but otherwise said nothing.

Eventually, he smelled that bitter herb again. She waved it in his face and he drifted back into sleep.

* * * * *

Migo wasn't sure how much time had passed. He was only aware of the moments when Katsi would feed or water him, or help him take care of his other, more embarrassing bodily functions. She left him alone a couple more times, always putting him to sleep with the terrible fumes before she left. Occasionally, she fidgeted with his body, but she said nothing through the whole process.

Time was immeasurable. It could have been several cycles for all he knew, but his body was starting to feel better.

"You're a vile person, you know that?" Katsi said. Her voice was soft, almost distant. He could imagine her turned away from him as she spoke.

Again, Migo was angered, but the solemn way that Katsi had spoken left him feeling more injured than he would have thought. She meant what she said. The worst part about her words was that Migo couldn't bring himself to deny them. In fact, he agreed. It was the major reason he wished he'd died.

"You executed some innocent people the other day. Their names were Bindom and Shali. I heard you didn't even give them a trial. The queen just ordered them dead, and you dealt the blow. You were supposed to be finding the murderers, but instead you killed the victim's friends. That's pretty messed up."

"What do you know of that?" Migo's heart started to pound. The shame was kicking in. He remembered the feeling he'd gotten right before be-heading the couple—the feeling that they were innocent—but he'd carried through with the execution anyway.

"I know they were friends with the people who got murdered. In fact, the family who'd been murdered were shamanfolk as well. Sounds pretty messed up that you were blaming shamans for killing their own people."

Migo shook his head. "No, that first couple, Kinay and Roda, were murdered during the Maedari by shaman fire."

"Even still, both families were working together. They were practically family. I think that's why the Bayvana Tribe decided to attack. They're getting sick of being victims while you murder innocent people."

"Perhaps they had a falling out. Even family members can hurt each other sometimes." Migo knew too much about that firsthand.

"Yeah, but do you think that's actually what happened? Aren't you supposed to look at the evidence? What evidence connected them to the murder? It doesn't make any sense."

Again, Migo was left without anything to say. How could he respond to that without acknowledging that she was right? *She can't be right.* Somehow, he knew that she must've been trying to deceive him, but he couldn't figure out why.

"You seem ignorant enough. For all we know, the queen set it up herself. Framing shamans for murdering people, trying to instill fear in the public by convincing them of a threat that *she* created. Whatever. You probably don't even care. I don't know why I bothered. I probably should have let you die." Katsi's voice had become muffled, and it picked up a tone of sadness.

"Why didn't you?"

Katsi took her time to answer. "I wanted to," she finally answered. "I almost did."

Migo waited for more, but she didn't add anything. "Well, don't think this means I'm indebted to you or anything."

"Right, because you *wanted* to die. You're probably overwhelmed with the guilt of all your injustices."

Migo's face burned. Not because Katsi was wrong, but because she was right.

* * * * *

Migo must've dozed. He was awakened by a new smell. Instead of bitterness, this new smell was savory, like meat fresh from the fire. His mouth burst with saliva. He couldn't help but ask. "What's that?"

"Nothing that concerns you. I had to roast this out in the sun for two whole marks before bringing it back in."

"You cooked meat under the sun?"

"Yeah, us Outlanders do stuff like that all the time. If you have a decent stone, you can face it towards the sun and lay the meat out in thin strips. You have to be a little further out into the Scorched Waste to do it though, so usually it's done by using a sort of roof oven since you have to stay underground without burning yourself too much." Katsi's voice was slightly distorted since she was eating the food as she spoke.

Migo gulped.

Katsi sighed. "You want some, don't you?"

Migo didn't respond.

Katsi laughed. It was a rich laughter, pure and unrestrained. It reminded Migo of younger years, back before Maedaris had become such a nightmare. He found himself smiling, but he wiped it away as soon as it appeared.

"Whoa! What was that?" Katsi's voice had gone shrill.

"What?" Migo asked, his heart rate increasing.

Katsi laughed more, easing the tension just as quick. "I think I saw a smile on your lips. I didn't know you could do that."

Migo scowled. "No, it was a cringe. Or a sneer. I felt a surge of pain right at that moment."

"Riiiight," Katsi said, her voice skeptical. "Here." She tapped his lip with a bit of food. Migo opened his mouth eagerly. He felt ashamed of himself for behaving like that—jumping to open his mouth for food like some kind of tableside animal begging for scraps. Still, when she placed the meat in his mouth, even though it was a tiny piece, the taste was well worth it. He savored the tiny morsel, chewing and sucking on it until the flavor was all but gone. It had been a long time since he'd savored food, despite Hatan's best efforts.

"Thank you." The words were out of his mouth before he could stop them.

"Careful, princeling. You're starting to sound like you don't hate me," Katsi said.

Migo clenched his jaws and swallowed hard. "I never said I hated you."

Katsi didn't respond, but she touched his cheek with a fingertip. "We can uncover your eyes now. I don't remember how long I was supposed to keep the ointment on there, but eight cycles is probably good enough."

"Eight cycles?" Migo couldn't keep from shouting.

"Yes, eight grueling cycles taking care of you. Now, are you ready to see if you can... see?"

Migo clicked his tongue. "Go for it." There was a slight sting as something peeled off both his temples. Katsi rubbed his eyes softly before pulling the covering away. Migo blinked his eyes open, resisting the powerful urge to rub at them. Everything was blurry and gray, and there was still something goopy around his eyes. He feared that he might have gone blind.

Katsi wiped gently at his eyes again, clearing away most of the goop. When she stopped, things gradually came back into focus. The first thing his eyes settled on was the face of a young woman, dark hair falling around her shoulders. She had a sharp jaw, but soft chin and cheeks. She bit her lip, her thin eyebrows curved into a frown as she looked down at him. Her eyes were the most striking feature, dark brown and outlined by long lashes. He tried to suppress the idea as soon as it occurred, but he couldn't help but think that she was quite pretty. The fact that she was looking at him with concern made it that much worse. The only person who'd ever seemed to look at him with concern was Hatan.

"Well, you're looking at me, so I take it you can see?" Katsi asked.

"Yes."

Katsi smiled. "Nice. I didn't know if I did it right. I've never had to use it before." She held up a tiny, empty vial.

"What was it?"

Her smile widened. "A potion. One of my father's concoctions."

"You've poisoned me?" Migo gasped. A million possibilities ran through his mind. He'd heard some wild stories about the effects of shaman potions, like mind control, paralysis, or pain. Perhaps this was the cause of his suffering and inability to move. As soon as he had the strength, he would rush her—strangle her if he had to.

Katsi groaned. "You are intolerable. Believe it or not, I actually want you to live."

"Why? I mean, you seem to hate me so much, why go through all the effort to keep me alive?"

Katsi slumped down to the stone wall. Looking around, Migo gathered that they were in some kind of cave. There was a distant, natural light, but there was also something glowing from the ground with a constant, yellow-white light. "This is going to sound crazy, but I need you to trust me."

Migo barked a laugh. "Good one. A captain of the guard should trust a shaman?"

Katsi gave him a scathing look. "Yes, that's exactly what you should do. And I'm not just some shaman. I don't associate myself with the Bayvana Tribe. I'm against killing, and that seems to be all anybody is interested in, so I left the tribe. I'm on my own—and I don't support you and them killing each other all the time. It's stupid." She spoke the words in a sputter, nearly screaming. "Why else would I tell you they were planning an attack? I didn't want any of the people to get hurt."

Migo had already considered this. "I'll listen."

Katsi's frown switched to a smile again. Smiling came too easy to her. "Of course you'll listen. You don't really have much of a choice."

Migo shrugged. The small motion wasn't as painful as it had been a few cycles back. He spared a glance down at his exposed chest and saw the cut that spread from one side of his lower ribs to the other. Some goop had been laid across it, and there were crude stitches, nothing like the kind he was accustomed to getting from his trained army physicians, but then Katsi only looked like she was sixteen. Maybe seventeen. Her smile made him look away, eyes back towards the roof of the cave. He was only wearing a cloth around his waist. He became suddenly aware that she'd been managing his near-naked body for eight cycles, and his cheeks flushed. "So, do you have a proposition?"

Katsi shrugged. "Not really. I guess I just wanted to share some information, expecting that you'd trust that I'm telling the truth so that you don't make further mistakes."

Migo nodded for her to continue.

"I heard you arrested a man named Damani. He's innocent. He's a really good person, and he was just letting me work on his land so that I could eat. He knows that I'm an orphan, and so he wanted to help. He's not shamanfolk or anything—you shouldn't hurt him or keep him in prison. It wouldn't be fair."

"This is about Damani?" Migo was flabbergasted. He'd expected her to want to hold him for ransom or something, not just try to convince him of somebody's innocence.

"Yes, he's a good man. He doesn't deserve any harsh treatment. You should let him go."

Migo shook his head. "The law doesn't work like that. He harbored a fugitive—an enemy."

"I'm hardly an enemy. What kind of enemy warns you about danger and even saves your life? It sounds like you have a worthless policy in place. He didn't even know I'm a shaman. He shouldn't be accountable for that. He was just helping me like he did dozens of other people."

"I don't know if I can do anything about that now. He confessed everything he knew."

"No." Katsi scooted over to Migo, rising on one of her knees. "You have to let him go. He's innocent, and I can't have anything happen to him because of me. It's not fair. Please." She was near to tears. He could see the water forming at the edge of her eyes.

She doesn't want somebody else to suffer because of her own mistakes. Migo knew a thing or two about that. He'd wager she was in love with the man. *She certainly doesn't know that Damani told me everything about her.* He could use that to his advantage. He hadn't died in battle, and since he had to return to the queen, he could at least bring one last shaman with him as a farewell gift before the queen had him assassinated.

"I'll have to think about it. What you're asking could be very difficult, but since you saved my life, I'd be willing to consider it."

The big, beautiful smile she gave him almost convinced him that he really *did* want to help her. Alas, he had a penance to pay.

Chapter Twenty-Nine

The Past

Cloth scraped against stone as Katsi changed positions. Her body ached. She could hardly believe that Migo had conceded to help her. To some degree, anyway. Two marks had gone by since he'd offered the consideration, and she was beginning to doubt. *Of course, I can't trust him.* This was the son of Queen Rikaydian. She murdered countless shamanfolk, and he killed several of them himself. The queen's policies all but eradicated every shamanfolk in the area before they could think to flee.

She had to anticipate that he would try to trick her somehow. That idea alone was exhausting. How to outmaneuver an expert shamanfolk hunter?

Migo had dozed off, but now he stirred. After a moment he spoke. "So, this is how shamans live in the wastes? In caves?"

Katsi shrugged. "For the most part. Caves like this one have bewitchments applied to them that help keep out the heat. Hiding from the sun is the only way to live in the Scorched Waste. I'm not totally sure how they do it over in the Frozen Waste. I've never had to spend any extended time over there."

"And you just go and forage in the Ring, then bring everything back here?"

"Sometimes. One place usually can't sustain a whole tribe for very long, so they rotate to different locations, stay for a few months, harvest the food, set up another harvest to grow, then move on."

"You can grow food out here?" He frowned at her in disbelief.

"Sure, though mainly pastes, herbs, and nuts. Not the kind of stuff you want to live off of for more than a few cycles. We have some potions that will help food grow in harsh environments. I hear it's even harder to get stuff to grow in the Frozen Waste though. Not a good place to live." She shook her head. It seemed weird that he was asking such simple questions, but Katsi found it refreshing. She was being completely honest with somebody—something she hadn't done for a while. She didn't even tell this kind of stuff to Damani. That frightened her.

"That's pretty amazing. People have talked about how only demons can live out here, but if magic is as robust as you say, it would certainly open up possibilities." Migo shifted, flexing the muscles in his arms as he stretched. He was regaining strength, which was another scary thing. He was even more massive up close, and his body rippled with muscles she didn't know existed. Eight cycles to recover did seem like a decent amount of time for him to function more normally. Part of her suspected that he was just waiting for an opportunity to spring up and strangle her. The sooner this arrangement was over, the better.

As he shifted, she noticed three short scars that ran across his jawline, just below his left ear. They were distinct, like something had clawed him.

"She hurts you, doesn't she?" She asked, the words coming out without a second thought.

"What're you talking about?" Migo looked up at her, his eyes igniting.

"You're mother, the queen. She hurts you." Katsi could remember when her parents had been murdered. The queen had been there, and she'd smacked a young boy that had sought refuge with her. It must've been Migo.

"You're full of it. I don't know where you get your information."

Katsi shook her head with a frown. "It's common knowledge. Everybody knows she yells at you and smacks you around. Besides, I've seen it."

Migo turned his head away from her, fuming. "What do you mean you've seen it?"

"When she had my parents murdered. You got nervous about it and went to hide behind her, but she hit you in the face and made you watch."

Migo's head popped off the ground, and he stared at her with wide eyes. He dropped his head back down and blinked up at the dark rocks overhead. "Wh-what happened? Where was it?"

Katsi slumped back against the stone wall and let out a sigh, preparing to tell him the worst experience of her life. She started into it hesitantly, but Migo listened intently, nodding, and blinking, but otherwise silent. He made no protest as she related every detail she could remember, from helping her father make the potion, to the song her mother had hummed. By the time she was done, she was surprised to find that she felt somewhat relieved.

"So I'm an orphan. All because your mother doesn't tolerate shaman-folk."

Migo was silent for a long moment before he finally spoke. "That was my first time witnessing an execution. I had just turned eight, and the queen wanted me to see it for myself, telling me that it would be my greatest duty to slaughter every shaman I could find."

Katsi noted how Migo referred to his mother as "the queen." Clearly not the happiest relationship. "Yeah, that sounds like the kind of thing an evil queen would do. Beat her child and tell him to murder people. Sand and ice, how did she become the queen to begin with? She's got some real issues."

"She has reason to act that way. She's been filled with nothing but anger and vengeance since my father was murdered by a shaman." He glared at her, eyes fresh with malice. His muscles strained. It was like a switch had gone off, activating a bestial instinct.

"Why are you looking at *me* like that? I didn't murder your father."

Migo growled, clenched his fists, and then pressed them against his temples. He squeezed his eyes tight as a couple tears trickled out, face twisted in pain that looked more excruciating than the wounds on his body.

Katsi had no idea what to do. She'd never seen anybody so distraught. Without a thought, her knife was in her hand, her back up against the stone. Something was wrong with him. Perhaps it was a spell or a curse. *Or maybe his mother just messed him up.* What was worse, no parents or an evil mother? Katsi felt like she was starting to put it together. Maybe Migo wasn't mad at her, but at himself.

"What's going on in there?" she asked, tapping her temple and keeping her voice as calm as she could make it.

Migo's breathing was still strangely irregular. She might've used the stonebark smoke to knock him out a little *too* much.

"It's my fault," Migo said, his voice barely audible.

"What do you mean?"

"It's my fault my father's dead."

"Did you give someone a knife and tell him to stab your father or something? How could it be your fault? I thought you were a young kid when it happened."

"I will not speak of it." Migo peeked at her through half-lidded eyes.

"Alright, keep to yourself then, but try to relax. Your wrist is bleeding where a scab peeled. I'll need you in decent condition to get back to the palace and free Damani."

Migo let out a long sigh. "She's going to kill me." His voice was a rasping whisper.

Katsi froze. "What do you mean?"

Migo looked at her, dark eyes piercing, etched with pain. "The queen. She's going to have me killed."

Katsi grunted. "I know she's evil, but why would she have you killed?"

When Migo didn't say anything, Katsi answered for him. "Because of your father again?"

Migo managed a nod.

Katsi placed her hands on her hips. "Enough with the mystery. Tell me why." The silence that followed was tense, but Katsi didn't mind waiting if it meant Migo would tell her what was wrong with him.

"Fine," he said, his voice deep. Katsi felt a thrill at the word, as if he was about to reveal one of the greatest secrets in all Malahem. His face became stone. Expressionless. "The queen wasn't always as she is now. The change happened ten years ago, when I was seven, after the Maedari when my father was murdered. I was playing outside when a Maedari came. My friend ran inside, but I was paralyzed, like an idiot. I got caught in the storm. My father came out to save me, but a shaman assassin was there waiting for him. They fought and... my father lost. It was my fault my father died. If I hadn't been so terrified, I would have run inside like my friend. My father wouldn't have come out at all. He would have been safe."

He cringed and turned his head away. "I'm surprised the queen hasn't ordered my death sooner."

Katsi's heart swelled. She resisted the urge to kneel beside him. To place a hand on his shoulder. "I'm sorry, Migo. That's a terrible thing to go through." She took a few more breaths before adding, "and this is why you and the queen hate shamanfolk—because one of them murdered your father... That's a nonsensical connection to blame an entire people for a single murder, but why would your mother want to kill you because of what happened? That doesn't make sense either." He was in pain, and yet she couldn't hold back the words.

"It was my fault. She hates me for it—just like I hate myself. That's why I deserve to die."

"That's not fair. You were just a kid! That's not your fault at all. If you blame anybody, it's whoever that assassin was. It sounds like he was just waiting for that to happen. It's almost like he knew the storm was coming."

"He probably created the storm to begin with! Now you see why we hate shamans? This is why we have to eliminate all of you." Migo's face twisted again with anger.

Katsi threw her arms to the side. "No, I don't see. This is probably the stupidest thing I've ever heard. If one of your own citizens had performed the murder, would that then mean that all of your citizens were worthy of execution? Of course not. One person's action does not make an entire people guilty. Magic isn't inherently evil—it all depends on the person who wields it."

"One of my own citizens *wouldn't* have committed the murder." His eyes glazed over. "They couldn't have either. Only shamans have the dark magic to create the Maedaris and then stormwade through them. That's what we need to eradicate. Without shamans, there are no Maedaris, no murders." Though he spoke with venom, Migo's expression had softened. He looked weary of the conversation. They seemed less like his own words and more like a script.

Katsi shook her head. She thought of her own strange power as a storm-caller. "Maedaris aren't caused by shamans, Migo. I don't know where you got your education, but they're clearly caused by a clash between the Frozen and Scorched Wastes. The heat and cold are always trying to claim each other's domain."

"I know the science—and those might cause the normal storms, but there's something different about Maedaris. Don't deny it."

Katsi knew exactly what he was talking about. Every Maedari, she could feel something different in the air—that something that reminded her of her parents—that tingling sensation that reminded her of magic. "Do you... feel the magic during Maedaris as well?"

Migo grunted. "I don't know about magic, but I do feel fear. Like a fist reaching through my chest and crushing my heart." He shook his head.

Katsi considered the idea. It wasn't too farfetched to believe that Maedaris affected ringdwellers differently. "Even if that were the case, which I'm not saying it is, then I still don't think that justifies the eradication of an entire people. I know I don't cause the storms, and the Bayvana Tribe doesn't do it. They're simply retaliating in order to keep themselves alive because you're threatening to exterminate them."

"You sound like my cousin, Hatan," Migo said, letting out a big breath.

"I didn't realize you had relatives that were capable of being intelligent."

"Look, can we not talk about this anymore?"

Katsi shrugged. "Sure, but on one final note, I still don't think you are to blame for your father's death. If your mother—the queen—blames you for it, then she's a fool. I don't think there was much of anything you could have done. My parents weren't guilty of killing your father either, but the queen executed them as innocent people. She seems to have a knack for blaming people for things they're not responsible for. You ought to be a little easier on yourself. Don't be like her."

Katsi left it at that and stepped outside, still under the shade of an outcropping of stones. Her cheeks were flushed, but not from the heat. The temperature above-ground was staggering, but it was still refreshing compared to being in a confined space with Migo Rikaydian. She wanted to go back in there and kick him in the chest to rip his wound back open. Her nails dug into her palms.

She'd saved the life of an evil man and one of her greatest enemies, and now she was trying to convince him that he didn't deserve to die. *What is wrong with me?*

Chapter Thirty

Removing Stitches

Migo wasn't sure how much time had passed, but it seemed like it must have been almost two cycles before he and Katsi spoke again. She'd been gone most of the time. The isolation gave Migo a chance to test his strength and check his injuries. Both of his legs felt stiff and swollen, so he'd started stretching them and flexing the muscles. His left wrist had been immobilized by a makeshift splint. The abrasions from sand and ice across his legs, face, and arms had healed up fairly well, though there were a couple spots that were more deeply injured. The wound across his chest was healing okay, and the reason they'd broken their silence was because Katsi had said it was time to remove the stitches.

Undoing the stitches took a lot longer than Migo would have liked. He stared up, refusing to watch, knowing that it would only reveal to him how amateur her abilities were.

"That should do," Katsi said, her voice monotone. She poked around the wound. "It seems to be holding well, but you won't want to twist around or bend back very much." She poked it some more, applying a bit of the gel from before. "Can you sit up?"

Despite her warning, Migo stretched, though only enough to feel the tug of the skin around the wound, getting familiar with the limitations of his flexibility. He nodded to Katsi. He almost expected her to help, but instead, she stepped back and placed a hand at her waist, as if holding something.

In all reality, it would be no problem for him to sit up. In his current condition, he would have been able to walk if he'd wanted. He sat up slowly, easing his legs up, holding on to his knees as he brought his torso up, looking Katsi in the eyes. She suddenly looked very small. He doubted her head would reach higher than his chest. Overpowering her before she could stop him would not be difficult. In the glint of the light however, he could see the tiny glimmer of something metal. She was armed.

"Before you get any ideas, you should know that I'm a very powerful shaman," Katsi said, as if reading Migo's mind.

"I've killed plenty of powerful shamans."

"I doubt that. I'm probably the only one you've met of my caliber."

"Whatever you say." Migo looked away from her dismissively. It was difficult to see this tiny woman as being powerful, and he hadn't seen any manifestations of said powers. He hadn't seen much evidence that shamans were very powerful at all. Aside from their weapons and their ability to stormwade, he wasn't sure they were as big a threat as people thought them to be.

"You know nothing about us." Katsi smiled and shook her head. "You ringdwellers call all of us shamans, but we're called shamanfolk. Only a select few of our numbers are truly shamans—the ones who are able to use magic."

Migo hadn't known that, but gave no indication. It sounded so simple. If it was true, how did he not already know that?

"Lie back," she said suddenly, shoving him to the floor with a hand to his shoulder.

Migo acquiesced without a second thought, the urgency in her voice dissuading resistance. She left her hand there as she inspected his chest.

"You started bleeding again. I'm sorry I'm not very good at stitching. I've only had to do it on myself a couple times—and on Damani once—but fortunately that was just a smaller cut. Nothing like this."

"Even I could have told you it was a terrible job," Migo said, relaxing against the floor. It seemed strange to have blood oozing from a wound, but not really feel a thing.

"Do you have to be so mean all the time?" Katsi asked, slapping something over the bleeding portion of the cut.

"Me? Is that a joke? You've hardly said a few words to me without slipping in some kind of insult." Migo was shocked to see that Katsi's eyes were watering, though she blinked it away before any tears fell.

"I've just been so sad, and lonely, and angry because of what your mother did. I hate her, and I've hated you. You've done terrible things." She shook her head, backing away from him. "I think I'm starting to understand, though. She's a vengeful monster with no idea where to direct her anger, and she's been using you to kill shamanfolk. She taught you to hate us so that you'd be her own pet monster."

Her words resonated with Migo so deeply that it struck him to the core. Chill bumps rolled across his skin like a wave.

"Or maybe I'm wrong," she said, regarding him with a sad expression, "and you'd choose to hate and slaughter us of your own accord. Something tells me that's not the case. I'm sorry about your father, by the way. It's a terrible thing to see one of your own parents murdered, especially when you were so young. I'm sure it filled you with the most torturous feelings for a long time."

Migo's fingers trembled. He regarded Katsi with widened eyes, trying to analyze her more deeply. She was snappy and sarcastic, but she was also very keen and intuitive, like she had some strange ability to see right through him. He didn't fail to notice the parallel she'd drawn. He'd watched his father murdered, and she'd watched both her parents get executed. For Migo, he'd been bent on revenge, but for Katsi...*She doesn't seem vengeful...does she really just want to save her friend?*

"I'm still responsible for my father's death," he said.

"Being blamed and being responsible are two different things, and you are *not* responsible. Even the queen has no place to hold you accountable for what happened. Form your own identity, not the one she assigns you." Katsi whispered a word and one of the glowing stones went out.

Another wave of chill bumps. He wondered if she'd used magic against him. Would he dare try to think of himself any differently? Would he dare try to forgive himself? He shuddered at the thought and couldn't fathom the idea of forgiveness. Despite how peaceful it sounded, he knew he didn't deserve it. He dropped his head with resignation, trying to force away the calm feeling that Katsi's words had slipped beneath his skin. "But she's right."

Katsi threw up her hands and said, "Have it your way," then strode out of the cave.

* * * * *

From the rear of the cave, Migo watched Katsi who stood near the entrance. The remnants of a small storm still roared outside as it began to dwindle. Katsi had been moving her hands and muttering to herself most of the time as if she were incanting some of her dark magic.

Under such circumstances, Migo might have normally shriveled into a ball, fear crippling him as he was under the power of a shaman, but the recent battle seemed to have changed him. Instead, Katsi's actions were somehow intriguing. There were a couple of times where he could have sworn that a pillar of sand swirled around her arm before shooting back into the storm.

Katsi rifled through her supplies before tossing a pomay fruit to him. It was a little past ripe, and he was about to complain, but Katsi started eating one that looked even worse. He ate anyway, avoiding the worst parts.

"Not the delicacies you're used to." Katsi smiled at him as she slumped against the wall opposite him.

"Delicacies were never my thing, to be honest. That was more for my cousin." *Hatan.* Migo nearly choked as he remembered his cousin, thoughts spinning as he considered the outcome of the battle. *Is Hatan even alive?* He needed to get out of here immediately.

Katsi gave a light chuckle as Migo coughed. "This is just like princeling food—has the same process. Chew, then swallow, but don't try to breathe and swallow at the same time. You'll get accustomed to it if you keep practicing."

Migo rolled his eyes, but the comment didn't ease his worry.

"Your cousin is Hatan, right? You've mentioned him before. He's one of the officers I see with you."

Migo gave Katsi a quick up-down look. She obviously knew things.

"I've heard the soldiers say nice things about him." She shrugged at his look. "I like to do my research."

"Apparently."

"And don't worry." She rose back to her feet and placed a hand on his shoulder. "I've heard good things about you too." She went to the mouth of the cave and muttered just loud enough for him to hear, "On the rare occasion." She slipped outside.

Migo heaved a sigh. His mind was under constant assault, and his gut felt like it could rip in half. Something about being with Katsi and living in the Scorched Waste gave him a sense of freedom, even though he hadn't moved more than a few feet in the last several cycles. Since she'd stopped insulting him, he'd even felt a semblance of peace. He wasn't watching his back. There was no pressure to perform well, no competing with the other captains, no festering about the queen's last scathing comment. Katsi was being so *real* with him. No malice, no hatred. *She makes me want to live.*

He blinked quickly and clenched his jaw as tears threatened to water his eyes.

He cleared his throat and looked away from Katsi. *But shamans are supposed to die. They* caused his pain to begin with. How could he forget that? *I can still kill her. Overpower her if I must.* The thought didn't carry the same resolve as it had a few cycles ago. It made him tremble. She appeared extremely fit, and she always kept that knife on her. Surviving on her own would have undoubtedly come with learning to fight. He'd need an opportune moment. Plus, there was the unknown factor about her magic. He sensed it was real but didn't know what she was capable of.

The downside to him wanting to stay alive was that it now kept him from doing anything too risky, otherwise he might have tried to kill her already. *But what do I do once I kill her? I'd have to run through the Scorched Waste and find my way back to the Ring to return to Jehubal where I'm a dead man anyway.* His other option would be to turn to Cataban. Queen Rikaydian probably thought Migo was already dead. He could start a new life elsewhere.

It was possible, but he'd need a way to either kill Katsi or shake her off. He could potentially fulfill her request and free Damani, but he refused to think about it.

Migo rubbed his temples and groaned. He knew in his heart that there was only one option: return to Jehubal. He could not flee, and he could not die here. He could not allow himself to fall to cowardice—not again. Either he would die knowing he did his best, or somehow convince the queen that he was still worthy of living.

Would killing Katsi please the queen? Was it even worth it to try? His head ached. What he was really afraid to admit was that he hadn't felt this peaceful in the last nine years.

Chapter Thirty-One

Touch

Dust swirled about her as Katsi entered the cave with a fresh supply of water. Migo blinked up at her as if he just woke up, but he didn't at all seem like he'd been sleeping. She'd noticed him flexing and stretching when he thought she wasn't looking. That wouldn't have been abnormal aside from the fact that he only seemed to do it when she wasn't paying attention. That automatically made it suspicious.

She popped her neck and strode to the far end of the cave, keeping one hand on her knife. Migo shifted, and she didn't fail to notice the definition of his muscled body in motion, though he made no move to rise. She was ever-cautious of the moment he would bolt to his feet and try to attack her, but as the cycles passed, she noticed she was starting to feel comfortable around him. She'd even started to think that his rippling body, deep-set eyes, and strong jaw were something *other* than frightening.

"Put this on," she said, throwing the remains of his undershirt to him. Covering him up would help.

Migo scratched his chin then did as she said.

She left the remnants of his armor on the ground, but placed his boots in front of him. Everything else went into her belt.

"We're leaving?" he asked.

"Yes. You should be well enough to walk about. We should try and at least move closer to the Ring. It's difficult to go all the way there and back. I never got a chance to check on Jehubal. Plus, we're getting close to the New Season. We don't want to be caught out here in a storm that could last more than two cycles." During New Season, there were a full two months where storms were frequent and could last as long as a whole week. Though they weren't as strong as Maedaris, the frequency of storms during New Season made it just as bad.

"How far from the Ring are we?" Migo said, carefully putting his boots on, trying to bend his torso as little as possible.

"Too far. The Maedari took us a long way. I'm familiar with the area, but I've only come this deep into the Scorched Waste on a couple other occasions." She didn't mention that both instances were only a few cycles ago through a canyon by Delirad Lake. On both those occasions, she had gone quite a bit deeper than they were now.

"You seem to have made it to the Ring and back a few times since we got here," he said. "So I assume it mustn't be too bad." He braced himself against the wall of the cave and slowly put his feet beneath him.

"It's never easy if that's what you're insinuating," Katsi said. She hesitantly reached a hand down to help him up. The other hand she kept on the hilt of her blade. He gripped her shoulder and rose to his feet. Their eyes locked as his body pressed against her. She couldn't look away. All the pain and anger in his eyes was gone, his pupils widening to soak her in.

"You know I could destroy you right now," he said, looking down at her lips. Their faces were so close, his breath blew across her forehead.

"You're welcome to try."

Her heart thundered as he put a hand around her neck and pulled her in. The suddenness struck her like lightning. Her movements felt sluggish as she lifted her knife to his gut. Instead of tightening his grip to strangle her, his lips pressed against hers, warm and gentle.

A flush of blood pounded through Katsi's body, like a warm bucket of water pouring over her head. The tenseness in her muscles melted away. She expected his lips to feel like iron, but they were soft. Tingling tendrils spread across her skin as he held her against him.

He let go of her and drew back just as quickly as he'd pulled her in. His mouth hung open, eyes wide, staring at her like he'd just been electrocuted. The kiss had been both miniscule and forever.

Katsi gulped, speechless, and let out a breath.

Migo looked down at his stomach and lifted his shirt just enough to reveal a bead of blood on a fresh cut.

Katsi still held the knife up. Apparently her movements hadn't been as slow as she'd thought. She'd stabbed him. She resisted the urge to inspect the wound more closely. Even though he'd just kissed her, the fact that he was towering over her and easily twice her weight instilled a deep sense of caution.

"One can never be too careful," she said, voice shaking, mind spinning. "Is it bad?"

He wiped the blood away with his hand. More blood came, but not much. "I don't think it's deep."

She placed her knife back on her belt and rifled through her things until she drew forth another bandage. She applied some adhesive and handed it to him. "Stick that on, then. It should be fine." She tried to ignore the burning in her cheeks.

What just happened? That kiss was amazing. It was like what her first kiss with Damani *should* have felt like. Her cheeks burned hotter. *Oh sands, what would Damani think?* They burned hotter still.

Unsure of what else to do, she walked to the entrance of the cave, taking gasps of the burning air. She avoided looking at Migo, afraid of what she'd see in those eyes again.

Migo moved to pick up his bronze chest-plate.

"Leave it. That won't help you against the Scorched Waste *or* shaman-folk warriors. The less you wear, the better, but you still want to cover as much skin as you can."

"What about you? You look like you're dressed for the Frozen Waste." He gestured to her padded clothing. He seemed to have recovered from his shock.

The heat outside seeped to Katsi's core. Her stormwading armor was more valuable than he could understand. "I'm a shaman. That makes me an exception. For you, trekking back to the Ring will be difficult to survive without me."

For the most part, that was true. Their location wasn't ideal for getting back to the Ring. The stone outcroppings didn't provide enough shade cover, and there was a large field of rough sand that they had to cross. If Migo simply sprinted back to the Ring, he'd pass out from heat exhaustion before he made it halfway. Katsi had been making good use of her new-found ability however.

"I've been using magic to get to the Ring and back more quickly. We'll have to go slower for you."

"All right. How do we do it?" Migo asked, stepping up behind her. The proximity made her skin tingle.

Katsi glanced back. Migo's dark eyes glimmered with the reflection of tan sand. A whole galaxy shimmered at her. She couldn't detect any emotion. "Stick close behind me. The first part of this is easier. It's worst right before we cross to the Ring. If things get really bad, I found another place we might be able to lodge, but it's not as good as this one. Let me know if you're not doing well."

Migo nodded. "Lead the way."

Katsi turned back outside. The landscape ahead of her shimmered in waves. She took the last few steps outside, passing the magic barrier that warded off most of the heat. They were covered from the sun by the shadow of the outcropping, but the temperature was intensely hotter. They were deep into the Scorched Waste. So deep that she couldn't even see the Ring.

She focused and spread her hands to either side, two bursts of sand flowing in response. She'd recently discovered that she could not only control wind, but the sand itself. She still had no idea how this all worked, but the elements merely responded as if they were a part of her. Controlling them was exhilarating.

The sand swirled overhead, shifting in a line that spread out over Migo. She watched him as he tensed up, but he otherwise remained still as the sand hovered over him. He first regarded the sand with a sense of awe, his mouth gaping open. He quickly snapped it shut and looked back at Katsi with resolve in his clenched jaw.

Katsi couldn't hold back the smile that followed. "This will provide some shade for us, but remember to stay close. It will move with me." With that, she hurried forward, rushing in the direction of the Ring. It would be best if they headed straight there in one go. She willed a light breeze to blow at their backs, but the hot wind did little to ease the temperature.

Ahead of them, the Ring quivered like a mirage. They'd made it about halfway across when Migo started groaning. Katsi immediately stopped and pulled the canteen from her shoulder, her throat rasping as she said, "Drink."

The desperation in his hurried grab made her add, "Not all of it."

She half expected him to slosh it all across his face, but he took a few careful swigs then handed it back. Katsi drank as well and continued walking. She wiped at her forehead, caked with salt. It was the only sign that she was sweating since it evaporated instantly.

Her feet sank into the sand as she strode forward. Migo trudged behind her with the occasional grunt. Despite all the water she'd just drank, she felt parched, her lips, mouth, and throat completely dry.

Katsi pushed some wind at their backs. Before she knew it, they'd reached the wall. She kept the wind blowing in case there was anybody watching. This would hopefully provide the illusion that it was merely a small sandstorm, which was not uncommon.

A boulder laid beside the wall in a pile of crumbled bricks. Katsi hurried over to it, ushering Migo ahead.

Migo struggled to crawl over the wall, but eventually they both dropped down into the Ring. He went straight to his hands and knees, elbow scraping against a prickly bush.

"Time for rest later," Katsi groaned, her voice cracking. She helped haul Migo to his feet.

He made no complaint at her urging and followed after her as she led him towards the jungle. Once thick trunks and big leaves covered them from the sun, the tension in Katsi's stomach eased. It was also a relief not to be summoning the sand and wind. How the magic worked and why it was draining was still unclear.

"We need to head straight for the well. Normally I wouldn't have to do this, but my canteen doesn't hold enough water for two people," she explained.

"Have you seen others on your previous visits while I was recovering?"

"Not a human soul, but the jungle has been active with wildlife. I only stayed long enough to collect food and water to bring back."

Migo pressed ahead. "Then we should hurry."

"Look, if the city got overrun, then on the bright side, maybe your mother is dead and you don't have to worry about her killing you."

Migo's expression was flat.

Katsi's smile was short-lived and her cheeks warmed as she said, "In all seriousness though, I don't hate you as much as I thought I would. The queen is the real monster. Once you get Damani out, I can help you get away, maybe take you to Cataban."

Migo shook his head. "At least you're honest."

Katsi sighed. "Alright, you want to know what I really think happened? That Maedari threw off the attack. Not even stormwading armor can help shamanfolk wade through tornados safely. I think they had to abandon the fight before they could murder enough of your soldiers. I saw plenty of your soldiers making it back to the city walls, and from what I could tell," she paused, a wave of nausea coming over her as she remembered all the dead bodies she'd seen, "a lot of the shamanfolk were killed. I don't know if they expected to lose that many. I'm betting Jehubal is still under Queen Rikaydian's evil clutches."

"That's also possible."

Katsi liked how she could call Migo's mother evil without him jumping to defend her. She almost smiled thinking that there was some redemption for him.

When they neared the well, they hid beneath some underbrush and waited. "Ambushing people at the well is all-too-common," she explained to Migo. He nodded with clear understanding. She realized that he'd probably used the exact tactic *against* people like her.

"We should rotate over to the north or south end," Migo said. "If there are people waiting for us, they'd be on either side. They leave passage from the wastes open. I say we swing around north, then move towards the well. That will help us catch any activity."

Katsi didn't argue, but raised an eyebrow at him. "I should have saved your life a couple years ago. Can you imagine all the amazing things we could have accomplished as a rogue shaman and captain of the guard?"

Migo rolled his eyes, but she caught the smirk on his face before he grunted and led the way. Katsi followed.

Together, they approached the well as stealthily as possible, but Migo's lumbering, injured body had difficulty hiding behind the smaller bushes.

Even still, they made it to the well and filled the canteen without any disturbance.

Migo drank an entire canteen full, and Katsi drank nearly the same. Once the canteen was replenished, Katsi led the way closer to the Frozen Waste. Unless it had already been salvaged, she knew a good spot where some wild fruit would be ripe.

The cooler air was a stark contrast to the blazing heat they'd been in earlier. Her body felt chalky with dry sweat. As with her previous visits, the jungle was thriving with wildlife, perhaps prompted into activity by the lack of people walking the road. It was an unusual atmosphere, and Katsi wasn't sure if she liked it.

When they reached the spot, Katsi checked the aboda fruit. Some of the higher hanging and lower hanging fruit was missing—probably ransacked by creatures—but most of it was intact and still ripe. "Eat your fill," she said, pulling a few of the red fruits off and putting them into her bag. "Who knows when we'll see more food in this condition, and we still don't know if we'll be welcome at Jehubal."

Migo plucked several off before plopping down at the trunk of a tree. The dozens of palm-sized abodas in his lap seemed like little more than a morsel for the large man. He dug into them, barely breaking the hard skin apart before throwing the soft, green insides in his mouth.

Katsi shook her head and sat across from him with her own small pile. She savored each aboda as she placed it in her mouth, the rich juices activating her tongue with little explosions of taste. They were perfectly ripe. This was the kind of sweetness Katsi liked—straight from nature in its purest form. She almost wanted to slap Migo for his lack of respect for such a delicacy. He hardly even seemed to chew them.

"Have you no respect for fine food?" she asked.

"Of course I do," Migo said, popping two more into his mouth. "I respect the way that it makes me stop feeling hungry." A bit of juice slipped out of the corner of his mouth, and he hastily wiped it away, smiling as he did so.

"Why is that funny? You think you're clever?"

Migo shook his head. "Though I am clever, that's not why I was laughing." He swallowed. "It's funny that some of it dripped down my chin. Something like that would never be acceptable in the queen's court. I'm appreciating the contrast of sitting in the jungle eating with a shaman. I don't have to worry about proper table manners at all!"

Katsi gave him a blank stare. "Well, you may want to reconsider that statement. *Some* manners are still appropriate." She smiled. "But I'm glad you can appreciate the benefits of living away from that demon-queen."

Migo sighed. "I'm enjoying the peace while I still can."

"Here, here." Katsi smiled at him and raised another peeled aboda to her mouth, but she pitied him. When was the last time he'd enjoyed life? She tried to convince herself that he deserved it for being a horrible person, but it wouldn't work. He was just another victim of Queen Rikaydian's cruelty.

"You could run away, you know," Katsi suggested. "After you help me free Damani of course. I know a good route you could use to sneak out of the city, and some good places to hide."

"I can't do that," Migo said, his face turning sour. "I can't be the coward the queen says I am. I must face my fate, whatever that may be."

Katsi shook her head. "Well I disagree with that. I think you deserve a fair shot at life, one where your future isn't determined by somebody who hates you."

Migo didn't respond, but he leaned back and looked at her—not with the anger or hatred she was used to seeing—but something different. Instead of his scowl, his features were softened, the hard lines smoothed away. It was like seeing a different Migo, one that actually had hope. It was gone in a moment as he got to his feet. "We should get moving. I'd noticed the angle you took to get us back to the Ring led us further south, away from the city. I assume this was to get us over the wall and close to the well, but it also means we're almost a half cycle away from Jehubal."

Katsi raised her eyebrow at him. "Clever. Your assumptions are correct." She stuffed a few more abodas in her bag. "We'll want to stop at the fringes of the jungle outside the city. I think it'd be a good time to rest. You especially will want to gather your strength in case we have to get away. You were stumbling around earlier."

"I agree," Migo said, flexing his fingers as they started walking north.

"Nervous?" Katsi asked, noticing his hands.

Migo threw up a hand. "I wish I had my weapon. I haven't been unarmed outside the city for years."

Katsi nodded. "I feel the same way whenever I come out without my stormwading armor on. Strange how tools become a part of us."

"Though mine is a weapon, and yours is armor. Maybe that says something about us."

"That may be the most profound thing you've ever said. I suppose you could take a few cycles just to contemplate that, perhaps even write an essay on it and send it to the Lahanawe Archivists for publication and acceptance into their library. Though I think you'd have to portray shamanfolk as demons in order for them to look at it."

"I don't know what's in those abodas, but I believe you just complimented me. You should have brought some back earlier."

Katsi shook her head and smiled, trying not to think about the kiss. The shocking tendrils that laced across her skin. The warmth of his body pressed against her. A moment passed in silence before she said something else. "Sorry to keep bringing her up, but do you really think the queen would have you killed?"

A flood of yellow streamed overhead as a flock of lizards flew ringright, abandoning the tree they'd been hiding in. Migo chewed on Katsi's question and said, "Yes. She has been disconnected from me for years. I doubt she even sees me as her son. I've had hopes of regaining her favor." He shook his head. "That time has passed."

"Could you buy more time somehow?"

"It's possible. I've been considering my options, but I think my best bet is to make her feel like I can still be used to eradicate shamans. Who knows, maybe the attack on Jehubal will make her feel that my services are still required. If I can convince her of that, then I may have enough time to help you free Damani."

"You're willing to try and free him?" Katsi said, a new bounce in her step.

Migo brushed back his black hair and sighed. "I understand what you mean by his ignorance. If he truly didn't know you were a shaman, then my own morality lets me believe that he could be let go."

"Well, I guess that's a start. If anything, he's only guilty of being a nice person. He's probably the greatest citizen in the whole city. It would be more of a crime to keep him locked up than anything."

Migo gave her a strange look before turning away. "You love him?"

Katsi's cheeks and neck flushed with heat. "What kind of question is that? I don't know about love, I'm seventeen, but he saved my life and helped me out for years. All from the kindness of his heart." Katsi tried to think what love even meant, but couldn't grasp anything. Though she certainly liked Damani and had sometimes thought about marrying him. "He's a great person."

Migo nodded but didn't look back at her as they ducked under some brush. His pace quickened. Why, by all the storms, did she feel like she didn't want him to think she was head-over-heels for Damani?

"Do you think I should die?" She asked, though she already knew the answer.

The muscles in Migo's jaw clenched. "You can command the Maedaris, can't you?"

"Sleet, no. Our magic can do some awesome things, but Maedaris seem way too powerful. Maybe if there were a thousand of us with really rotten intentions, then I suppose something like that could be possible." Katsi rolled her eyes at him. His perception was still fogged up by ringdweller superstitions about the Maedaris being caused by shamans. Though it was true that magic was in the Maedaris, there was no evidence that *people* were behind it. "You saw what I did back there, churning sand overhead and blowing wind. It was very directional. The Maedaris are way too sporadic to possibly be something that could be controlled by somebody."

"But there's still the potential," Migo countered. "Storms are already common enough—maybe some shamans throw magic into the mix to make them even worse."

"Well, I guess I don't know, but maybe. What's the point?"

"Katsi, that kind of power is... terrifying. Every day, people could die if a Maedari suddenly decided to show up and blow through the city. Not every city is like Jehubal with advanced constructions like we have. Do you have any idea about the kind of destruction the Maedaris cause?"

Katsi scratched her neck. "I guess I don't know. I've lived in a cave by myself most of my life."

Migo nodded. "Well, it's not good. People die from them all the time, just not so much here because of our engineering designs and the stone imports from Cataban. The kind of power to create a Maedari is a terrible weapon." His eyebrows creased, and his face darkened. "I don't think it should exist."

"Well that's not fair!" Katsi shouted, heat rising in her cheeks. "I've never hurt anybody with my powers before. Am I suddenly guilty because of my potential? Maybe everybody that could hold one of your glaives should be put to death for the *potential* of them hurting others."

"I agree with your outburst," Migo said with a pained sigh.

Katsi slipped on a patch of damp moss and slammed an elbow on the ground as she went down. Migo offered a hand, but Katsi ignored it as she popped back up to her feet. She was so shocked by his response that she wasn't sure if she should be angry. "What do you mean?"

"I mean you aren't a bad person." Migo's right hand seemed to be grasping for his lost weapon again, and he frowned at the ground. "Independently, I don't think you should die, but at the same time, I don't think your power should exist." He gripped his forehead with one hand. "That complicates things."

"I'll say, and if we're being honest, it's nice to hear that you don't think I should die. That's about the nicest thing you've said to me since I *saved your life.*"

Migo shook his head, and gave her a small grin. "I excel at flattery."

Katsi laughed so hard that she snorted. The fact that he'd never been sarcastic with her made it that much funnier. "You've taken a page from my book."

Migo's smile broadened for a heartbeat before disappearing, and he kept walking. It was like he'd recognized that he was being happy, so he hurried to bury it away. Katsi shook her head and followed. He was struggling, but perhaps there was redemption for him after all.

Chapter Thirty-Two

The Captain Returns

A light breeze awakened Migo. When he saw the leaves and branches hanging overhead, he sprang to a crouch, grasping for his glaive. It wasn't there, of course. He'd lost it in the Maedari. It took another moment for him to collect his bearings. He felt groggy, like he'd slept five marks straight.

After popping his neck, he crawled out from under a collection of rockberry bushes. He took a peek at his chest and ran a finger across the scar there. The wound healed nicely. Despite Katsi's lack of medical training, whatever poultice she'd used had a remarkable reparative quality. *Healed by magic.* He shook his head, still baffled by the idea. He wondered if other people even knew that shamanic magic could be used for good things.

The fresh stab wound was the only thing left to worry about, though he'd suffered several similar injuries without too much trouble. The stab wound he'd gotten for kissing her. His mind spun at the very thought. He didn't know what had overtaken him. Was it the caring look in her eyes? The compassion? The ability her words had to pierce him with a sense of clarity and freedom? Her raw, unfiltered beauty? He wanted to slap himself to clear the image away. Even thinking of the kiss left him feeling like he was wrapped in a soft, warm blanket.

He flexed and looked around. His body felt great compared to yesterday. He spotted Katsi out towards the Frozen Waste. It almost looked like she was dancing as she practiced her magic, arms swaying, body winding. Dirt flew by as gusts of wind occasionally burst in his direction. Her veil was down, revealing her soft features, dark brows furrowed with focus.

Migo rose to his feet and walked closer, stopping against the trunk of a tree. Watching her use magic gave him the same feeling as when he'd first started learning to ride rangolas: it was scary and electrifying at the same time. She'd said that she couldn't create a Maedari, and he believed her, but she was young. Perhaps she could develop that with more practice.

Katsi had removed her thin robe, revealing the leathers she wore beneath, the mystical garb she'd referred to as stormwading armor. It didn't look very mystical, more like plain, dark leather that had hardly any padding, if any at all. It was tight against her body in some places, and loose in others, like it wasn't properly fitted. On the positive side, it was well-crafted, if a little old and worn in some spots. Even though it wasn't fitted, Katsi wore it well.

"You know, I've had people stare at me plenty before, but never so blatantly," Katsi said. She slowed to a stop and regarded him with her brown eyes. She flicked her black hair behind her back and started tying it.

Migo refrained from rolling his eyes. "The magic is intriguing. I don't know anybody like me who's ever seen it this close before."

"Mmmhm. I'm sure watching my body gives you such a profound understanding." She arched one of her dark eyebrows at him, then grabbed her robe and swung it on.

Migo grumbled. If he didn't know better, he'd say she was being flirtatious. He turned away and clenched a fistful of his shirt. Of course she wasn't. She was trying to implore his help to free her *boyfriend*.

He changed the subject and asked her about food. Relying on her for such things made his brain twist. It was even more strange to have such mixed feelings about her. On one hand, he respected and admired her. He'd never met somebody so complex and intriguing. On the other hand, she was a shaman, and she portrayed the very power that haunted his nightmares and caused a shiver of fear to run down his spine with every boom of thunder or strong gust of wind.

His old hatred flared, but it was diminished, as if something were holding it back. For a moment, he wanted to lose himself in that hatred, as he'd done many times before. He wanted to embrace that familiar sensation, drowning in self-loathing at least for a brief time, but found the desire weak. Getting to know Katsi had done something to change him, and sharing his story with her had somehow made him feel more comfortable with her.

It was a disturbing realization.

"Back to brooding, eh, princeling?"

Migo blinked at her.

Katsi flicked away an aboda peel. "You frown too much. It makes you look like you're thirty. You could use some gratitude."

His brow furrowed deeper.

"You know, gratitude for me saving you, for having food to eat. That kind of thing."

"You want me to express gratitude to you?"

Katsi shrugged. "That's up to you, but I'd much rather you *feel* the gratitude. Life's happier that way."

Migo gulped down a crunchy root as he thought. He'd been planning to die, fully hoping that it would happen, even excited about the prospect of not having to live in his terrible state anymore. But right now, he didn't want to die. "Thanks," he said, forcing the words out.

Katsi choked on the food in her mouth as if with surprise, but she was clearly faking. "Amazing. I think this moment should go down in history. Prince Rikaydian thanks a shaman girl for saving his life and taking care of him." Katsi coughed a laugh, popped to her feet, and patted Migo on the shoulder as she walked by. "I think you're ready to go home. Shall we?"

Migo threw the rest of his aboda on the ground and strode after her. He was prepared to accept whatever may have happened to Jehubal. Most of all, he was anxious to see if Hatan was alive.

He stopped short. Something was off. The sounds of nature had ceased. He held a hand up to Katsi, but she too was still, eyeing the jungle. Instinctively, they both took a step towards each other.

A shaman dropped from a tree ahead of them. Others emerged from behind the foliage. They were surrounded.

"Katsi Danan." A figure stepped out to the front, an older woman. "Do not shame yourself by standing with a ringdweller. I did not think you would stoop to harboring the prince himself. Turn him over and there may yet be redemption for you. You cannot fight us."

The shamanfolk brandished their weapons, each armed with the deadly seculas.

"No, Mashe," Katsi said.

The glares Migo received as he looked at the shamanfolk burned to his soul. Their hatred was hot. Their muscles tensed.

"Let's gut him!" one shouted.

"We do not wish to hurt you, Katsi. Step away from him," Mashe said.

"No," Katsi screamed. The ground beneath them trembled. "You will not touch him."

The air hummed as it came whistling through the trees in a warm breeze. Her power was palpable, like a lightning bolt ready to strike. It raised the hair on Migo's skin.

Mutters ran through the shamanfolk.

"Katsi, do not aid them," Mashe said. "You must use your power wisely."

"I'm *aiding* all of us," Katsi said.

"We have decimated their armies," Mashe said, voice laced with anger. "We're on the verge of regaining our lands."

Katsi clenched her fists and the wind grew stronger, swirling around them in a circle. "We do not have to return blood for blood. I will bring peace, but I need him. Now step out of my way." She took a step towards the old woman, who held her ground, but the others backed away. They feared Katsi. Or revered her. He wasn't sure which.

Mashe shook her head. "We are prepared to destroy the city, Katsi. How can you hope to bring peace now?"

Migo was stunned by the boldness. Could the shamanfolk really take the city? The casualties among his people must have been terrible. Guilt grabbed him by the throat. It had to be his fault somehow.

"I have a plan," Katsi said. "The seer showed me a way."

Mashe's nostrils flared as she let out a long breath. "The future is never certain. You have until the end of the next Maedari. If you have not resolved things by then, the city is ours."

Katsi strode on and Migo stuck right behind her. The crowd of shamanfolk parted, but their glares, sharp as daggers, needled at Migo. He glared back, ready to defend himself if they decided to attack.

Slowly, the shamanfolk disappeared into the jungle, and Katsi's power faded away.

Migo kept looking over his shoulder until they reached the end of the jungle. Katsi didn't look back once. Despite knowing the city hadn't been overrun by shamans, the tenseness in Migo's muscles only intensified. Maybe assassins would be waiting for him as soon as he entered the city.

A few farmhouses came into view. "I can't believe they let me walk out of there alive," Migo said, voice barely over a whisper.

"I wouldn't have let them try anything," Katsi said. She looked back at him with a smirk. "Our tribe hasn't had a stormcaller in generations."

"A stormcaller?"

Katsi groaned and snuck up behind a farmhouse. "It's the kind of magic I'm proficient in. I'm not about to go into all the details of the different magic systems."

There were no sounds ahead, but they slowed their pace, keeping to cover as they proceeded. Not a single person came into sight when they snuck around the back of a farmhouse. Katsi bit her lip—something he'd noticed her do from time to time. He found a hooked rod and picked it up, catching a scrutinizing glance from Katsi, but she made no protest.

From there, they went straight across the farmlands, not even bothering to head to the main road. Some of the crops they passed looked ready for harvest, and Migo almost expected Katsi to take some pickings, but she made no attempt.

When they reached the smaller jungle that stood between the marshes and Jehubal, they slowed their pace, Migo following Katsi's lead. Lizards and insects clamored about, but no people.

Migo's grip on the rod grew sweaty. They could see the fringes of Jehubal's walls when Katsi stopped and folded her arms. Soldiers' voices echoed from the walls.

"You're going to have to come up with a good story," Katsi said, pulling her knife out and pointing it at him.

"What do you mean?"

Katsi raised an eyebrow at him. "You're going to show up two weeks after a battle, wearing none of your armor, and carrying no provisions. It'll seem strange."

Migo looked down at himself. He was utterly filthy. There wasn't a time in his life where he'd ever felt so disgusting. "Perhaps I escaped custody."

"There's no way you would have been able to escape," Katsi said, shaking her head. "Rescued, maybe." She used her knife to tap her left temple. "It needs to be something more natural that fits in with what happened. The Maedari picked you up and threw you into the Scorched Waste, and you lost your weapon. You were stuck out there for a few marks while the storm kept going, unconscious as you'd fallen among an outcropping of stone." Katsi kept going with the story, her words picking up speed after the lie gained momentum. "When you gained consciousness, the Maedari was dying down, but it was hot, so you stripped off your armor and dragged yourself back towards the Ring.

"You managed to climb over the same spot we did, and then hid yourself in the cleft of a tree. You had some bad injuries, so you couldn't get around while you were healing, and you considered yourself a fugitive behind enemy lines, so you laid low. You got hungry and thirsty enough that you just started looking around and found a batch of low-growing moss with soft roots and decided to eat the roots. They're called Kajina Roots, but it'll sound better if you pretend like you don't know—"

"Okay, okay." Migo had to cut in. "That's very good. I get where you're going. I think I can come up with the rest from there."

"You didn't let me finish!"

"You didn't need to. I get it. Sands, do you make up stories like that a lot?"

Katsi shrugged. "It helps to get out of tight spots sometimes. I give myself a fake background all the time when I have to mingle with the people. It ensures I'm ready when people start asking too many questions."

Migo glanced at her satisfied smile. "Am I supposed to believe anything you've told me about yourself, then?" He wondered if she'd created a fake story about her parents getting murdered in order to create some kind of sympathetic relationship with him.

"I wish a lot of what I told you *wasn't* true," she said, looking at her feet, "but unfortunately for me, I didn't lie to you about my past."

Migo nodded. He wasn't sure how it had come to this, but he actually believed her. "Right, well," he paused and took a breath, looking back towards the city. "I'll head back in. I'll find out what I can about Damani."

There was enough evidence to convict Damani as a shaman sympathizer, a crime punishable by death. Queen Rikaydian's laws were completely merciless regarding anything to do with shamans, but Migo and Hatan were the only ones who knew about that. As long as Hatan was still alive, anyway.

Migo was a captain. Would it be right for him to release a guilty man, even if that man was just being a nice person? The only reason he was considering releasing Damani was because a *shaman* had asked him. It was twisted, and it made his chest clench just thinking about it.

"Katsi, what's this plan that you have? How will you bring peace and prevent the tribe from attacking?"

Katsi flashed a smile. "I'm still working out the details, but don't worry, it'll be flawless."

Migo felt no sense of assurance. "What about Damani. Where do I take him once he's out?"

"He'll know where to go. Just make sure he's free."

"I can try that."

"Get to it, then," she said.

Migo grabbed a fistful of his shirt again. "Katsi, about the kiss—."

Katsi held up a hand to silence him. "Just forget about it."

He knew he couldn't. The memory settled on him like gravity. It would forever pull at him, influencing his every movement. A law he could never deny. He swallowed hard then moved to leave. Katsi's hand stopped him, grabbing him at the elbow.

"And don't die, okay? Miraculously enough, you've convinced me that you don't deserve that."

A tingle went up his spine. Migo didn't move, but stared back into her dark eyes, feeling somewhat mesmerized by the look of concern that she gave him. It wasn't just that she was trying to use him to save her friend, but the way she spoke and looked at him gave him the impression that she actually cared about him. It was a foreign concept, but something he didn't mind.

"One more thing," Migo started. "Did you try to assassinate the queen? Before the battle?"

Katsi groaned. "No, I was trying to free Damani. That obviously failed." She gestured at Migo. "That explains our current arrangement."

Migo only nodded, afraid to voice his next thought.

Katsi jerked her head towards the city, patted his arm, and disappeared into the jungle.

Shaken from the spell, Migo clenched his jaw and took a resolute stride towards the city. Migo still held the farming rod in his hand as he entered the clearing before the city, eyes scanning the walls and towers.

Figures moved along the parapets with greater activity than normal, and they wore the maroon and beige colors of the Rikaydian soldiers, although an occasional uniform looked different. Those were the hired soldiers belonging to merchant lords or even mercenaries from northern provinces. The queen was probably wasting her money on the latter.

Shouts erupted from the wall as soon as Migo emerged. Heads popped up over the walls, but the gate to the city remained closed.

He made it within a few steps of the gate before someone hesitantly called down to him. "Captain?"

* * * * *

Katsi watched from the bushes as the gates opened before Migo. Soldiers shouted and cheered for their returning captain. She huffed and withdrew a few paces once Migo was out of sight.

She could hardly believe that she'd just nursed Migo Rikaydian back to health, and then escorted him to safety. *This serves a purpose*, she reminded herself. Still, the whole idea made her nervous, to say the least. She was gambling on the hope that she could somehow trust Migo—a man who'd been hunting her for weeks.

She had no plan to bring peace. How could she possibly hope to make the queen recall the extermination order?

This was simply an idea to get Damani out before the tribe ravaged the city.

Guilt gnawed at her stomach. What about the other farmers? What about Migo?

She veered towards the road and reached beneath her robe, hand searching amongst the pouches at her belt. She drew forth a letter, folded over multiple times. It had crumpled up a bit over the last couple weeks, but it was still undamaged. She unfolded the creases until it was fully revealed. She scanned the single page with a quick glance, but there were, of course, no words or images on the aged sheet. Those words would only come at a cost.

After spending some time with Migo though, it was a price she was even more willing to pay.

Blood.

It would change everything she'd stood by for a long time, but it seemed as if everything had been pointing to this anyway. She folded the letter back up and stuffed it in the pouch, double-checking to make sure it was still there after placing it in.

She had an idea. It was rash. It was insane. There was no way it could work, but with her powers... maybe there was a chance. She needed some of her father's old potions, stashed away at their hideout in the Scorched Waste.

She'd have to move fast. Who knew how long it would take for Migo to release Damani? Worst still, how long until the next Maedari came?

Soft moss squished beneath her boots, and the scent of blooming castletrunk leaves wafted in a calm breeze. The respite of nature contrasted her unease and made her lips curl in disgust. She shook out her hands and took off at a run.

Chapter Thirty-Three

Betrayal

Migo swelled as he entered the city, holding back a smile as applause and cheering echoed off the stone walls. People flooded into the streets to catch a glimpse of their prince.

"We thought you were dead!" A soldier shouted at him from atop the wall, almost giddy with awe.

Another soldier had tears glistening in his eyes as he came and bowed before Migo. "Thank you, Lord. You saved my life." The soldier's arm was still in a sling. Migo vaguely recognized him from the battlefield.

It was a slow procession as Migo made his way up the road toward the palace. He'd never seen the citizens so happy before. It was like he'd just been married and everyone had been promised free food and drinks. More than a few people called him the "Hero of Jehubal." Despite all the smiles, Migo kept a close grip on the farming rod. Who knew—any one of these people could be his assassin—but they crowded around him so tight, there was no getting around it.

Maybe his original plan would work. Maybe the queen would love him now. He swallowed the thought, forcing it down. He didn't dare to be so optimistic. Not yet.

He was halfway to the palace before Hatan emerged from the crowd. Relief washed over Migo as he jumped forward, hugging his cousin, not caring what anybody would think.

"I knew you had to be alive," Hatan said. They kept walking toward the palace, Hatan shaking his head every few steps. "They even held a ceremony in your honor. The queen herself shared a few words. You wouldn't have believed it."

Migo truly *didn't* believe it. Maybe it had been for show.

"Over forty soldiers say that you're the reason they're alive." Hatan clapped Migo's shoulder and leaned in closer, lowering his voice so it wouldn't be heard over the continued cheering. "I'll want to know how you survived, and why you even came back." His tone was serious.

Migo nodded in acknowledgement, grateful that Hatan was still being cautious. The queen would confront him, of that he had no doubt. And when she did, would he be forgiven, or would he still be condemned?

He needed a strategy, and he still felt unsure about releasing Damani as Katsi had asked.

"They call you the Hero of Jehubal," Hatan said.

"So I heard," Migo said, gripping his farming rod tighter. "Though we aren't safe yet."

Hatan narrowed his eyes and nodded. "Are you hungry? You look thinner."

"You have no idea. I've been living off fruits and roots for two weeks."

A few blocks later they were ascending the path to the palace where the streets were mostly clear of pedestrians and the cheering had died down.

"How did you survive the tornado?" Hatan ventured to ask.

Migo shook his head. "Technically, I didn't. I got flung out into the Scorched Waste. It knocked me out. When I woke up, I was barely alive." He figured he could share his fake story now. There were enough soldiers around that they would pick up on the minor details. Gossip would spread quickly, like it always did. "I ditched my armor and crawled back to the Ring."

Every soldier saluted as Migo and Hatan walked by. Migo had never seen such respect in all his years. Even as a captain, Migo had often only been respected by his own soldiers.

"What about you?" Migo asked. "How'd you get back to safety?"

Hatan sighed. "I helped a couple other groups of soldiers just after we parted. As a group, we tried to help others, but once the storm started coming, we had to run for it. We were almost back to the wall by the time the tornado started." Hatan's eyes dropped. "We lost nearly three-hundred lives. Captain Seba among them."

Migo staggered and leaned up against the wall just outside the door to the palace. "Their plan worked then," Migo said breathlessly. He should have trusted Katsi's warning.

Hatan nodded slowly, placing a hand on Migo's shoulder. "I'm afraid so." He glanced inside. "Come, let's talk more inside and get you something to eat."

Migo pushed away from the wall and entered the palace. Without his armor, the air was too cold. He checked every corner as they walked, constantly wary of an assassin emerging. This was his home, and yet it made his skin crawl. He faced his fears during the battle by staying, despite the Maedari, and fought to save his soldiers. But here, in the halls of Rikaydian Palace, his greatest fear had yet to be challenged.

But if he'd learned anything in the last two weeks, it was that he wanted to live. If somebody came after him, he would defend himself. He bounced the farming rod against his palm.

Hatan stopped a servant. "Arrange to have a soldier's ration brought to my room for Lord Rikaydian," he said to her.

She smiled at Migo before running off.

"You never told what happened once you got to the Ring," Hatan said.

"Right," Migo said, raising his voice so that anybody else in the halls would hear. "I figured I was behind enemy lines, so I laid low. I was covered in injuries and my skin was raw from the storm. I spent most of my time recovering. I lived off whatever fruit or root I could find, then made my way back towards the city." They passed a couple more soldiers, then went up a flight of stairs. "I had to sneak by a group of shamans near the farmlands, but didn't see anybody else until I reached the gates."

At the top of the stairs, three soldiers stopped dead in their tracks at the sight of Migo. They bowed in unison. "Welcome back, Lord Rikaydian." Eyes sparkled in wonder.

Migo couldn't help the smile that followed, and he nodded back to them. He waited until they got inside Hatan's room before saying, "Everyone has been calling me Lord Rikaydian, instead of captain."

"Yes," Hatan said, locking the door. "Everyone thought you were dead. Falshon was appointed captain in your stead."

"At least they picked a good man," Migo said.

"Except for the part where Tarahan was appointed Senior Captain."

Migo ground his teeth. "The turd."

A suppressed smile slipped across Hatan's face. He opened a cabinet and withdrew a sheathed knife. "There's still the question of your potential assassination. I don't know if the queen intends to carry on with the plan. There are several mercenaries within the city." He handed Migo the weapon. "Take this, at least. So you aren't unarmed."

Migo hooked it to his belt on the inside, under his shirt. The metal was cool against his skin.

Hatan dropped to one of the two chairs in the room and folded his arms. "Tell me then, Migo, how did you really make it back here alive."

Migo stroked a hand through his hair and plopped down opposite Hatan. This was the one person he could trust completely, but he still struggled to find the words, chewing his tongue a moment before finally speaking. "The tornado did throw me out into the Scorched Waste. I should have died, but... someone saved me." He let out a long breath and lowered his voice. "It was the shaman girl. Katsi."

At first, Hatan cocked his head, but then slapped his knee and burst out in laughter. "Truly?" he asked.

"I know, it might sound hard to believe, but it's the truth. She has magic over the storms—though just enough to keep the Maedari off me after we were blown into the Scorched Waste. She dragged me to a cave and used potions to care for my injuries." Migo lifted his shirt to show Hatan the new scar across his chest which was even smaller than he remembered. "She brought me food and water, and helped me get back to the Ring once I was well enough to move."

"Did she... ask for ransom money or anything?" Hatan scratched at his chin. "What was the motive?"

Migo shrugged. "That's the interesting part. Her friend, the informant." Hatan nodded knowingly. "She wants me to release him."

"So she saved your life, one of the most hated enemies of the surrounding shamans, hoping that you would return the favor by releasing her friend?" Hatan smiled and shook his head.

"No." Migo's cheeks and neck burned. "Boyfriend. She loves him. She feels guilty for being the cause of his arrest."

"Hm." Hatan narrowed his eyes. "Is she... beautiful?"

Migo stared at Hatan flatly. "She's a shaman, Hatan. What kind of question is that?" The image of her returned. Her warm, brown eyes. Black hair. Soft brown skin. The feel of her lips. The lightning that coursed through his veins whenever she touched him.

"It's relevant."

"Sands, Hatan, she wasn't trying to seduce me. She could hardly talk to me without insulting me the first week." He leaned back in his chair and folded his arms.

"Expert tactics, then. Start off mean, then soften up. I know their schemes too well—probably why I'm not married."

"Could we stay on topic?"

"Right. So, if I understand, she let you come back so that you'd free her boyfriend?"

"She helped me come back regardless, there was no formal agreement. Though I did tell her I'd try."

Hatan shook his head. "That seems suspicious. It seems like a ploy set to deceive you into releasing somebody of importance to them. The shamans attacked shortly after he was taken prisoner. How can you be sure there isn't any correlation?"

"There isn't. Katsi disbanded from the tribe because she doesn't agree with some of their standards. She's acting of her own accord. In both warning us before the attack, and saving me afterwards, she was obviously moving against them. The tribe even tried to stop us from entering the city, but she convinced them to let us go."

Hatan leaned forward, hands on his knees. "Can you trust her?"

Migo grunted and closed his eyes. It could all be an elaborate ploy. All his training taught him to expect nothing but deception and lies, but his gut wouldn't buy it. Katsi was too real. Too innocent. Too... He opened his eyes. Maybe she was playing him. Her kindness, her mercy, her compassion. It wasn't because she cared about him, it was because she wanted Damani free. Even still, part of him wanted to release Damani just to spite the queen. "Yes and no. I think she's lying to me about some things, but I still believe she's acting independently of the tribe."

Hatan's eyebrows rose. "Anybody who can win even a fraction of my cousin's trust must be remarkable indeed."

A knock at the door came abruptly.

Migo shot to his feet and Hatan snatched up his glaive, fanning Migo behind him. Migo drew the knife and took up a position behind the door while Hatan approached, unlocked the door, and cracked it open.

"The food you requested, sir," came a woman's voice.

Migo relaxed.

"Ah, I'll take that, thank you," Hatan said, taking a tray.

"Also, the queen requested that Lord Rikaydian attend her in the throne room at fifth mark."

"Very well, thank you." Hatan closed the door and set the tray on a small table.

They looked at each other in silence for a moment.

"That gives me, what, two marks?" Migo asked. His mind spun, searching for answers.

Hatan nodded.

"Do you think she'd have me killed between now and then and scheduling the appointment is an alibi of sorts?"

"I wouldn't put anything past her." Hatan leaned his glaive against the wall and folded his arms. "I recommend you eat up, maybe get some rest. Stay in my room. I'll escort you to the throne room and wait outside."

"Agreed." Migo sat and started eating.

"Do you think the shaman girl is the murderer you were hunting? Now that you met her."

Migo waved a hand and swallowed. "No. I don't think she's the kind of person who'd murder anybody, or even hurt them for that matter. In fact, she seemed to agree with your own theories about the murders and the wars. She annoyingly reminded me of you sometimes."

Hatan barked a laugh. "Well, I'd say she sounds like a great person, but she must have a few tricks up her sleeve to be wary of."

Migo took another spoonful of food. The rations were dense, filled with nutrient, lacking in flavor. How paradoxical for a nation that grew its wealth by producing food. "The shamans plan to attack the city by the end of the next Maedari unless we somehow bring peace."

"Is that a reasonable threat?" Hatan popped his fingers.

"I believe it," Migo said between bites. "There must have been hundreds of them at the battle. They had soldiers on both sides. They outnumbered us. There could have been anywhere from 700 to 800 of them. Even with the extra mercenaries and private merchant forces here in the city, there are probably somewhere around 700 soldiers within our walls, spread all about. Did we have anybody check the battlefield to see what their losses may have been like? Or did we retrieve any of their weapons? It would have been good to analyze them."

"A marvelous idea—one that I'd had only a few cycles ago. This is why we need you here and alive. By the time our men scoured the battlefield however, it seemed that the shamans had cleared the area. None of their dead or armaments were found."

"So we have no idea how many there are, but they have significantly superior equipment, and they're confident in their ability to take the city." Migo took another bite.

"And we're already due for another Maedari any moment now," Hatan added.

Time was short. Migo would die soon, but perhaps Migo had already proven himself a worthy successor. Perhaps winning another battle would earn his mother's love.

Chapter Thirty-Four

Prisoners

Katsi had just gotten back to her hideout and lighted one of the Linara stones when she heard scraping and shuffling of sand from outside. Her heart fluttered with panic for a brief moment, but it was quickly replaced by resolve. She'd known this time would come, she just hadn't known when to expect it.

She'd been discovered.

Trapped. She always considered the danger of living in a small cave as a deathtrap, but there'd been no other solution.

She quickly grabbed the potions she came for before turning off the Linara stone and facing the entrance to her home. The shuffling noises from outside ceased, and a swirl of dust curled up from the entrance. Her breathing stilled in the silence. With both her knife in hand and her magic at the ready, she wondered what method they would use to flush her out.

In answer to her question, three smoking balls were hurled through the entrance. Because of the slant, they stopped short, and didn't make it very far. Katsi smiled and, with a gust of air, pushed all three of them back outside.

The response was a flurry of coughing and curses. Some of the smoke from the balls must've remained inside, however, because Katsi's eyes started to water.

Their next attempt came in the form of several men rushing through the entrance. Katsi tried another gust of wind, but from inside a small cave, she didn't have much to work with. The men were hardly slowed down as they charged in, growling at her as they came as if they were more animal than human.

A couple of them carried torches, casting a feral light into the dwelling.

Katsi didn't bother fighting back. What could she do against ten men? Even if she managed to stab one of them, the others would be more merciless against her. She'd have to play it smart. She sheathed her knife, dropped to her knees, and raised her hands. "I demand a trial for this," she said, but the men gave no response. For a moment, she feared they would merely hack her down.

To her relief, one of them grabbed her hands and shackled them behind her. As a prisoner, she could still hope to escape.

When they dragged her out into the sunlight, she was only half surprised to discover that her assailants were soldiers from the Rikaydian guard. Anger boiled inside her. She never should have trusted Migo.

* * * * *

Migo smoothed down his vest before clipping his maroon cape onto his shoulders, regarding himself in Hatan's mirror. In just a few minutes, he would approach the queen.

Hatan had brought in warm water so Migo could clean off, some of Migo's clothes, and another meal. He felt well and healthy. All that was missing was his glaive, but the weapon was long gone.

"Ready, lord?" Hatan asked, checking the sand dial for time.

Migo clenched his fists. One last fear to face. Hatan's knife was still sheathed against his skin. "As ready as I can be."

Hatan grabbed his glaive and opened the door. Two more soldiers waited outside and fell in behind them as Migo took the lead. Their boots echoed down the hallway and Migo's heart thundered in rhythm. Each step brought him closer to fear. He could feel the queen's nails, dragging across his cheek, peeling his skin apart, exposing him for the weakling he was.

No.

He clenched his fists. He was strong. He was brave. He'd already proven that. The queen wouldn't be able to deny it.

When they reached the throne room, they were greeted by two of the queen's guards with their blue shoulder cuffs. They opened the doors. "Lieutenant Padarro, the queen said you may enter as well," one of them said to Hatan.

Together, their whole procession entered the room.

The queen sat on her throne, legs crossed, wearing a black dress smothered in golden embroidery. Her black hair was pulled back and pinned with golden chains. One hand rested in her lap, another was draped over the armrest. Her plump, beaming red lips curled into a smile.

She said nothing as Migo approached the dais. He stopped at the bottom step and dropped to one knee, bowing his head before her. His ears burned. His hands tingled. Clenching them into fists was the only thing keeping them from trembling.

Silence permeated the air.

Migo stayed in position, biting down on his lower lip. He would only raise his head when the queen acknowledged him.

"My son," she said.

Emotion flooded across Migo's body like warm water. It dripped down the hair of his head and down to his toes. His eyes stung with tears, but he blinked quickly and gulped down the lump that rose in his throat.

She hadn't called him her son in years. Not since before the king died.

He rose to his feet and let out a shuddering breath as he lifted his eyes to look at the queen. His mother. "Your Majesty."

"We're glad to see you've safely returned," she said, her melodic voice a calm wave flowing through the room. "The battle was hard-fought. I heard many reports of your bravery in the field." Migo thought he could detect a hint of moisture glistening at the edges of her eyes. "They say you stayed behind to fight while others fled."

Migo bowed his head. "I vowed to defend our people, Your Majesty."

A frantic knock came at one of the doors.

Queen Tilayna Rikaydian rose to her feet, brow dipping into a frown. "Who dares knock unannounced?"

Two of the queen's guards went and threw open the door. It was Senior Captain Tarahan. Captain Falshon was right behind him, dragging a gagged and chained prisoner.

"What have you brought me, Captain Tarahan?" Tilayna said.

Tarahan placed a hand over his chest and bowed before speaking. "It was Captain Falshon, Your Majesty. His men captured a shaman." His eyes strayed to Migo, widening at the sight of him. He fumbled over his next words. "It is the shaman that Prince Migo was after. Purportedly the one responsible for breaking in at Wajek Manor and also breaking into the palace."

The queen's smile was vicious. Feral. "Captured alive." She traced a finger across her own neck. "Delightful." She pointed to a curtain at the far side of the room. A servant bustled over and pulled it aside, revealing a set of cages. Their metal bars were laced with silver, specifically designed for holding shamans.

Migo's hands flexed. He wished for the companionship of his glaive. He fixed his gaze on the prisoner. Katsi stared back at him, eyes wide. She screamed into her gag and pulled against her restraints, stepping toward him as if she might try and strangle him.

Two soldiers stepped up and grabbed her under the arms to haul her forward.

"She hasn't been this energetic since we caught her," Falshon muttered under his breath as they walked to the cages.

"The prince has her riled up," Tilayna said. "I'd love to hear what she has to say to him."

Migo's jaw tensed as the soldiers shoved Katsi into the cage and removed her gag. He couldn't look away.

"Migo, you liar," Katsi screamed. Her face twisted in pure rage. He'd never seen such an expression on her face, and it filled him with dread. "I shouldn't have trusted you. I saved your life. Tell them!"

Tarahan chuckled openly and turned to Migo. "Well this just got interesting."

Migo clenched his fist. This wasn't part of the plan. He hadn't expected Katsi to get captured. She didn't deserve to be here. "Yes," he conceded, voice deep. "She's the reason I survived after the Maedari threw me into the Scorched Waste."

Katsi clanged up against the bars of her cage, her stare so intense it burned Migo's heart, but he couldn't avert his eyes. He needed to play this situation to his advantage. "I used her expertise to get back to the city in exchange for peace."

Tilayna released a melodic laugh. "And yet you stayed true, Migo," she said. "This is an expert tactic of theirs to try and sway us to their side. They often tried this sort of thing on your father."

"The shamans are intent on attacking the city directly, Your Majesty," Migo said. "With our decimated forces, they are confident they will achieve victory. Whether or not that is true, if they attack, hundreds will die, if not thousands. Soldiers and civilians. They can enter homes easily. The attack will come at the conclusion of the next Maedari. They said they'd only call off the attack if we offer a peaceful resolution. No more killing."

"Migo," Tilayna said. Migo tore his eyes away from Katsi to regard his mother. She shook her head at him, golden earrings swaying. "Your father sought peace, and they still killed him. The shamans don't want peace. They want us to let our guard down so they can sweep us away like one of their storms. I raised you for one thing, Migo. To kill shamans. They can never be trusted. They will always try to manipulate you."

Katsi screamed rebuttals. "It's not true! We're sick of the killing! Please!"

Tilayna pointed at Katsi with her chin. "Replace her gag."

Katsi gave a muffled scream as the gag was replaced.

Tilayna came down one of the steps, staring down at Migo. "You know now that the shamans are to be eradicated. This is the only way we can achieve peace. You know not to sympathize for them. Think of all they have taken from you."

The fire had ignited in her eyes. The hatred. The fury. His first instinct was to flinch, but he straightened his shoulders and nodded. Like Katsi said, a shaman may have killed his father, but that didn't mean they were all guilty. The queen was looking for compliance. He nodded his head.

"Everything I have done for you is so that you would be strong," she continued. "This is why I let you believe that you would be assassinated. So you would prove your honor. Your loyalty."

Migo's mouth opened. Hatan looked like he'd just been slapped.

Tilayna's smile was devious. "Don't worry, I knew all about Hatan's spies. They never heard anything I didn't want them to. But to your credit, neither of you acted against me." She stepped down to the floor.

Migo felt difficulty breathing. How could she do this to him? She claimed the shamans were manipulating him, but she'd just admitted to manipulating him into hating and distrusting the shamans. Katsi had never done anything to hurt him.

"Now," Tilayna said. "If we are going to be attacked soon, we need to plan our defenses. Captain Tarahan."

He came forward and bowed to her. He reached out a hand as if to take hers and kiss it, but she withdrew her hands and placed them behind her back.

Tilayna blinked at Tarahan, expressionless. "Assemble Captain Akailen and any other available officer so we can coordinate our efforts."

Tarahan placed a hand to his chest. "Very well, Your Majesty. I will gather them in the meeting hall."

"Migo," she said. "You will attend as well." She turned away, leaving with her personal entourage of two women-in-waiting and two guards.

Migo looked back at Katsi. She sat slumped in the corner. Defeated. He hadn't expected any of his soldiers to remain posted outside her home. He'd completely forgotten that three of his men had been posted there to keep watch for when she'd return. Despite the battle, they hadn't left their post.

It was because of Katsi that Migo's self-loathing had practically dissipated. She had experienced some of the same loss he did, and yet she hadn't grown angry and bitter. It was because of her that he'd regained his will to live. The queen had been the one to take it away. She'd done nothing but use and abuse him. As tears trickled down Katsi's cheeks, his fists tightened.

Katsi was worthy.

The queen was not.

There was *one* way to bring peace. And it didn't require bloodshed. Not very much blood anyway. Migo smirked. The calm that settled over him solidified his resolve.

The queen needed to die.

Chapter Thirty-Five

Key

Katsi slumped at the back of her cage, head resting back between two bars. She was defeated. Numb. Her throat was ragged from yelling. She only wondered who would die first, her, or Damani. Would she even get to see him again? Part of her didn't want to. She'd failed him.

Migo had used her. She was merely another tool. He must've lied about his mother wanting him dead. She was cruel, certainly, but Katsi had really believed that she might kill him. It was all a lie to gain her sympathy.

She struggled against her restraints. The rusting magic she used last time wouldn't work. Silver was somehow resistant.

The single hope that remained was that the Bayvana Tribe would attack soon, take over the city, and set her free, but the thought of that happening made her sick. Thousands would die. The tribe would be whittled down. So many of her cousins had already died. She wondered for a moment if Shinaseh had survived the last battle. It wasn't right. People like her shouldn't be out fighting wars.

Hot tears came to her eyes and she gritted her teeth. She thought she was done crying, but new pitiful thoughts kept coming. She forced the tears back and let out a long breath. The soldiers guarding her didn't deserve to see her cry. She looked up at them. There were four still in the room after the queen and all the officers left.

What she wouldn't give to have her hands free just to see what her magic could do. Did she even need her hands? It didn't seem necessary. It wasn't like the magic was stuck to her fingertips, but it certainly helped direct the flow of things, especially when calling up the sand or wind.

Migo. Her thoughts kept going back to him. She should've been cursing his name, but the memory of all his pain from back in the cave kept coming back to her. It couldn't have just been for show. And the look he kept giving her, when his stony facade cracked and his pupils widened, turning into a whole galaxy of stars.

And the kiss. The way his hand traced a tickling line across her neck.

It was horrible. Disgusting... Electrifying. Passionate.

Heat rose in her cheeks.

The very memory made her blush.

Sands. What had Migo done to her?

He'd made her care about him. Maybe even something more. Yet here she was. A prisoner. And she hated him for it.

Her throat was dry. She needed to pee. Her jaw ached from the gag. She must have been in here for two marks now. Maybe three. She kicked her foot against the ground in frustration and a couple guards cast a lazy glance in her direction.

A door slammed open and Migo came stomping into the room, maroon cape trailing behind him. "One of the keys has gone missing," he announced, heading straight to Katsi's cell. "Has anyone else been in here since she was locked up?"

"No, lord," answered one of the guards with blue patches in his shoulder.

"We need to check her cuffs," Migo said. "Has she moved much since she's been in there?"

"No, lord," said the guard right next to Katsi's cage. "The cage is coated with silver. This hasn't been an issue with any other shaman we've caught. Is there really a problem?"

Migo gave the man a scathing look. "She's a stormcaller. Have you ever heard of that kind of shaman? A silver cage won't keep her from calling the elements."

The guard stammered a response. "U-understood."

Katsi rose to her feet as Migo closed in. She *wished* her hands were free if only to hit him in the face once before her execution.

"Show me your hands," Migo said quietly, stopping in front of her cage, planting his feet as if expecting her to charge at him.

All four guards were watching. They raised their weapons and stood at the ready.

Did they really think she could do anything? Anything at all?

She bit down on her gag and glared back at Migo, refusing to turn around.

He groaned in frustration. "Come closer, and show me your hands," he repeated.

She wanted to yell back at him, but then she saw it. His voice was harsh, but his eyes. They had the same softness she remembered during those bright moments when he seemed like he didn't hate the whole world. Something glinted at her from between two of his fingers, held at an angle that only she could see.

Sleet and sand. It was a key. He was trying to break her out.

Katsi gasped and stepped towards him.

The door banged open again. This time, Captain Tarahan entered with two more soldiers at his back. His laugh was shrill, dripping with raw amusement. "Migo! You almost made it."

Migo turned to face Tarahan. "You will address me as Prince Rikaydian." He backed up, holding the hand with the key behind him.

"I think not," Tarahan said.

Kasti immediately hated the man's nasally, demeaning tone.

"Traitor might be a more fitting title, wouldn't it?" Tarahan gave a single gesture and all six soldiers came together, turning their weapons on Migo.

No. No, this couldn't be happening. Katsi shook her head.

"What are you doing?" Migo said.

Tarahan shook his head. "The missing key, Migo. You're the one who took it. The queen told you she was testing you. Seeing if you'd remain loyal. You were so close! She had me keep an eye on you. We left that key unguarded just to see if you would try something. Sure enough!"

Migo took another step back towards the cage. His hands were nearly touching it, but a glaive poked him in the back, forcing him away.

Katsi wanted to scream. She would call up enough magic to level the whole palace. Her arms flexed and tugged at her restraints.

"Keep him away from the shaman," Tarahan ordered. The guard nearest them sliced his glaive down behind Migo. Migo skipped forward to avoid being clipped. "Hand over the key, Migo. It all ends here." All seven men came and surrounded Migo, seven glaives pointed directly at him.

The muscle in Migo's jaw twitched, but he said nothing.

"Open the other cage," Tarahan said. "Throw him in."

The soldiers did as they were ordered, but not before they wrested the key from Migo's grip. Migo didn't fight back. One wrong move and a glaive would slice him apart. The gate to his cell clapped shut with a hollow bang.

A dry sob escaped Katsi's throat. Migo hadn't betrayed her. He was still trying to help, and he'd gotten caught for it. She was a fool. Did she really think this plot would get Damani free? Now she'd brought about Migo's downfall as well. She was a curse to everyone around her.

If only she'd listened to Damani when he'd asked her to stay instead of running off to steal that stupid armlet. What good was her magic now? She couldn't save Damani. She couldn't save herself. She couldn't save Migo. And now her tribe and all of Jehubal would crumble.

Migo stared at her from his cell, but she turned away. She couldn't bear to look at him.

Lightning flashed across the westward windows and thunder immediately reverberated throughout the throne room. Everyone looked up. The lightning and thunder didn't stop.

The Maedari was upon them.

"Is this your doing?" Tarahan said, stepping up to Katsi's cage. "Migo called you a stormcaller. If you hope the shamans will save you, you're wrong." He unlocked her cage. "They won't reach you in time. I'm going to kill you. Now." He gave a wicked grin. Maniacal.

Fear was a rare emotion for Katsi, but now it flooded her being. As soon as the door was open, she tried to run past him, but he grabbed her by the hair and threw her to the ground. Her head crashed against the stone.

"Tarahan," Migo bellowed, his voice like the roar of a rangola.

Tarahan kicked her in the gut, then two soldiers picked her up and dragged her to the front of the queen's throne.

"TARAHAN!" Migo shouted again. His cage rattled. She managed a glance at him. The anger on his face was worse than anything she'd ever seen. His muscles strained against the metal bars, trying to pry them aside to no avail.

Something throttled Katsi in the ear and all air escaped her as pain overtook her senses.

They dropped her to the floor and cold metal pressed up against her neck. Tears blurred her vision. She'd failed them. All of them. Her pacifism had earned her nothing.

Here she would die. At the foot of the queen's throne.

Chapter Thirty-Six

Treason

"Tarahan. Duel me. Now," Migo said, voice grating like rocks. An inferno raged inside him the instant Tarahan grabbed Katsi's hair. Anger burned him. Scorched his skin. Dripped from his fingers like liquid flame.

Earlier, when Tarahan caught him trying to release Katsi, he'd been too hesitant. He'd been tempted to fight back—but he was their prince—these were his own soldiers. But after seeing them hurt Katsi, there was only one reasonable solution left.

Kill them. All of them.

It would also mean that Migo's treachery wouldn't escape this room. But first, he needed to goad Tarahan into a duel.

"The queen doesn't love you, Tarahan," Migo said.

Tarahan kept the blade of his glaive against Katsi's neck, but he spared a look back at Migo. "What did you say?" he said, his expression incredulous.

"She doesn't love anyone. I've seen the way you look at her. Believe me, she does not share any interest."

"Shut your mouth, you whelp," Tarahan said, eyes widening.

It was working. Migo would say anything, do anything, to keep him from hurting Katsi.

"Duel me," Migo said. "You've always wanted to. This is your only chance. When those shamans pour through our city, we'll all die anyway."

"You do not have enough faith in our people," Tarahan said, withdrawing his weapon from Katsi's neck as he took a step toward Migo.

"Well, I'm our best soldier, and yet you've locked me away before the battle."

Tarahan shook his head. "You are far from the greatest warrior."

"And yet they call me the Hero of Jehubal, and you... when was the last time you even fought a shaman?"

Tarahan's scowl deepened.

"Duel me," Migo repeated. "Tilayna's love is reserved for the strongest. How can you claim to be worthy when she hears that you refused to fight me? You would be a disgrace in her eyes."

"I would belittle myself to accept a duel with a traitor."

"You know that's not true," Migo said, squeezing the bars of his cage. "You're afraid. I can see it in your eyes. The slight twitch. The dilation. But don't worry, I'll make the duel fair." Migo pulled Hatan's knife from under his shirt. They hadn't even bothered to pat him down before tossing him in. Fools. "You keep your glaive. I'll duel you with this." Migo smirked. "Come on. Don't you want to be the one who strikes me down?"

"I would prefer you use a glaive, but if you insist on a knife, that's your own stupidity."

Ailon, one of Tarahan's soldiers, spoke up. "You don't have to duel him, cap—"

"Shut up," Tarahan said through his teeth. "You'll be the one scrubbing the prince's blood off the stone." His eyes grew dark. "Release him."

The soldier who'd taken the key from Migo hesitantly approached.

"You're the one she doesn't love, traitor," Tarahan said. "She is only bitter because you survived and her husband did not. With you gone, her bitterness fades."

Tarahan's words were meaningless. Right now, there was only one thing on his mind. Saving Katsi. After that, if he survived, perhaps then he could save the city.

His gate was open.

Migo stepped out. "You've just made a mistake, Tarahan. Hatan isn't here to hold me back this time."

"He's not here to *save* you. It's fitting that you'll die holding a knife, a weapon reserved for vagabonds and thugs, rather than a soldier's glaive."

The other six soldiers in the room backed up, forming a circle. Two of them threw Katsi against the steps of the throne and remained by her side.

Migo took a serious gamble. No matter how skilled he was, a knife against a glaive gave him horrible odds, but that was probably the very reason Tarahan accepted. But Migo knew all the stances. All the tricks. All the routines. For years, he spent half his waking marks training, dueling, and running drills. There was nothing Tarahan could try that Migo hadn't seen before, even if he was young.

He already knew the tactic Tarahan would use before he set his feet apart, slid his hands toward the bottom of the haft, and lowered the blade to the floor. Snake stance. It would allow him to strike from below and keep his distance. Migo's knife wouldn't even get close enough to graze Tarahan's fingers.

"To death," Migo said. He charged forward.

Tarahan lashed up. Migo jumped back to avoid the blade. Tarahan didn't fight defensively like most Migo's duelers had. He was bold. He followed through with two more swings, driving Migo back. He'd be up against the wall in no time. The fight would be over as soon as it started. The other soldiers quickly cleared away.

Migo ducked low to dodge a jab. He punched the flat side of the glaive and tried to roll in to get closer, but Tarahan simply stepped away and swung again. He had complete control of the space.

Migo rotated in a circle as he dodged attacks, anything to keep himself away from the walls. He tore his cape off his shoulders and wrapped it around his left arm. He deflected a swing of the glaive with his knife, but that was risky. The small blade wasn't built to block.

Tarahan became more aggressive. His strokes were quicker instead of strong. Even if it wasn't a killing blow, he wanted to draw blood. But Migo knew what to expect. Each movement was almost completely anticipated. And Tarahan didn't change his stance. Migo couldn't win. Not like this. Getting closer was the only option. It would take a bold move.

The glaive clipped Migo across the shin as he tried to move. He'd seen the attack coming but was too slow to avoid it. The crowd of soldiers, silent until then, let out muttered cheers. They were still unsure. Clearly they'd all thought the fight would have been over in seconds. Migo wouldn't be able to last much longer. Not like this.

Thunder rumbled around them.

Tarahan swung up in a sideways arc. Migo dodged to the side. Tarahan followed with a high slash. Instead of backing away, Migo ducked. This was it. He knew what was coming next. Tarahan stabbed straight at Migo's midsection. It would strike home. Migo stepped into it. Using his cape-wrapped arm, Migo smacked the back of the glaive's blade, sliding his arm down the length of the weapon. He grabbed the haft, just below the blade, and pulled hard.

Tarahan's jaw and eyes widened. He didn't let go of his weapon, but tried to hold his ground, tugging back, but he stumbled forward. Migo rushed in, keeping one hand on the glaive. He sliced the knife across Tarahan's hand, severing at least two fingers.

To his credit, Tarahan was unphased. He pushed the haft of the glaive forward, striking Migo in the jaw, but the blow wasn't enough. Nothing would keep Migo from achieving victory. Migo stabbed with the knife, catching Tarahan on his upper arm. It tore through muscle. Tarahan lost grip of the glaive.

Migo adjusted his grip on the glaive and swung hard. Tarahan tried to skip backwards, but the glaive caught him straight in the inner thigh with a meaty thunk. Migo followed through with a stab in Tarahan's clavicle, just to the side of his silver shoulder plate.

Tarahan collapsed with a pained groan, his blood dull against the dark stone.

The duel was won.

Phase two.

He struck at the nearest soldier—one of the queen's guards. A one-handed slash with the glaive cut the guard right across the throat.

The soldiers were too shocked to react quickly enough. He charged the two nearest Katsi, one of them was Ailon. They swung at him in unison. He jumped, pushing the weapons down with his glaive. He stabbed one of them, a queen's guard, in the face with his knife. He hooked Ailon's glaive with his leg on the way down, buying himself the precious enough time to cut across the back of Ailon's leg with the knife.

Ailon screamed, shifted his grip, and tugged his weapon away, but Migo stabbed him in the thigh before he could get away.

The other three soldiers rushed in as Ailon stumbled. Migo popped up to his feet, sheathing the knife and wielding the glaive with both hands. He deflected attacks from the first two soldiers to arrive before giving a quick counterattack, severing one of their hands at the wrist.

His success relied fully on taking them out as quickly as possible. If this dragged out, he would easily lose.

From behind him, Katsi gave a muffled scream. A sharp pain lanced through Migo's side as a glaive sliced across his rib. Ailon had come at him from behind. Migo skipped away. He couldn't get surrounded or they'd hack him to pieces.

Smiling, Ailon limped towards Katsi. She rose to her feet and tried to run, but he rammed her in the stomach with the butt of his glaive.

The flame in Migo's gut reignited. "Don't touch her!" His voice echoed louder than the thunder. He spun, swinging the glaive in a wide arc that skimmed the top of a soldier's head, piercing the helmet. He sprinted at Ailon. The stupid smirk on Ailon's face vanished. Migo deflected a single swing from Ailon before lunging at him. His head smashed into Ailon's chin.

Ailon stumbled away. Migo cracked him in the face with a swift punch with such force that blood exploded from Ailon's nose. The glaive came next, hacking into Ailon's chest. He fell.

Migo was in his essence. This is what he was made for. Did the soldiers understand? Had they been raised the same way as him? Of course not. Their parents probably loved them. Probably saw them as something more than mere weapons. He faced them. He didn't hate them, but respected them for trying to kill him. It was what any honorable Rikaydian soldier would do, given the circumstances. These were brave men doing the right thing.

But they had to die.

A necessary evil for the sake of the whole kingdom.

The soldier with the severed hand hadn't backed down. Though his face was streaked with tears and twisted in pain, he knew that if he didn't help the others kill Migo, he would die anyway.

Migo stepped forward, standing between them and Katsi. He deflected several attacks, but pressed against them, keeping them on their toes. They weren't aggressive enough. They feared him. They'd seen what he was capable of.

One of them, bleeding from the wound in his head, had to wipe the blood from his eyes. Migo took advantage, lunging in with an upward swing that cut into the man's underarm. His scream of agony tore at Migo's ears.

The remaining two soldiers both swung at him, one high, one low. He ducked, dodging the high attack, and dropped his glaive, deflecting the low attack. He kicked the one-handed soldier away and batted down another swing from the other soldier. He withdrew the knife and stabbed it into the man's neck in one swift motion.

The last soldier clutched his severed wrist against his chest, sobbing as he held his weapon out towards Migo. "My prince," the man said. "Please."

A coldness washed over Migo's body. He looked at the massacre around him. His doing.

But no. All of this could have been avoided if the queen had only wanted peace. Instead, she wanted the destruction of all their people. She was to blame.

As much as it pained him, nobody could know what happened in this room.

He marched to the remaining soldier, knocking the weapon aside. He thrust the knife straight into the man's heart and watched as the life went out of his eyes. Migo would remember him.

Migo rose and found one of the keys, then helped free Katsi. He removed her gag first. She said nothing as he unlocked her cuffs and dropped them on the floor with a loud clang.

Katsi stared at the bodies.

Migo's face burned with shame. "I had to ensure there were no witnesses to my treachery for letting you escape," he said.

She only nodded.

There was so much more he could explain, but he needed to get them out of the room, away from the scene.

"Come," he led her behind the throne. The palace was laced with secret passageways, reserved specifically for the royal family. Migo had often used them as a child, despite his father's warnings that they were only to be used for emergencies.

Now was one such occasion.

He pulled aside three layers of tapestries to reveal a small recess in the stone wall. A hard shove swung it inward.

A door to the throne room creaked open behind them. Migo ushered Katsi inside, but they were spotted.

"Migo?"

Migo turned. It was Hatan. He blinked at the room in utter surprise.

"He betrayed us," Ailon squeaked. Apparently he was still alive.

Migo strode over to Ailon.

"What happened here?" Hatan asked, frozen in place.

"Is anyone with you?" Migo said, ignoring the question.

"I'm alone."

Migo kneeled down beside Ailon. "The idol you found in the shaman's home. Did you place it there? Were you framing them?"

Ailon spit blood on Migo's face.

Migo stabbed the knife into Ailon's side. The man didn't last long after that.

"Migo. What did you do?" Hatan asked.

"I killed them all," Migo said just as Ailon's thrashing body went still.

"Why?"

"I had to." *Because they hurt her.* He wouldn't voice the words. Not to Hatan. As soon as Tarahan hurt Katsi, that was Migo's tipping point. He would have been content going to his grave, but not if he knew he had a chance to free Katsi.

Migo rose to his feet. "I will explain everything, Hatan. I promise. Pretend you didn't see this. See if you can keep others from stumbling into the room. But right now, I have one last thing to do." He left Hatan standing there amidst the carnage and entered the narrow passageway where Katsi still waited. A tiny window high above provided the only light once Migo closed everything behind them.

"Your things are all here," Migo said, reaching into an aged basket and pulling out a sack. "I moved it here before I came to release you."

Katsi chewed on her lip as she looked up at him. She accepted the bag wordlessly.

Migo sighed. "I know. What I did was... shameful, but necessary. I'm sorry you had to see it."

Katsi shook her head. "No, I'm just trying to understand. You turned against your own people. You risked your own life. I was afraid you would die. All to save me? What reason do you have?" She reached a hand out and grabbed his arm.

Migo chewed his words. He stood so close to her. Her brown eyes blinked at him, searching. If he could freeze the moment he would. To keep her there, breathing the same air, each inhalation filling him with warmth and comfort. She didn't hate him. She wanted to understand him. The pain of his injuries was washed away as his heart beat, each pump filling him with a sensation so powerful it could only be called one thing. But it was a word he dared not think.

He took a half step closer to her. Her breath warmed his neck as her lips parted and she looked up at him. "I don't know what magic you used on me... but whatever it is, you've changed me. I would kill for you. I would bleed for you. I would die for you. I would defy the whole empire to keep you safe."

"Hold off on that dying part," she whispered with a faint smile.

He breathed a laugh. "I'll try my best, but we're not done yet. If we can't bring peace before the storm ends, everyone dies." He placed a hand behind Katsi's neck. "We have one option. I need to become king. Then I can make arrangements with the tribe. We can call off the war."

Katsi started removing things from the bag and placing them back in her belt and pockets. "And for you to become king that would require..."

"The queen needs to die, Katsi. It's the only way."

Katsi shook her head. "I'll do it."

"Katsi, what? Have you ever killed someone before?"

She clapped him on the chest. "I said I'll do it. Where do I go?"

"This is a passage," Migo said, still unsure how to respond to Katsi's sudden resolve. "I'll lead us there." He traced the wall with one hand and walked further into the distance. Instinctively, he reached for Katsi's hand to lead her behind him. She took it, her hand feeling small in his own. Her skin was almost as equally cold as the stone wall.

"The queen went to her room after our meeting. She'll have at least ten guards outside her door," Migo said. "And she's trained as a warrior."

"Stop trying to dissuade me," Katsi said, her voice hard, giving his hand a squeeze as they shimmied through the dark. "Point me in the right direction. I'll do it all myself."

They'd fail. Their chances of success were slim. Katsi had never killed somebody before. She wouldn't get past the ten guards. Even with Migo's help, he doubted they'd be able to do it.

"She's not immortal, Migo," Katsi said.

"I never said she was."

"But you don't think I can kill her."

Migo answered hesitantly. "I think you lack experience. It will not be easy."

"Maybe it will be easier than you think. Last time we talked, I didn't have a plan. I do now. It'll work. It has to."

Migo came to a stop as his hand hit a corner. Another door waited on the other side. "We're here." Their breathing echoed in the stale passageway. "You can still run away, Katsi. Outside this door, to the left, there's a door that leads outside. You'd just need to lift the stormguard to open it. You could get away in the Maedari."

"I'll use it when I'm done."

There was no dissuading her. He sighed. "Katsi, please. I didn't just save you from Tarahan so that the queen could kill you instead."

"I have to do it," Katsi said, voice sharp. "Alone."

Migo rubbed a hand through his hair. "Why alone? I don't understand."

"Because I'm not going to kill the guards, and you need to get out of this mix without being suspected of leading a coup. As king, you'll need the loyalty of your people. I'm going to kill the queen, and only her. I have a plan this time. I came prepared. You should stay away from the room until things are... done." She whispered the last word and let out a shuddering breath.

Migo shook his head and placed a hand on her shoulder. "I don't know why I'm agreeing to this. I wish there was another way. I trust you to do what's right. I'll draw attention to the throne room as a distraction to make sure you see no surprises. The queen's chamber is around the corner to the right. You'll recognize it by the ten guards posted outside."

"Migo," Katsi whispered. "Thank you for saving me." She pulled him into a tight, warm hug. A tingle shot up his spine as he embraced her, fingers lacing through her thick hair. Then Katsi slid from his arms and squeezed his hand again.

This was something worth fighting for. Not hatred or anger. Katsi.

Migo pulled the door inward, a bit of light filtering through. "Here we go."

Chapter Thirty-Seven

Blood

Katsi slipped out from behind the curtain and proceeded down the hallway to the right. Now that she wasn't standing with Migo, her resolve melted around her. The world spun. She placed a hand on the wall to steady herself. He'd just killed six of his own people and she saw the way it pained him, but he still did it. How? She could barely stomach the idea of killing the vilest person in the kingdom. The woman who needlessly executed her parents and countless others.

It had to be done.

She checked her inventory again. The key components were there, including the two metal vials containing the potion she'd need, as well as the blank letter from the seer. The circumstances were perfect. Katsi couldn't deny that old shaman woman's predictions now. It made her sick. She took a big breath and rubbed her forehead.

She had to do this. She had to succeed. Migo's life was on the line. *Damani's* life was on the line. As well as the entire city of Jehubal and all of her fellow tribespeople.

Her feet moved fast with the silent step of a practiced criminal. She didn't see a soul, though she did hear a door slam somewhere behind her. A glance back revealed an empty hallway. She slowed her pace when she neared the end of the hall. If Migo was correct, then Queen Rikaydian's room was just to the right.

Her heart pounded, not only from the sprint, but from the anticipation of the task that lay before her. She never would have imagined that she would be in such a position. She hadn't thought that she could possibly go through with something like this. But she didn't save Migo just so he could die at the hands of his mother. She peeked around the corner. Fifteen soldiers stood outside the door. Definitely not ten.

The air was uncomfortably humid. She chewed her cheek. There was a shout from far down the hallway behind her, and she looked back to see a man running away from her, shouting that he'd sighted a shaman.

It was now or never.

Time to make a king.

She secured her veil over her face. Hands trembling, Katsi pulled out one of the potions. Fingers slick with sweat, she unscrewed the lid and stepped out into the hallway. Willing her magic forth, a flush of white vapor flew from the potion and into the soldiers.

Most fell instantly. A couple soldiers made it another step before collapsing. Weapons clattered to the floor.

Katsi held her breath and forced the remaining vapor down the hallway. The whooshing of the wind was lost to the sounds of the storm. She waited a moment before breathing. The sudden stillness was eerie.

A shiver went up Katsi's spine as she stepped around the bodies. *Steady yourself*. She wiped her hands on her thighs, angry that they were still sweating. She pulled the second vial out and readied it before turning the knob on the queen's room. The room beyond was dark as she stepped inside.

Queen Rikaydian was waiting.

The queen stood across the room near a massive bed. A sneer marred her beautiful face. She flung her arm, something flashing from her hand.

Katsi spun. A searing pain burned across her arm. The weapon had pierced her armor. She tried to open the potion, cursing herself for not doing it before. She ducked to dodge another hurled weapon that grazed her finger, loosing the potion from her grip. The metal vial clattered to the floor.

The queen charged at Katsi, a javelin in hand. Katsi tried to dodge, but the queen stabbed the javelin at her, piercing through the stormwading armor that hung loose by Katsi's waist. The cold metal barely cut Katsi's side, but the javelin stuck into the wooden doorframe, pinning her in place.

"I was waiting for you," the queen said, her voice filled with an almost unnatural malice. Her nostrils flared and she pulled a knife from somewhere in her sleeping dress. "Did you think this was the first attempt on my life?"

Katsi jerked at the javelin, trying to loose it from the frame, but the queen held it in place, her muscles flexing. She was strong. Why did Katsi think she could do this? Surely Queen Rikaydian, of all people, would be most prepared to thwart an assassination.

The queen's perfect lips curled back, revealing her sparkling teeth. Katsi drew her knife, half expecting the queen to gnash at her like a rangola.

Instead, she withdrew the javelin and stabbed at Katsi again.

Katsi dropped to the floor and used her magic to push the queen sideways with a burst of wind. A drape ripped from the wall and whipped at the queen who batted it away with the javelin. This gave Katsi enough time to roll across the floor and snatch up the potion.

Realizing the danger, the queen hurled her javelin at Katsi. With a burst of sharpened senses, Katsi spun to her knees and slapped the javelin to the side. The weapon clattered on the floor.

The potion opened a heartbeat later. She hurled it at the queen, using her magic to empty its contents. Vapor encompassed the queen in a cloud, her eyes widening with horror just before she collapsed.

Katsi gasped. She looked at her forearm, blood slowly dripping from a cut. The spiked, metal disk lay on the floor. Silver. The javelin was probably the same. That certainly wasn't something she'd been expecting. Both her arm and hip stung where she'd been cut. She looked up.

The queen.

The air wasn't cold, but Katsi shivered. Her body trembled. She stepped closer.

Queen Rikaydian had fallen on her back. Her eyes were open, staring up at the ceiling. Now that the queen was paralyzed, her face was relaxed. She looked calm. Peaceful. It was the first time Katsi had seen Queen Rikaydian without a scowl. It made her seem like less of a monster.

Katsi's guts squirmed. She took a shuddering breath and drew out her knife. An empty vial was in her other hand.

What would my parents think of me now?

The thought brought tears to her eyes.

And the tribe?

She'd spent the last four years living by herself because she disagreed with the tribe's methods. Violence was not the answer. But now?

She kneeled beside the queen. She pulled back the beautiful, silky hair that had fallen across her neck. The skin beneath was warm and soft. A vein pulsed with steady life.

Katsi groaned and clenched her jaw. *I have to do this.* She held the vial at the ready and placed the knife on the queen's throat. A wave of disgust weakened Katsi's grip. The handle burned her palm with spite. Like Migo said, this was better for everyone. She was saving lives by taking one. *Sharp and swift. Like killing an animal.* She clenched her teeth, biting back the bile that rose in her throat. She pressed the knife harder. One quick jerk was all it took.

Chapter Thirty-Eight

The Price of Freedom

Migo threw the doors back and emerged from the throne room at the main entrance. Two startled guards blinked at him from either side of the hall. "Did you not hear me call for you?"

They shook their heads. "No, sir. The storm."

"We've been attacked. Traitors in our midst," Migo said, assuming command. "They tried to have me killed. Secure the room. I need to check on some others."

"Yes, lord." They clambered into the throneroom, cursing in alarm as they saw the scene.

Migo turned down the hall and headed to the guardroom. He needed to tie up any loose ends. The glaive bounced in his hands. Few others walked the halls. Most people bunkered down during Maedaris.

He came to the guardroom door. It was open. Two soldiers stood inside, taking inventory.

"Why is this door open?" Migo demanded.

The soldiers saluted. "Lord, we've just returned to the room. Captain Tarahan had instructed us to carry some supplies to the training hall."

"And you left this post unmanned?"

"No, lord." The soldier's eyes were wide as he shook his head. "Captain Tarahan left another man here in our stead, but he was gone when we got back."

"Well," Migo said, voice grave. "I just had to kill Captain Tarahan for murdering some of our own people and releasing a shaman prisoner. Is there anybody at the training hall who could attest to your delivery?"

"Y-yes, lord."

Footsteps charged down the hallway and came through the door.

Migo turned and saw Captain Falshon leading a few soldiers toward the throne room. Falshon stopped as he saw Migo.

"Lord, it's good to see you safe," Falshon said through panting breaths. He blinked at the blood on Migo's clothes, and then at the four dead bodies strewn through the room.

"What has you in a hurry?" Migo said.

Falshon clapped a hand over his helmet. "The queen is dead."

* * * * *

Katsi wasn't sure how much time had passed as she huddled against a tree north of Jehubal, weeping until the Maedari had dwindled into a warm rain. Part of her felt like she'd betrayed herself, betrayed her parents. How could she murder somebody? It had been her own choice. It wasn't self-defense. She had gone out of her way to reach the queen and end her. There was no going back from that point.

She punched the ground, hard sand grinding against her skin. *Come on, I did the world a favor. Queen Rikaydian was the evilest person on the planet.* Nobody deserved to die more. This was the same person who'd murdered her innocent parents. She saved Migo's life by doing it. She had to believe that killing the queen would give the Bayvana Tribe a reason to find peace, especially with Migo as king. She'd done the right thing, but the horror of slitting the queen's throat was sickening. Haunting.

Peace had been purchased with blood.

"Enough," she said aloud. "What's done is done." She wiped her eyes and pulled out the blank letter. In her other hand, she held one of the metal vials that had previously contained a potion she'd used earlier to get by the guards. She undid the lid and poured the contents onto the unfolded letter. The blood of Queen Rikaydian dripped out, spattering across the parchment before it soaked in as if sucked by a sponge.

Black lettering appeared at the top of the page. Katsi tried some of her own blood before, but that hadn't worked. She'd even tried a little of Migo's blood when he was unconscious, but that had failed also. This was different.

As the old shaman woman had promised, the words could only be revealed with the blood of the dead queen.

The lettering on the paper became clear. *Well done. You have succeeded where many have failed. You've slain the evil queen. We've made our bargain. Meet me at the mouth of the scar during Aivar's peak. Then, if you are still committed, you may find the answer you seek.*

Aivar. The shamanic name for the moon. The scar meant the canyon.

Katsi touched the magical armlet, still secured on her arm beneath her stormwading armor. *Some solutions. Some answers... come with a heavy price.*

Chapter Thirty-Nine

King

Light? Relieved? Migo wasn't sure how to describe what he was feeling.

Migo cleared his throat. He stood before a gathering of soldiers. With the queen dead, they all assumed his rule. "Get word out to all the officers immediately. Send every runner. The queen is dead and we offer an immediate truce." He clapped his hand once. "Go."

The soldiers and messengers sprinted off to fulfill his order. The Maedari had reduced to a mere drizzle. If the shamans were going to attack, the time was soon upon them.

Migo nodded to Hatan and Captain Falshon and together they entered an office beside the throne room.

"We've got the full reports," Hatan said.

Migo sat heavily on a chair. Migo's lie was spreading. That he'd single-handedly thwarted an attempted coup by Captain Tarahan. It was Tarahan who released the shaman girl.

As soon as he'd heard about the queen's death, Migo ordered a lockdown on the palace grounds. He had to play the part, though given the reports, he knew full well who'd executed the assassination. And he'd been the one to commission it. He kept the smile from showing on his lips. The queen had been raising him to kill his enemies. That's exactly what he'd done.

"All the soldiers posted outside the queen's room reported the same thing," Hatan said. "They were assaulted by a female shaman." They shared a knowing look. "She threw some kind of vapor at them that instantly paralyzed their bodies. They drooled on the floor as she walked past them straight into the queen's chamber. They heard a bit of a struggle from inside the room. A short moment later, the same woman ran out and went outside into the storm. They were all still lying on the floor when they were found about halfway through the eighth mark. Some of them are still recovering, but most have little or no paralysis remaining."

Hatan paused in his report and nodded to a woman who entered the room, Lady Yada Fasam. She had been Hatan's informant from inside Tilayna's court. She wore a crisp dress and held a roll of parchment in one hand.

Once the door was closed behind her, Hatan continued the report. "The next thing we did was investigate the room. The queen must've been more prepared than the guards outside. She was able to throw a couple of her throwing discs, and one of them had traces of blood on it, so she at least struck the assailant once before the queen was incapacitated. She was stabbed in the chest once, and her throat had been slit. There's little doubt who the culprit was there."

This was the part that worried Migo the most. The queen was formidable, though Migo never knew how much. Katsi must have been lucky if she got out alive. Whatever vapor she'd used to knock out the soldiers probably got the queen too. It was a tactic he'd never heard of, but it was ingenious. He wondered if it was the same kind of thing she'd used to knock him out while healing him.

The chair Migo sat on was warm. Comfortable. Even despite its plushness. He couldn't remember the last time he'd felt comfortable on anything.

Maybe this was the peace Katsi talked about. He didn't feel the urge to constantly grip the pommel of a weapon.

Peace. Thanks to Katsi. He sighed within himself, thinking he'd probably never see her again.

Migo cleared his throat. "There were also seven dead soldiers in the throne room, including Captain Tarahan." He met Hatan's eyes. "This is how the report should read: I went there and found Captain Tarahan and two of his men had just killed the last of the guards after I came to help. When I questioned Tarahan, he attacked me. I killed Tarahan before he would speak, but Ailon revealed a few things after he was injured.

"He admitted that Tarahan planned his own coup. They made a deal with the imprisoned shaman: her freedom for killing the queen. With me and the queen dead, he was planning on assuming the throne himself. That's all I was able to get out of him before he bled out."

"What do we do now?" Falshon asked.

Hatan arched an eyebrow. "First things first." He lifted a finger. "We need to order some pastries from the market." He held up another finger and pointed it at Migo. "Second, we need you to take your place. As the king."

Migo stood from his seat. "Then I need to make arrangements with the Bayvana Tribe. War is not necessary."

Hatan grunted. "There will be many people who won't be happy to make peace."

"Then it's a good thing I'll be the king," Migo said and handed Hatan back his knife. "There's one more thing I need to do." He left them behind in the room and made his way down to the main floor and the entrance to the dungeon.

Nobody questioned his authority as he passed the guards. The cavernous dungeon echoed with dripping water as Migo commanded the prison sergeant to accompany him.

Migo stopped before a single cell. "Damani," he said.

Damani emerged from the darkness. "Is it time, then?"

"Open the cell," Migo ordered. The sergeant unlocked it.

Migo entered and grabbed Damani by the shoulder, escorting him out. "That is all, sergeant. Return to your post."

"Yes, sir." He left Migo and Damani there.

"What's going on?" Damani asked.

"I'm letting you go."

Damani blinked back at him.

"On one condition," Migo said. "If Katsi comes to you, you must turn her away. You betrayed her to me. You don't truly love her and you don't deserve her loyalty. If I get the word that you take her in or pretend you care for her, I'll put you right back here. Understood?"

Damani closed his eyes and nodded.

"Good." Migo led him towards the stairs. "I'll escort you out myself."

Chapter Forty

Alone

Warm rain drizzled softly over Jehubal as Katsi slunk through the streets. Her veil was wrapped tightly about her face, and her breath felt sticky and humid. She couldn't wipe away her tears from earlier. It was like they'd stained her cheeks. Thoughts of what to do battled in her mind. She was afraid. Afraid of what she'd done, and afraid of what she could still do. She'd changed since she first found the artifact, and that scared her even more. All she wanted was peace and safety, but what did it cost?

She gritted her teeth. The smell of baked sweets drifted past her nose as she made her way to the sleephouse on the other side of the street, smashed between two factories that processed fruit sugars. Despite the rain, the streets were busy. Word about the queen's murder and the peace declaration was spreading quickly, and Katsi wasn't the only person rushing to get somewhere. She assumed the tribe had spies throughout the city. Otherwise, they would have attacked already.

This section of town was crowded with farmers who'd been hiding in the city since the battle near their homes in the southern marshes.

Inside the sleephouse, Katsi had to walk almost shoulder-to-shoulder in order to get around. Talk of returning to their farms, moving elsewhere, and the queen's murder were heavy on their lips, but above it all, the real tension was in their whispers about shamans. Katsi's heart pounded faster as she sensed the fear in their words. She'd always felt safe around the farmers before, but now that sense of safety felt threatened.

Best make this quick. She scanned the faces of each patron. It was a shot in the dark, but this was the most likely place she knew to look. She'd made it to the back of the building before she saw him seated at a small table, three empty seats around it. His light brown hair and blue eyes made him easy to spot. A warmth spread through Katsi's chest just to see him alive and well. She barely kept herself from leaping at the sight of him.

"Damani," she said, dropping to the seat beside him. One of his hands held a drink, his other was loosely set on the table. She reached out to grab his free hand, but he snapped it away and regarded her with wide eyes.

Katsi tried to brush aside the awkwardness. "I'm so sorry, Damani. How are you?"

Damani blinked at her, his body shifting away ever-so-slowly. "I always feared what you might be." His voice was so soft, Katsi could barely hear it over the other patrons. "That's why I could never ask you."

Katsi shook her head. "You're okay now, I got him to let you free, but things are crazy here now. We could go—."

"We?" Some of the contents of Damani's drink splashed out as he snapped his hands down to grip the edge of the table. He leaned his head forward. "Katsi, I almost died. I was nearly beaten to death because I tried to protect you, and you're a…" He shook his head and glanced at the crowd.

Shaman. Katsi finished his thought.

"And you're the one who did it, aren't you? The queen? They said it was a young woman."

Katsi said nothing. The way Damani spoke frightened her. New tears threatened the edges of her eyes.

Damani shook his head. "Revenge then? For killing your parents, I get it."

"It was more than that. I've changed things for the whole city. The war is over. I won't be hunted here anymore. We could be normal."

"You don't get it. A shaman killed the queen. How does that dissuade anybody from hunting shamans? It was revenge, Katsi. Maybe you should go back to the rest of the murderers in your tribe." Damani's eyes widened, and his features softened after he spoke, but the damage was done.

His voice had been a little too loud, and Katsi noticed a couple people start to stare over at them with questioning looks. It was time to go.

Katsi bounced out of her seat and dashed into the crowd, avoiding those who'd looked at her. A shout of alarm went out, but nobody could think fast enough to react. She shoved her way free of the sleephouse and sprinted into the outside rain. Tears flowed freely beneath her veil, blurring her vision.

She'd lost her home. She'd lost Damani. She was more alone now than she'd ever been. With Migo as king, she wasn't sure if things would change at all. Was peace only temporary? It seemed like something was working against her—against her whole people. There really was only one place left to go from here. She'd return to the shaman woman and hopefully learn more about her powers. If the power could help her maintain the peace she'd purchased, she was willing to do it. The price had already been paid.

But there was a final stop she needed to make before leaving the city. It was a longshot, but she had to hope anyway. Rain muted the sound of her feet as she wove through the streets. The clouds above reflected yellow in the sunlight. Sorrow clung to her chest like cold fingers, weighing her down, but each step brought her closer.

She stopped in a plaza. At the center of the plaza rose a castletrunk tree surrounded by coral bushes. She crouched in front of it, scanning the ground for any sign of movement other than the dripping water. She checked her surroundings. Anybody else in the plaza had their heads down, hurrying to their destinations.

"Scales," she whispered. Only the pattering rain answered her. "Scales," she repeated, louder this time, digging around in her bag for any food. There was none. She stayed for several minutes, repeating his name. She dropped her head in resignation, sniffing past the loneliness that enveloped her like a cold blanket.

A high-pitched croak pierced through the plaza.

Katsi snapped her eyes up, looking to the source. A lizard came gliding down from a nearby roof and alighted atop a coral bush directly in front of Katsi, splashing in the bit of water that had collected there.

"Scales," Katsi said, heart bursting as she held out her hand. The lizard tilted its head, scales shifting to a shade of turquoise and hopped onto Katsi's hand, snuggling down against her wet palm. "I told you I'd come back. You're bigger! Didn't I say this was a great spot." She lifted him close to her face. He was easily twice the size he'd been when she left him.

"You were gliding," she said, scratching under his chin. A low, bubbling croak emitted from his throat. His webbing had developed, but it was different than anything she'd seen before. Two new spikes protruded from his shoulders and webbing extended from the tip of the spikes down his back. She touched one of them and he folded it down against his back, blinking up at her as he did.

Scales flexed the seemingly new appendages for her, folding them up and down. He bounced in her palm then leapt into the air, webbed spikes pumping as he tucked his legs against his body. He flitted up to a low branch of the tree and gave Katsi an excited garble. She started to question if he was even a scaila, or something else. Something she'd never seen before. "You're more than a scaila, aren't you?" He jumped back down and landed on her hand.

Katsi released a laugh, the tension and loneliness leaking out of her like steam. Fresh tears watered in her eyes. "Oh, how could I have ever thought I was a failure, Scales. Not when I've saved you so you could fly." He sat back on his haunches and tilted his head at her. "And I'm more than just a shaman. I'm a stormcaller." She took a deep breath, filling her lungs. "And I intend to learn exactly what that means."

Afterword

Thanks for reading—if you enjoyed the story, I'd always encourage you to leave a review. You can do that by heading over to Amazon https://mybook.to/scornedprince

The story continues in book 2, Cursed King: https://mybook.to/CursedKingBH

Did you know there's a prequel novella? It shows the moment the planet became tidally locked (500 years prior to the evens in Scorned Prince). You can get the novella for free by joining my newsletter here: https://dashboard.mailerlite.com/forms/407793/86100098983921586/share

Glossary

Time on Malahem:

Cycle: The moon rotates around Malahem. A single rotation of the moon around the planet is called a cycle. This is the Ringdweller's alternative to a day.

Mark: roughly 2 hours. There are 10 marks in a cycle

Malahem: the planet

The Ring: the habitable zone between the Scorched Waste and the Frozen Waste

Frozen Waste: the dark side of the planet

Scorched Waste: the side of the planet facing the sun

Scaila: a small type lizard with webbing between its legs and colorful scales

Marem: a person born outside of shamanfolk lineage

Ringdweller: a person who lives in the Ring

Sunward: in the direction of the sun

Rangola: large feline animals, sometimes tamed as mounts.

Waheshi: humans that have been mutated into creatures by forcing them to drink a potion. Appearances vary based on the blood of the animal used in the potion.

Aivar: the shamanic name for the moon

Sleephouse: A place of temporary lodging. Also commonly serves food

Ganaueh: board game

Chama-fen: wrestling game

Maedari: the magical storms that sporadically ravage the Ring

Varman: Large, thick-hided oxen. Domesticated ones tend to have their massive horns clipped.

Tidal locking: This is when the orbital body (ie, Malahem) rotates around its axis exactly once during its orbit around the star (or sun, in this case).

Shaman Classes
Bleeder
Stormcaller
Mixer
Earthmelder
Seer
Enchanter

Pronunciation Guide

Ailon: Ah-ee-lawn

Akailen: Ah-kah-ee-len

Banadil-Atar: Bah-nah-deel-Ah-tahr

Bayvana: Ba-ee-vah-nah

Bindom: Been-dohm

Cataban: Kah-tah-bahn

Damani: Dah-mah-nee

Deliran: Deh-lee-rahn

Gendin: Gen-deen

Hatan Padarro: Ha-tahn Pa-da-row

Jehubal: Je-hoo-bahl

Kajina: Kah-jee-nah

Katsi Danan: Kaht-see Dah-nahn

Kidem Rikaydian: Kee-dem Ree-ke-dee-en

Kinay: Kee-na-ee

Maedari: Meh-dah-ree

Malahem: Mah-la-hem

Manahae: Mah-nah-ha-eh

Mashe: Mah-she

Migo Rikaydian: Mee-go Ree-ke-dee-en

Nedro Wajek: Ne-dro Wah-jek

Seba: Seh-bah

Scaila: Ska-ee-la

Shali: Shah-lee

Shavarani: Shah-vah-rah-nee

Shinaseh: Shee-nah-seh

Rangola: Rahn-goh-la

Roda: Roh-dah

Tarahan: Ta-rah-han

Tilayna Rikaydian: Tee-le-nah Ree-ke-dee-en

Yavasu Roqaya: Yah-vah-soo Row-ka-ya

About Author

Brady was born in a stronghold at the base of the Rocky Mountains. He currently resides there with his wife, their three daughters, and a few domesticated house lions of a rare breed. He set out with the goal to write fantasy that anybody could read with characters who face real life struggles. Everyone deserves to feel like there is hope.